Wizard Defiant

Book One

Intergalactic Wizard Scout Chronicles

Rodney W. Hartman

Books by Rodney Hartman

Intergalactic Wizard Scout Chronicles

DEDICATION

This book is dedicated to my wife and best friend, Karen.
She is my safe harbor in the stormy sea of life.

ACKNOWLEDGMENTS

This book could never have been completed without the assistance and support of family and friends too numerous to mention. However, I would be amiss if I did not give special thanks to my wife, Karen Hartman, for her support and encouragement in this project.

CHAPTER 1

[Begin Transmission]

Richard hid behind what little remained of a broken stone wall. His passive scan confirmed the presence of two life forms nearby. He pressed his back so hard against the stone that he could feel the metal rivets of his leather armor digging into his flesh.

At least two members of his team had been taken out already. His team of four—or quad as it was called in wizard scout jargon—was opposed by a quad of enemy soldiers. He had no idea if his remaining teammate was even still in action. Richard doubted it. The recent sound of enemy fire off to his right had been replaced by silence. That didn't bode well for his quad and didn't bode well for him either. The two soldiers stalking him would undoubtedly be getting reinforcements soon.

A drop of sweat dripped perilously close to Richard's right eye, but he dared not move to wipe it away, sensing the soldier approaching cautiously just a few meters away on the far side of the wall.

Take your time, Richard told himself. *The second guy is bound to be behind cover providing support for this one.*

Richard's plan was simple. He would use his phase rod to take out the first soldier. Then he'd grab the soldier's weapon and use it on his companion. If he was lucky, he could remove these two soldiers from the fight before their help arrived.

Risking a glance at his phase rod, Richard made sure it was

hidden behind his left leg. Even in stun mode, small red arcs of plasma energy crept up and down the entire meter-long length of the weapon's brerellium shaft. If he wasn't careful, even the dim glow of the phase rod would give away his position in the early-morning twilight.

Richard wished he had a pistol or rifle, but the phase rod was all he'd been provided so it would have to do. The modified riot baton was a battering weapon, so even if the soldier's armor resisted the stun effects, Richard was hopeful he could disable his opponent with a few well-placed blows.

A shuffling noise came from the far side of the wall. The source of the sound was even closer than he'd thought. Richard forced himself to relax his grip a little on the phase rod's handle. He'd been told repeatedly that too stiff a grip would break his wrist if an enemy's armor was supplemented with a force field.

Unless things are totally unfair, Richard thought, *they should have leather armor as well. The phase rod should do the job easy enough.*

The noise came again. This time it was accompanied by a small pebble skittering along the ground. It was time. Another step and the soldier would clear the wall. Richard gathered a small amount of Power with his mind and wrapped it around a loose, fist-sized stone sitting on the top of the wall across the stone path. He pulled with his mind, and the stone slid off the wall and clattered loudly on the rocky ground below.

A series of green plasma rounds erupted from around the corner of the wall, spraying in the direction of the falling stone. Richard spun around the wall and swung his phase rod at head height as he went. Instead of encountering a light leather helmet as expected, Richard's blow struck a heavy metallic face plate. The phase rod rebounded off with little or no effect. The only thing his blow had accomplished was to draw the soldier's attention.

Crap! He's wearing full armor!

Richard wasted no time in reflecting on the unfairness of the situation. For whatever reason, he was apparently expected to match his flimsy set of leather armor against an enemy equipped with full-body armor, reinforced with a low-level force field. It was a nearly impossible scenario, but Richard knew he'd just have to deal with it.

The soldier tried to backpedal in an attempt to bring his plasma rifle to bear.

Richard stayed in close and matched him step for step. He stuck his useless phase rod between his opponent's legs and tripped the already off-balanced soldier, who fell heavily to the ground. Richard used his knee to roll the soldier over until his enemy's face was in the dirt, then placed all his weight on the soldier's back. The maneuver would only buy him a couple of seconds, but he needed time to think. He had no hope of overpowering the soldier with brute force. His muscles were no match for the hydraulic-assisters of the soldier's body armor. As if to prove the point, the soldier began to rise in spite of Richard's full weight.

Richard caught a glimpse of movement to his front. The soldier's buddy was running towards them. A plasma rifle was aimed at Richard's head. He jerked the already rising soldier below him into a standing position just as the running soldier fired. The struggling soldier in his grasp absorbed a half dozen quarter-strength stun rounds to the chest. While dangerous to his light leather, Richard doubted they'd have any effect on the well-armored soldier he was holding. The second soldier must have thought the same and started firing a steady stream of green plasma rounds in Richard's direction. But luck and a little skill were on Richard's side. He pulled back on his human shield and used his hip to leverage the soldier's waist into the stream of green energy. One of the plasma rounds hit a stun grenade attached to the soldier's ammo pouch.

Boom!

When the grenade exploded, both Richard and the soldier were thrown back several meters. As they fell, Richard managed to yank the soldier's plasma rifle out of his hands. He rolled out from underneath his opponent just before they hit the ground.

The soldier's armor absorbed most of the force of the exploding stun grenade. However, at least some energy must have penetrated the armor, because the soldier appeared momentarily stunned.

Always one to build on success, Richard brought the acquired plasma rifle to bear on the second soldier and held the trigger down for full automatic. A seemingly solid stream of green energy struck the soldier's armor, ricocheting off in all directions. Tweaking his aim slightly, Richard directed the stream of green to the second soldier's ammo pouch.

Boom!

A stun grenade exploded and sent the soldier flying backward.

Richard jumped to his feet and aimed the plasma rifle at the first soldier who was just rising up to a sitting position. Richard fired a single shot at the remaining stun grenade on the soldier's waist.

Boom!

The soldier was thrown back once again, this time legs jerking convulsively. The first grenade had weakened the armor's force field a little.

Knowing he had only seconds, Richard released the plasma rifle and let it hang by its strap. Grasping the base of his phase rod, Richard twisted the end cap off and slid out the isotopic battery. He broke a third of the battery off and dropped the larger piece on the ground. Grabbing hold of his plasma rifle, he spun to face the second soldier.

Although still lying on the ground, the soldier's right hand was clawing for a plasma rifle.

Richard didn't give him time to complete the maneuver. He pulled the trigger and sent a dozen rounds of green energy towards the soldier's waist.

Boom!

The force of the second grenade exploding sent the soldier head-over-heels backward into a pile of broken rubble.

That should buy me eight to ten seconds, Richard thought.

Kneeling beside the stunned soldier at his feet, Richard jammed the small piece of isotopic battery into a convenient crevasse in the armor near the soldier's neck. The soldier's armor was not the close-fitting armor of a wizard scout. Instead, it was the bulky armor of a line soldier. It had an abundance of places in which to wedge the battery so it wouldn't fall off.

Richard took two steps back. Aiming his plasma rifle at the isotopic battery attached to the soldier's neck, he said, "This is going to hurt, buddy." Before Richard could pull the trigger, alarms sounded and the entire area was bathed in bright lights.

A loudspeaker blared, "Abort! Abort! Simulation terminated! Abort!"

Richard immediately dropped both the plasma rifle and phase rod to the ground. He threw himself against a nearby wall and faced forward at stiff attention. Within seconds, a dozen white-coated technicians came running into view. A couple went to each of the downed soldiers and began removing their armor. Another pointed an instrument at the broken piece of isotopic battery lying on the ground where Richard had dropped it.

"Careful with that piece of battery near the neck, Jacob," said one of the technicians to the two who were removing the fallen soldier's armor. "It's near critical mass. I don't think it would take much to set it off."

"Cadet 832!" yelled a squat, toad-faced man in the silver and black of an academy TAC officer as he walked briskly towards Richard. "You'd better stiffen that brace up, cadet. And don't let me hear you utter a single word. Anything you say can and will be used against you in a court martial. I swear, I'll have you up on attempted murder charges before the day is out if I have to go straight to the admiral myself."

Richard had no trouble complying with his TAC officer's command to keep quiet. From two long years of association with TAC Officer Gaston Myers, he knew it would do no good to say anything. Like all cadets, Richard was a worm. No, he was less than a worm. And TAC Officer Gaston Myers was the Intergalactic Wizard Scout Academy's local god.

TAC Officer Myers thrust his face in front of Richard until the brim of his instructor hat was jammed into Richard's forehead. "You crossed the line this time, 832! If you've permanently hurt cadet 215, I will personally make sure you don't even make it to your court martial. You're a disgrace to the Academy, and a dozen of you wouldn't be worth one cadet 215. How you ever wormed your way into wizard scout training is a mystery to me. You've obviously got friends in high places, but they won't be able to help you this time. Your scrawny little butt is mine, 832, and you're going to rue the day you ever met me."

I already rue the day, Richard thought. *And if I've got friends in high places, I wish you'd tell me who they are so we'd both know.*

TAC Officer Myers had hated Richard from the moment he'd stepped out of the space shuttle with the other cadets two years ago. Richard had never figured out why he'd targeted him, but Myers had made his life a living hell ever since. He could never do anything well enough to prevent a caustic remark from the TAC officer. If he was the fastest disassembling a weapon, Myers would give him a tongue lashing for being too fast and not taking the time to do it properly. If he won a sparring match against four opponents, he was chewed out for sloppy techniques. If he took the time to give a detailed reconnaissance report, he was chastised for being too slow. After a few weeks, Richard had learned to train and do things to the best of his ability for his own edification. He let the TAC officer's comments slide off like water from a duck's back.

By this time, the technicians had removed the helmet from the nearest soldier. The technicians helped cadet 215 to her feet. She seemed a little shaken, but otherwise unhurt.

Richard was glad. He liked her. She was a hard worker and probably the best cadet in class. If given the chance, she would make a good wizard scout. Richard wasn't sure she'd get the chance now. The simulation was the final test to determine advancement to the next four years of training at the Academy. Richard's class had started out with eight hundred and thirty-two students. After two years of pre-Academy training, the class had been winnowed down to four hundred and thirty-two cadets. In this final simulation, two quads of four cadets each had entered the training zone. The rules were simple. Whichever quad defeated their opponents would continue on to four years of training at the Academy. The cadets who were unfortunate enough to be defeated were immediately transferred out of the training brigade. They were shipped off to standard line units as buck privates unless they had prior military service. Richard didn't think it was a very fair system.

"Cadet 832," said TAC Officer Myers, "you will turn in your equipment and confine yourself to your room until further notice. Do you understand, cadet?"

"Sir! Cadet 832 understands, sir!"

Richard picked up his phase rod and double-timed to the equipment turn-in point. He hastily removed his leather armor and laid it on the vehicle's tailgate along with his phase rod.

"You broke my phase rod," said Sergeant Hendricks good-naturedly. "Now what'd you go and do a thing like that for?"

"Sir! Just the battery, sir!" Richard answered, standing stiffly at attention. He liked Sergeant Hendricks. Rumor was the old noncom just liked being an armorer. Every time headquarters tried to promote him, he'd do something to get busted back to sergeant so he could stay in his beloved armory. In any other unit, he would probably have been thrown in the brig or kicked out of the military. Sergeant Hendricks was renowned for creating unique weaponry for wizard scouts. As a result, the upper-echelon officers pretty much left him alone. Even the TAC officers tried to stay on his good side. After all, a wizard scout with a defective weapon was a dead wizard scout.

"Well, 832," said Sergeant Hendricks, "isotopic batteries are expensive. I'd mark it on your record for pay deduction, but since cadets don't get paid, I'll just put it down as a training loss."

"Sir! Thank you, sir!"

"Don't mention it," laughed Sergeant Hendricks. "Once you graduate and start making major credits as a wizard scout, I'll remind you of the favor so you can buy me a drink or two. Now you better get a move on before one of your TACs sees you lollygagging around."

"Sir! Yes, sir!"

CHAPTER 2

Hours later, Richard stood in the doorway of his room watching cadet 215 walk down the hall with a large duffle bag hefted over her shoulder. She stopped in front of Richard.

"You caught me good, 832," she said. "I was too trigger-happy. I should have cleared the wall with a stun grenade first. I knew you were close."

"I'm sorry it was you," Richard said sincerely. "You'd have made a good wizard scout. Do you know where they're sending you?"

"Back to my old unit," she said. "I was a shuttle pilot before I got selected for wizard scout training. Didn't know that, did you?"

Most cadets were tightlipped about their lives before the Academy. While many of the cadets were new to the military, a few had prior military experience.

"A shuttle pilot?" Richard said. "I'm impressed. You'll make a good ship's captain one day."

Richard expected her to continue down the hallway, but she remained standing in front of his door with a thoughtful look on her face. Richard had never really paid much attention before, but suddenly realized cadet 215 was quite pretty. Her blue-steel eyes, short blonde hair, and freckles made for a nice combination. He wondered if the fact she was no longer a cadet made a difference on how he viewed her.

There was an awkward silence for several seconds. Finally, she set her duffle bag down and looked at Richard with a serious expression on her face.

"Were you trying to kill me?" she asked bluntly.

Richard hesitated only a second before replying. "No. I only put a third of the battery in the crease on the neck seal of your armor. It would only have cracked the seal. I just wanted to remove your helmet so I could knock you out. I won't lie, it would've hurt. But you wouldn't have been seriously injured. I give you my word of honor. I wasn't trying to kill you. I was only going to disable you."

She seemed to mull over Richard's answer for a few seconds. Then she thrust out her free hand and said, "I believe you, 832. If by some miracle TAC Officer Gaston Myers lets you become a wizard scout, take a hard look at the pilot whenever you're on a shuttle. You might see a familiar face."

Richard gave her a strong handshake in return and said, "Good luck, 215."

"No," she said. "Not 215. I'm no longer a wizard scout cadet. I'm worthy of having a name again, and my name is Ensign Elizabeth Bistos. You can call me, Liz. I know you're still a cadet lower than a worm and not worthy of a name," she said with a grin, "but if you did have a name, what would it be?"

"My name would be Sergeant Richard Shepard," he said with a grin of his own, "formerly of the 43rd Marine Recon Detachment." Then more seriously, "The Academy's system for filtering cadets is screwed up in my opinion. You've been in the top of the class in just about everything we've done during the last two years. To DFR you based upon one simulation is wrong. I'd say it's not fair, but nothing involving TAC officers is fair. But it's still wrong. I don't even understand why our quads were matched against each other. My quad was in leather. Your quad was in full-body armor. The whole basis behind the simulation is for everything to be equal except for the skill of the cadets. I think someone made a mistake, Liz."

Liz looked at Richard a moment. "I'm not a cadet anymore, so I'll let you in on a little secret. I mean, what are they going to do to me? They've already kicked me out of the Academy."

Her comment piqued Richard's curiosity. "What secret is that?"

"I think the whole thing was a setup from start to finish, Richard. We had four hundred and thirty-two cadets who were supposed to be randomly divided into one hundred and eight quads of four cadets each. I had cadets 212, 87, and 316 on my quad. All modesty aside, we were probably the four top-performing cadets in the class. You're normally rated somewhere in the middle of the class. I personally think you could do a lot better, but I've always had the impression you could care less about scores."

Richard shrugged his shoulders.

"In any regard, you were teamed with 114, 187, and 605. Don't get me wrong, they're good. No one gets into wizard scout training unless they're good. But they were consistently the bottom three cadets in combat scores. What do you think the odds are that the four highest-scoring cadets would be randomly teamed together while the three lowest-scoring cadets would be randomly teamed with you?"

"Pretty low, I guess," said Richard.

"Astronomically low," Liz said. "And on top of that, my quad had full-body armor, phase rifles, and grenades. Your quad had light-leather and quarter-power phase rods, which were incapable of penetrating my quad's armor. Doesn't that seem suspicious?"

"Well," Richard said noncommittally, "it's like I said. Somebody made a mistake."

"No one made a mistake," Liz said emphatically. "You were setup. You were supposed to lose. Unfortunately for me, whoever set you up misjudged your combat abilities. I don't mind telling you that when we were told you were a member of the other quad, we got very concerned. Scores aside, most of the cadets take it for granted you're the best in the class at combat. If not the best, you're certainly the luckiest. It was just my bad luck to get matched against you in the simulation."

"You were told who you would be fighting?" Richard asked, a little astonished. "It's supposed to be a secret in order to simulate real combat. Who told you I was in the other quad?"

"It was on my heads-up display," Liz said. "I had access to full specs on everyone in your quad. The only thing I didn't know was your exact location."

"Why would anyone want to stack the deck against me?" said Richard. "I guess I wouldn't put it past TAC Officer Myers, but the quads for the simulation are determined by the central computer via the tele-network. I don't think Myers has the resources to hack into the system. I know he hates me, but I doubt he hates me enough to beg, borrow, or steal the five million credits it would probably take to hire a team capable of hacking the selection program."

"I've said my piece," Liz said, "so I'll leave it at that. But let me give you a bit of advice even though you haven't asked for it. You should try to be a little friendlier with the other cadets every once in a while. They're good people. You've always seemed a little standoffish. One day you may regret not having friends. They come in pretty handy sometimes."

Richard thought about her comment for a few seconds. It was true he wasn't the friendliest of cadets. It wasn't that he was unfriendly, but just that he didn't go out of his way to get to know the others. If truth be known, he was probably scared to get close to people. During his short twenty-two years of life, it seemed like every time he got close to someone, that person either died or had to leave.

"Liz, I understand what you're saying, but friends can be a liability at times. I had two good friends in my last unit, and both of them were killed in front of my eyes. Cadet 647 was a good friend during our initial training, but she got DFR'd in our sixth month here."

"I've lost friends in combat too," Liz said. "But being Dropped From the Rolls is not the end of the world. You'll probably see cadet 647 again someday. Almost anyone with prior military experience has lost friends. You're no exception, and neither am I. Just because there's a chance you could lose a friend doesn't mean you shouldn't let someone get close."

"Life's strange, isn't it?" said Richard. "We've talked more today than we have in the past two years. I'm sorry we didn't get to know one another. I have a feeling you'd have made a good friend."

"I'm just DFR'd. I'm not dead," Liz said. "We were cadets together. If we ever meet again, I hope you'll consider me a friend and buy me a drink. You owe me, after all, for getting me kicked out of the class."

"I'll buy you all the drinks you can handle, Liz."

Liz laughed. "You may regret saying that. I can handle a lot." Then more seriously, "Goodbye, Richard." With that, she picked up her duffle bag, turned, and walked down the hallway to the stairs.

"Goodbye, Liz," said Richard. He continued watching the stairs long after she disappeared from sight.

CHAPTER 3

Late in the afternoon, two security police came to Richard's room and escorted him to the commandant's office on the far side of the parade field. It was a nice day, but the field was empty. The last of the failed cadets had departed earlier in the afternoon. The TAC officers had rewarded the winning cadets with a twenty-kilometer road march. Such was the life of a wizard scout cadet.

Richard knocked on the frame of the commandant's door. The door was already open, but no one who wanted to keep their head on their shoulder's ever entered the commandant's office without an invitation. The commandant was Wizard Scout Thomas R. Jacobs. Wizard scouts had no official rank other than wizard scout. But everyone in the Academy, and even the Interstellar Fleet, knew where Wizard Scout Thomas R. Jacobs stood in the military command structure. He was allegedly the oldest living wizard scout at ninety-three years of age. He had been on active duty for almost seventy years. Considering many wizard scouts didn't acquire more than five years of active service, the commandant's age alone demanded respect. However, his near deity status among wizard scouts came from his battle record during the fifty-two-year-long Teton war. After the defeat of the Tetonian Empire, he had been assigned to his current position as Commandant of the Intergalactic Wizard Scout Academy.

"Enter," said the commandant.

Richard marched into the office and hit a stiff brace two paces in front of the small field desk. He didn't salute. Wizard scouts rarely saluted.

The commandant's office was Spartan, to say the least. The commandant didn't believe in fluff or comfort. Besides the desk and chair, the only other furniture in the room was a high-carbon plastic chair located in front of the desk. Out the corner of his left eye, Richard noticed TAC Officer Gaston Myers standing at parade rest against the wall.

"Sir! Cadet 832 reporting as ordered, sir!"

The commandant looked up from the computer display in his desk long enough to acknowledge Richard's existence. Like all wizard scouts, he appeared the same age as the day he'd gotten his DNA baseline taken. Richard guessed the commandant's apparent physical age was in the late twenties. Mid-twenties to early thirties were pretty typical physical ages for wizard scouts. With an actual age of ninety-three, Richard knew the commandant was nearing the end of his lifespan. A wizard scout's self-healing could maintain youthful looks, but it couldn't stave off eventual death. Richard had a feeling the commandant would remain at his post until his last breath unless he was removed from office by the higher ups. Considering the commandant's war record and political friends, Richard doubted that would ever occur.

"Take a seat, 832," said the commandant. He had a short, gruff voice. Instead of being intimidating, it gave the impression of someone who took care of business quickly and fairly.

Richard sat down while keeping a stiff brace. He could feel the eyes of his TAC officer drilling into his back. Richard knew he would hear about even the slightest departure from proper military protocol later. Assuming, of course, he was fortunate enough to leave this office still a wizard scout cadet. Richard wasn't sure he would be.

"Let's set the rules, 832," said the commandant. "This is an inquiry. It's not a court martial so we'll do away with any legal mumbo jumbo. However, you may stop answering questions at any time and request legal counsel, should you desire. My only other rules are that you answer honestly. Also, I want you to forget for the time being that you are a wizard scout cadet. That means I don't want to hear two 'sirs' when you address me, and I want you to relax in that chair. Your back is so stiff I could bounce a plasma round off it."

"Yes, sir," Richard said, forcing himself to drop the first 'sir.' He tried relaxing his back a little but failed miserably. His half-hearted attempt to relax was even more uncomfortable than the stiff brace had been.

The commandant watched Richard's attempt to relax. He looked like he wanted to smile. "Ah, yes," he said. "I guess that's about the best we can hope for with your TAC officer burning holes in your back. Be that as it may, we will proceed. Margery will be recording the proceedings, and TAC Officer Myers is here as a witness. Is that acceptable?"

"Yes, sir," Richard said.

Margery was the commandant's battle computer. Richard noticed the commandant's battle helmet sitting on the corner of his desk. Margery would be embedded in a hardened, brerellium-steel shell deep inside the battle helmet.

"TAC Officer Myers," said the commandant. "You've made a charge of attempted murder against cadet 832. Is that correct?"

"Yes, sir."

"That's a very serious charge," said the commandant. "Present your evidence?"

"Sir, a review of the simulation's video files will show that cadet 832 removed the isotopic battery from his phase rod and placed it on the neck armor of cadet 215. He was preparing to detonate the battery with a phase rifle when we declared an emergency and stopped the simulation."

"I've already reviewed the video file," said the commandant. "Your charges against cadet 832 also include a lesser charge of cheating."

"Yes, sir. During the course of the simulation, the technicians detected a use of Power to perform telekinesis on a rock in order to distract cadet 215. Since cadet 832 hasn't been trained in telekinesis, the technicians believe he must have smuggled a mind booster into the test environment. I concur."

"Was any unauthorized equipment found on the cadet?" asked the commandant.

"No, sir. However, the technicians haven't yet completed a full sweep of the simulation area. They should be finished by 2100 hours."

"Cadet 832," said the commandant. "You've heard TAC Officer

Myers's account of the incident. Is it accurate?"

"Sir," Richard said. "TAC Officer Myers's account is partially accurate. I was preparing to detonate part of an isotopic battery on the neck seal of cadet 215's armor when the simulation was stopped. It would have cracked the seal on the cadet's armor, but wouldn't have seriously injured her. As to the lesser charge, I didn't smuggle any unauthorized pieces of equipment into the simulation area. Nor did I break any test rules during the course of the simulation."

"The detonation of even a small portion of an isotopic battery can be deadly," said the commandant. "Are you saying your technical skills are so high that you can accurately judge to the milligram, the amount of battery required to crack the seal without injuring the person inside? Were you somehow connected to the tele-network and receiving detailed specifications from the central computer?"

"No, sir," Richard said.

"Then explain," said the commandant. "Otherwise, I'll have no recourse except to recommend a court-martial."

Richard hesitated a moment. He was getting into a gray area. A misstep would get him kicked out of the Academy at the least or sent to military prison on Diajor at the worst. All cadets were connected to a Power reserve else they wouldn't have been selected as a wizard scout cadet. However, it was unusual for cadets to use their Power before receiving training. It happened, but it was unusual.

"Sir," Richard said. "I saw the amount of energy stored in the portion of the isotopic battery that I broke off and placed on cadet 215's armor. I saw how much energy it would take to crack the seal without causing injury to the cadet."

"Wh—" began TAC Officer Myers from behind Richard.

A stern look from the commandant cut him off. "I see. Are you claiming you're a diviner?"

A diviner was a rare type of wizard scout who specialized in manipulating Power links. Their abilities allowed them to 'see' the Power in objects, as well as the Power links and energy, flows between objects. Only one out of a thousand wizard scouts were diviners, and it normally took years of post-Academy training to develop their skills to a useable level.

"I don't claim anything, sir," Richard said. "I'm merely saying I was able to determine the size of the battery required to break the seal on the armor based upon what I could see."

"TAC Officer Myers," said the commandant. "You look like you're bursting to say something. Out with it."

"Sir, cadet 832's records don't indicate a potential for diviner abilities or any other advanced skills. Additionally, with the possible exception of combat training, his scores during the past two years of pre-Academy training will show cadet 832 barely meets the minimum required to stay in wizard scout training. As the commandant knows, it would take years of diviner training to obtain the proficiency level required to accurately determine that a broken-off piece of isotopic battery would be non-lethal."

"Cadet 832," said the commandant. "If you had any indication of diviner abilities, it should have been listed on your application for the Intergalactic Wizard Scout Academy. When you volunteered for wizard scout training, the members of your review board undoubtedly drilled you. They would've documented every nuance of your abilities that you had ever noticed during your life. Did you fail to tell them about an ability to see Power links?"

Again, Richard felt as if he was on the edge of a very dark pit with a bottom that could only be his doom. He'd known things were different for him but never mentioned it. He really did want to be a wizard scout and hated to stir up trouble.

"Sir, I never filled out an application for the Academy, nor did I volunteer for wizard scout training. Additionally, I was never reviewed by a board or anyone else. My commander called me into his office two years ago and told me I had orders to report for pre-Academy training. I was escorted by security onto a space destroyer heading for Velos that very afternoon. I was put into deep sleep immediately upon boarding. I woke up two months later in a shuttle just as it was landing at the pre-Academy barracks. Other than a Power reserve test that first day at pre-Academy, I've never been tested or questioned about any skills or abilities."

The commandant looked past Richard. "TAC Officer Myers. What does cadet 832's application and records indicate about his abilities?"

"Sir, cadet 832's records prior to his assignment to the pre-Academy are restricted access. I'm unable to affirm or deny cadet

832's claims. I can verify that his Power reserve test upon assignment to the pre-Academy shows he has the smallest Power reserve of any previous or existing wizard scout cadet."

The commandant said, "Didn't you think it strange a cadet's records were restricted access?"

"Yes, sir, but I assumed he had political backers who had used loopholes to get him into wizard scout training. His Power reserve test meets the minimum requirements, but a standard review board would never have approved him for the Academy."

"Hmm. We'll soon see," said the commandant. "Margery, pull up cadet 832's application and previous testing records. Are there any indications of diviner abilities?"

"Unable to comply, Thomas," said a soft, feminine voice from the battle helmet's external speakers. "Access is restricted."

"Nonsense," said the commandant. "Use commandant override."

"Insufficient override authority, Thomas," said Margery. "Records are marked council-restricted."

"Bullsh..." the commandant began before he caught himself. He paused for a few moments, then said, "Margery, are you connected to the tele-network?"

"Yes, Thomas."

"Then place a priority message to Councilwoman Janice Deluth. She should be in the Aloran planetary administration building on the planet Risors."

After a dozen heartbeats, Margery said, "I have contact with Councilwoman Deluth's battle helmet. She is presently in a meeting, but I'm assured she should be out shortly."

Richard was astonished at the turn of events. Councilwoman Deluth was an old wizard scout who'd went into politics after her Power reserve was irreparably damaged during the Teton war. She'd gone on to hold a position on the Imperial High Council. It was the highest political office ever held by a wizard scout.

The commandant looked at Richard and said, "You must have some high-level friends to get your records restricted from the Academy's commandant. You'll find I have some high-level friends as well."

Richard kept his thoughts to himself. *Why bother trying to explain? I could tell them I was raised in an orphanage and that the few friends I made in the military are all dead. I could tell them I'm mystified why my records are restricted. In the end, what would it matter? They'd never believe me anyway.*

Four minutes passed without anyone saying a word. Finally, the commandant stiffened in his seat and said, "Yes, Janice. It's Thomas. ... It's good to hear your voice too. ... Yes. It has been a long time."

It took Richard a moment to figure out Margery was somehow silently transmitting the councilwoman's part of the conversation to the commandant while he was replying aloud. After a few more pleasantries, the commandant said, "Well, Janice, I have an unusual situation here. One of our cadets has his application and testing records marked council-restricted access. ... Yes, that's what I think. It has to be a mistake. ... Yes, if you would be so kind. He's cadet 832 of the 637th cohort. ... Yes, I'll wait."

After about thirty seconds, the commandant said, "Are you sure? Everyone has to have an application and testing records. ... No, I believe you, Janice. It just seems strange. ... Is there anything else strange in his records? Any help would be appreciated. ... Pretty generic, huh? ... Yes, I understand. ... That would be great. If you find out anything, please let me know. ... Same to you. ... Bye, Janice."

The commandant said nothing for a long time. Both Richard and TAC Officer Myers remained silent. Richard had a feeling the commandant was in deep conversation with his battle computer. After almost a minute of silence, the commandant turned his attention to Richard and stared at him intently.

Richard saw a small line of Power move from the commandant towards him. When the Power touched him, he felt a tingle at the base of his neck. Richard didn't need anyone to tell him he was being probed. After a couple of minutes, the tingling stopped, and the line of Power withdrew back to the commandant.

"Who trained you in shields?" said the commandant.

"I don't understand, sir," Richard said.

"You have a stealth shield up. It's pretty crude, but I doubt you could create it without training. Who trained you?"

Richard had no idea what he was talking about. *What the hell is a stealth shield?* "Sir, I'm not familiar with the term 'stealth shield.' I haven't been trained by anyone, to the best of my knowledge."

The commandant looked thoughtfully at Richard. Finally, he said, "TAC Officer Myers, you will confine cadet 832 to his barracks until I make further inquiries."

"Yes, sir," said TAC Officer Myers.

Richard thought he detected a note of disappointment in his TAC officer's voice and figured he'd hoped the commandant would convene a court martial that very evening.

"As for you, cadet 832," said the commandant. "I'm curious. Why didn't you mention to your TAC officer or anyone else that you didn't apply for wizard scout training? Didn't you think it was unusual?"

"Sir, yes, sir!" said Richard. He added the second "sir" since he figured the inquiry was over. Apparently, he was still a wizard scout cadet. "Sir, this cadet assumed it was a mistake, sir. However, I've never quit anything in my whole life. Since I like challenges, I figured I would see if I had what it takes to be a wizard scout. Sir!"

The commandant looked past Richard. "Apparently, cadet 832 enjoys challenges, TAC Officer Myers. If by some miracle I decide not to kick him out of the Academy, maybe you can help him find some."

"With pleasure, sir," said TAC Officer Myers.

"You're dismissed, cadet 832. Report back to your barracks." With those words, he looked down at the computer display on his desk. Richard was just another worm again.

Richard jumped to his feet, stood at attention, and said, "Sir, yes, sir!" He did as near a perfect about face as he'd ever done and marched at the double out of the commandant's office.

CHAPTER 4

Richard woke up and glanced at the clock on his desk. It displayed 04:59 in glowing green numbers. He strained to hear the sharp footfalls of a TAC officer walking down the hallway towards one of the four common latrines. They almost always checked to make sure none of the cadets were trying to cheat the system by getting up early.

The clock's glowing display changed to 05:00. Almost immediately, the hallway's bright overhead lighting snapped on. Richard heard the sound of two hundred and fifteen other cadets scrambling to be first to one of the common latrines. Richard eased himself out from underneath his blanket in a well-practiced maneuver to keep the well-starched sheets from being wrinkled and reached into his wall locker for his physical training uniform. With two quick pulls, he had his shorts and sweatshirt on. They were quickly followed by socks and exercise boots. Dressed, he turned back to his bed. With a few well-practiced tugs, he had the sheets back in tight, regulation order. Richard glanced at the clock again. 05:02. He grabbed his shaving kit and sprinted for the nearest latrine.

When he'd first arrived for pre-Academy training, he'd thought there was a misprint on the daily schedule. Richard had been in the military for almost two years before he'd arrived for training. Anyone with prior military experience knew it was impossible to wake troops up at 0500 hours and expect them to be in formation at 0505 hours, fully shaved and teeth brushed. He'd been wrong.

21

Not only did the TAC officers expect it, but woe-be-unto any cadets who were even a second late for morning formation.

By the time Richard got to the latrine, it was already starting to clear out. The first wave of cadets had already run back to their rooms to make last minute adjustments. Richard normally liked to have first shot at the sinks, but not today. Since he was still confined to the barracks, he was exempt from morning formation. He figured he'd take his time this morning. Besides, the other cadets needed the extra time more than he did. Richard made a quick swipe with his razor, ran his toothbrush under the faucet to get it wet, and headed back to his room while scrubbing his teeth. He walked briskly. Although he wouldn't be in formation, the TAC officers would still expect him to be standing in front of his room, ready for inspection.

"It's four minutes after," someone yelled from down the hallway.

As Richard turned into the doorway of his room, two hundred and fifteen sets of running feet were racing for the stairwells leading outside. Richard placed his razor and toothbrush in their proper positions in his wall locker, then stood at attention beside the door of his room.

Beep. Beep. Beep.

The fifteen-second warning alarm sounded in the deserted hallway. That is, deserted except for the presence of TAC Officer Gaston Myers.

"You're off confinement as of now, cadet 832," yelled TAC Officer Myers. "You'd better not be late for my formation or you'll be sorry you were ever born!"

Richard cursed Myers under his breath and raced for the stairs. He took them four at a time.

Beep. Beep.

The five-second alarm sounded. Richard raced out the door in a futile attempt to get to his spot in the company formation. He knew he'd never make it in time.

Beep.

The final alarm sounded at 0505 hours.

"You're late, 832!" shouted a nearby TAC officer. "Everybody can thank cadet 832 for some extra calisthenics this morning. Formation is a group effort. If one cadet is late, every cadet is late.

Now everybody down and give me thirty!"

Some of the nearby cadets made half-hearted grumbles at Richard, but nothing serious. They all knew the TAC officers would always find some reason for extra calisthenics. The bad news was that it was a weekend, so there were no classes. The TACs had all day to give the cadets their undivided attention. The morning wore on with one torturous exercise after another. The only break was when they got the privilege of running from one end of the parade field to the other. It was 0830 hours before the TAC officers finally ordered them back into formation.

"I hope you're awake by now, cadets!" said TAC Officer Myers. "Today is a special day. We're going to call it Cadet 832 Day. It seems cadet 832 told the commandant he liked challenges. Well, TAC officers like challenges too. So for this special Cadet 832 Day, we're going to strive to help all of you get all the challenges you can handle. Next formation is at zero nine hundred with full field gear. Too bad you missed breakfast, but since cadet 832 didn't make our little road march yesterday, we're going to do it again today. You can eat when you get to the top of hill 3025. That is, assuming you get there by noon. Dismissed!"

Richard ran back into the barracks with the other cadets. Many of them let him know how much they appreciated the opportunity to participate in Cadet 832 Day. "Thanks, 832!", "Idiot!", "What the hell were you thinking?", and "Why don't you just DFR?" were some of the nicer comments.

Richard let the snide remarks roll off his back. They were just being used in one of TAC Officer Myers's mind games. Next week, a different cadet would probably be the company scapegoat.

As Richard approached the door of his room, he spied a few of his personal items strewn in the hallway. His heart dropped to the pit of his stomach. He knew what to expect even before he entered his room. It had been exploded by one of the TAC officers. His tightly made bed was overturned and the bedding was tossed across the room. Every item in his wall locker had been thrown helter-skelter from one end of the room to the other.

It's going to be a long day, Richard thought as he turned his bed upright and straightened the mattress.

"They've got you zeroed in this time, 832," said a voice from the doorway.

Cadet 147 was Richard's acting platoon sergeant, at least for this week. Leadership positions among the cadets rotated frequently because the TAC officers had a habit of taking out their wrath on the acting leaders whenever their cadets screwed up. Cadet 147 was an exception to the rule. He'd been acting platoon sergeant for almost three months. That was a lifetime in pre-Academy terms. Richard had a lot of respect for him. He was an older man, probably in his mid-thirties, and a good leader. Richard was certain he was prior military. Probably a senior officer, but 147 had never acknowledged such. Why a senior officer would want to go through the misery of a worm school like the Intergalactic Wizard Scout Academy was beyond him. He figured everyone had their own little secrets.

"Yeah," said Richard. "Myers is unhappy I didn't get kicked out of the Academy yesterday. By the way, 147, I'm sorry about 215. I know she was your friend."

"So am I," he said. "But the way attrition is going, we'll probably all be DFR'd before we can graduate." 147 looked around at the mess in Richard's room. "Why don't you get your field gear ready and then go shower. Once some of the others in the platoon are ready, we'll help you get your room back in shape."

"Thanks, but that's not necessary. I can handle it."

"Nonsense," said 147. "Cadets stick together. You'd do the same for us."

Richard wasn't sure that was true but kept quiet. He'd been raised in an orphanage until he was fifteen, then spent three long years living hand-to-mouth on the streets. Those were rough years. He'd learned the hard way you had to look out for yourself because no one else was going to give you anything for free. When he turned eighteen, Richard joined the military and discovered he had skills and abilities that were valued by his peers. After his initial boot training, he'd been assigned to a coveted position in marine recon. His eighteen months there were the most rewarding and happiest time of his life. Of course, the downside was the numerous enemies of the Intergalactic Empire trying to kill him on occasion, but nothing was perfect.

With the help of several other cadets, Richard's room was back in shape quickly. This was not the first time TAC officers had exploded a cadet's room. Richard made a silent promise to assist in the cleanup the next time a cadet was on the receiving end of a TAC officer's wrath.

Liz was right, Richard thought. *I haven't been very friendly or helpful to the other cadets, but I'll force myself to do better. Too bad she had to get DFR'd for me to figure out friends can come in handy.*

The TAC officers were in rare form during the road march to the top of hill 3025. Every few hundred yards, they had the formation stop at a hastily improvised torture device. In one location, the cadets were divided into teams of ten and forced to hold a five-meter long wooden pole at arm's length. In another location, a huge pit had been dug, and all two hundred and sixteen cadets were put in the pit at the same time. Then they were told the last one out would be excused from the remainder of the road march. It didn't take long for the smaller cadets to team up against the largest cadets and toss them out of the pit. After five frantic minutes, cadet 303 was the sole remaining cadet in the pit. She was a short native of the planet Cremia, but feisty and never gave up. She laughed and waved playfully at the other cadets as one of the TAC officers drove her past them while they were marching up the steepest part of the hill.

Richard smiled. It was hard for anyone to get mad at 303. She seemed to be eternally good-natured, and most of the cadets in the company protected her as if she were their own sister.

Eventually, they reached the top of the hill and were fed a well-deserved lunch. No cadets had fallen out during the march, but many of them were hurting more than they would like to admit. Richard was in better shape than most since he'd missed the march on the previous day.

After a short lunch, the TACs marched the cadets to an open area swarming with technicians. They were busy setting up three-meter-high posts to form thirty-meter-squares. Richard counted three rows of seven squares. The TAC officers divided the cadets into teams of ten with the six odd cadets being spread out among the other teams. TAC Officer Myers personally took charge of Richard's team and double-timed them to the farthest square.

"This is different," panted 303. She'd rejoined her squad when they reached the top of the hill. As it so happened, 303 was assigned to Richard's team.

"They're holo-squares," said 147, who had also been assigned to Richard's team. "They're only used for advanced training because they're so expensive. I guess we've joined the big boys now."

"What's that?" said 303 with a mischievous smile. "You mean the big *girls*, don't you? You are aware since the last simulation, we females outnumber you males?"

"I hadn't noticed," said 147. "Had you, 832?"

Richard rarely participated in the friendly banter cadets used to vent their stress. However, fresh from 215's chastisement to be friendlier, Richard took advantage of the opening. "Well, to tell the truth, 147, I've never really paid attention. Are there females in our cohort?"

"Oh," said 303, sounding a little surprised. "Cadet 832 does talk outside of a classroom. Well, 832, you can't fool me. I happen to know cadet 647 and you had a few hookups before she was DFR'd. So don't try to tell me you don't notice females in the unit."

Richard turned a little red at the mention of 647. They'd been pretty close during their first six months of training, but he thought they'd been discrete. Apparently, they hadn't been as discrete as he'd assumed.

"Oh, ho!" laughed another cadet in their team. "I think cadet 832 is actually blushing."

Several of the other members of the team laughed good-naturedly.

"Silence in the ranks!" said TAC Officer Myers. "We'll see if you feel like laughing after a few minutes in the holo-square."

They reached the square formed by metallic posts. All but two of the technicians had departed.

"Is it ready?" said TAC Officer Myers.

"Yes, wizard scout," said the senior sergeant. "We've got it hooked up into the tele-network. Your battle computer should have no trouble controlling the training scenarios."

"Fine," said TAC Officer Myers. He removed a rounded piece of dull black plastic off his hip. As he flipped the elongated plastic in his hand, it expanded into the shape of a wizard scout battle helmet. He placed the close-fitting helmet on his head.

The sergeant hadn't moved.

"Is there something else?" asked TAC Officer Myers.

"Wizard scout," the sergeant said. "The specs for this holo-square were different than the others. Those are full-force rays on the holo-posts. The specs were specific, and they were signed by Imperial High Command. But I'm concerned. Full-force rays can be deadly if not handled correctly."

"I'm well aware of the specs for this holo-square, sergeant," said TAC Officer Myers. "All is as it should be." When the sergeant didn't move, TAC Officer Myers said, "If you have any concerns, you should address them with Imperial High Command. In the meantime, you're interrupting our training. That will be all."

The sergeant hesitated. Wizard scouts weren't officers, but then again, they weren't enlisted soldiers either. They were a strange, gray area between officers and enlisted. Still, they were skilled specialists, and most military personnel gave wizard scouts well-deserved respect.

"As you say, wizard scout," said the sergeant. "I'll be sending a protest up the chain of command."

"You do that," said TAC Officer Myers to the back of the retreating sergeant. With that, he turned to the cadets. "As you may have gathered, our training is going to be a little different this afternoon. If it's a little tougher than normal, you can thank cadet 832 and his preference for challenges."

Richard felt nine sets of eyes turn to him. He was beginning to hate the word 'challenges.'

"A holo-square," said TAC Officer Myers, "is an advanced, simulation device used to train special operation teams in scenarios that would be deadly if attempted under actual conditions. It's a very expensive piece of equipment, but you'll be seeing a lot of it during the next four years. In spite of my protests to the contrary, the higher ups believe you're now ready for actual Academy training. As such, you're going to be introduced to scenarios reflecting actual combat conditions. Are there any questions?"

Silence. No one ever asked TAC Officer Myers a question. He was not one of those who believed there was no such thing as a stupid question; quite the contrary. TAC Officer Myers believed every question asked by a cadet was a stupid question.

"Fine," said TAC Officer Myers. "Then since you're all experts, I think we can begin. Cadet 303, since you missed the last part of the road march, you can go first." Pointing to a pile of black leather-looking clothing on the ground, TAC Officer Myers said, "Put it on."

"Sir! Yes, sir," said cadet 303. She ran to the pile of black clothing and started to pull on a pair of pants over her training shorts.

"No, you idiot!" said TAC Officer Myers. "That's a wizard scout training uniform. You have to be bare-skinned."

"Sir! Yes, sir," said cadet 303 as she hurriedly began to strip off her clothing.

Stripping naked in front of other cadets was not that big of a deal. They'd all shared common latrines and showers for the last two years. Still, Richard couldn't help but notice 303 had a very nice body. She was small but well-shaped. 303 turned a light shade of pink as she removed her clothing. It was one thing to not have the protection of clothing when everyone else was naked. It was a little different out in the open air with nine other cadets staring at you. Apparently, TAC Officer Myers thought so as well.

"What are the rest of you waiting for?" yelled TAC Officer Myers. "Don't you see the other piles of clothing? Do I have to hand feed you idiots everything? Find the pile with your number on it and get dressed."

Richard ran along with the other cadets as they hurried to find the pile with their number. He had a feeling the last one dressed would feel the wrath of TAC Officer Myers. But in spite of his efforts, he did not find anything with his number. Soon, all the available piles were occupied by other cadets.

"Well, 832," TAC Officer Myers said as Richard looked around confused. "I don't believe you'll need a training uniform. They provide far too much protection for someone with your high skills and abilities. This training wouldn't be a challenge for you if you were wearing armor. All you'll need are these goggles. Put them on." TAC Officer Myers tossed a pair of goggles in Richard's direction.

Richard caught them with his left hand, then donned the goggles. Two ear plugs dangled from the strap, so he placed them in his ears. The ear plugs were lightweight and didn't seem to affect his hearing, although he did hear what he thought was the sound of a stiff breeze. He was surprised when he looked back at the holo-square. The area inside the square was no longer the open area of the hilltop. Instead, it appeared to be a frozen, wind-blown wasteland.

The wonder of holograms, Richard thought.

The other cadets were soon dressed in their training uniforms. They weren't actual wizard scout battle suits, of course. Those would be issued later, once the class had been reduced further. Instead, the pants, top, and boots appeared to be made out of thick black leather. The helmet appeared similar to a wizard scout's battle helmet, but Richard doubted it had any of the advanced electronics. They were just too expensive to waste on first-year cadets. However, they did have full-face visors, which each of the cadets pulled down. Richard assumed they served the same purpose as his goggles.

"Cadet 303," said TAC Officer Myers. "I believe the best way to learn is through experience. Enter the holo-square."

As cadet 303 moved to a nearby gate in the square, a utility vehicle with a large red cross surrounded by blue stars drove up and parked near TAC Officer Myers. Two medics got out carrying bags.

"This is serious crap," whispered a nearby cadet to her buddy.

"You'll go next, 422," said TAC Officer Myers. "This is so obviously boring that you have to carry on a conversation with your buddy. You'll go after her, 815, since you had time to listen."

Neither Richard nor any of the other cadets said another word. As he watched 303 enter the holo-square, Richard noticed her training uniform take on the look of an actual wizard scout battle suit. He'd never seen a wizard scout in a full battle suit in real life but had seen them in plenty of training videos, so he knew what they looked like. Cadet 303's battle suit included a utility belt with a phase rod on her left side and what appeared to be a hand blaster on her right hip. Richard watched as she removed the blaster and looked at its battery indicator. She must have liked what she saw because she placed it back in its holster. Next, she removed her phase rod and performed a function check. A meter long shaft of metal was thrust out of the handle, and small, red arcs of energy climbed up and down the shaft.

It looks like a full-powered phase rod, Richard thought. *What's Myers up to?*

Richard didn't have to wait long to find out. Through his ear plugs, he heard a series of howls. He looked at the far end of the holo-square. The distance did not appear to be limited to the actual physical thirty meters. Instead, Richard thought he could make out a dozen white shapes in the distance moving low to the ground and heading in 303's direction. She saw them too. She ran to a shoulder-high boulder and quickly scrambled to the top. Cadet 303 then drew her blaster and stood facing the oncoming creatures. Richard thought she looked impressive standing defiantly on top of the boulder with a blaster in one hand and a phase rod in the other. The tight-fitting training uniform highlighted her feminine figure. Like all cadets, there wasn't an ounce of fat on her. Two years of pre-Academy training had hardened her into a deadly killing machine.

As the creatures drew closer, they took on form. They were all white except for their black noses and fiery-red eyes. They were about half a meter high at the shoulder, and they had six legs. While they weren't huge creatures, Richard could see impressive fangs protruding from their open mouths. Every once in a while one of the creatures would raise its head in a blood-curdling howl. They approached 303 at a dead run. When they were about fifty meters away, she began firing her blaster. She dropped three of them quickly. The survivors started weaving in and out among each other as if they were trying to confuse her aim. Whether intentional or not, the tactic worked. Cadet 303 missed several shots before she was finally able to drop two more of the creatures. Then they were on her, gathering at the base of the boulder and jumping up to snap at her legs. She took out two more with the blaster before one of the creatures bit one of her legs and pulled her off the boulder. Cadet 303 slammed the creature in the head with her phase rod as they fell. Its yelp of pain cut off abruptly as its head burst open in a spray of green liquid.

Cadet 303 rolled as she hit the ground and made two quick swings with her phase rod as she gained her feet. Her strokes failed to connect with the fast moving creatures, but it did keep them at bay long enough for her to fire a round from her blaster. She hit one of the creatures in the chest knocking it backward. As if on command, the three remaining creatures charged 303 simultaneously. She shot one in the head with her blaster and hit another in the side with her phase rod. The energy of the phase rod must have destroyed the insides of the creature because it flopped motionless to the ground. The third creature didn't falter. Its jump carried it straight at 303. It grabbed her throat in its big mouth. Cadet 303 was carried over backward by the momentum of the creature's charge. They both hit the ground hard, but the creature was able to maintain its grip. The creature shook its head violently from side to side in an apparent attempt to break 303's neck. She had lost both the phase rod and the blaster during her fall, so she beat the creature's head with her gloved fist in an attempt to free herself from the its grip.

"Sir! Stop the simulation, sir," pleaded cadet 147 who'd seen all he could stand. "It's killing her."

"Silence!" said TAC Officer Myers without looking at 147.

Richard continued watching the grim scenario to his front. One of 303's flopping hands grabbed hold of a rock on the ground. She slammed it into the side of the creature's head. It made a muffled yelp, but it didn't release its grip. Cadet 303 slammed the rock into the creature's head again. This time it gave a yelp of pain and released its grip. It backed off a couple of steps whimpering. Cadet 303 dove at the creature and slammed the rock into its head once more. It fell to its knees. She repeated the process a half dozen times until the creature's head was just a bloody splatter on the ground. With the obvious death of the creature, 303 dropped the rock and fell on her back.

The holo-square wavered. The frozen wasteland was replaced with the grass-covered top of hill 3025.

"Medics," snapped TAC Officer Myers.

The two medics ran into the holo-square and removed cadet 303's helmet. They worked on her for a minute or so. Before long, one of them said, "She'll be all right, wizard scout. She's bruised, but her neck isn't broken. The creature's teeth didn't penetrate the armor around her neck."

"Take her to see TAC Officer Shatstot by the mess tent," said TAC Officer Myers. "Have him give her the once over. Then get back here. I've no doubt we're going to need you again."

The medics helped 303 to their vehicle. As she limped by, Richard thought he saw blood flowing from a hole in her leg armor. He assumed the creature that grabbed her on the boulder must have penetrated the armor as it dragged her off. Richard wasn't overly concerned for 303 since her neck wasn't broken. TAC Officer Shatstot was a healer. From what he'd been told, many wizard scouts had healing abilities in addition to their normal wizard scout ones. While all wizard scouts could heal themselves, TAC Officer Shatstot was able to heal others. Having seen soldiers die due to lack of medical care, Richard thought the ability to heal others was a mighty useful skill set to have.

Richard felt his biggest concern was the seriousness of TAC Officer Myers's training scenario. Pre-Academy training had been tough over the last two years. They'd had their share of injuries, and even one death, but none of their TAC officers had ever gone out of their way to seriously harm the cadets. Richard was concerned the rules had changed. From the expressions of the other cadets on his team, he wasn't the only one with concerns.

Myers isn't playing around this time, Richard thought. *The guy is out for blood, and he's already got some.*

Fortunately, cadet 303 had survived her training scenario, but just barely. Richard wondered what was going to happen when it was his turn to enter the holo-square. He wouldn't have the advantage of armor. *I'll bet Myers won't even allow me to have a weapon.*

Once the medical vehicle drove off with cadet 303, TAC Officer Myers turned to cadet 147. "You are relieved of command, 147," he said. "You are to report to the TAC officer on duty tonight for punishment."

"Sir! Yes, sir," said 147.

"Cadet 303 will now be the platoon sergeant," TAC Officer Myers said. "She's shown she is resourceful and doesn't quit or whine under pressure. You could all learn from her." When no one said anything, he said, "You're up next, 422. Enter the holo-square."

Each of the cadets took their turn in the holo-square. Having seen 303's encounter, 422 did better and was able to kill the last of the creatures before any could drag her off the boulder. After her success, TAC Officer Myers upped the ante a little by adding an extra creature each time a new cadet entered the holo-square. During the next two hours, three more cadets had to be transported by the medics to see TAC Officer Shatstot. One of the cadets was seriously injured with a compound fracture.

Cadet 147 was next to last in the holo-square. As he was preparing to enter, cadets from some of the other teams were marched up by their TAC officers and positioned around the perimeter of the holo-square. As soon as 147 entered the holo-square, a series of howls sounded. A full score of the creatures charged in 147's direction. Cadet 147 climbed the boulder just like the previous cadets, but instead of immediately firing his blaster, he kept it holstered. With both hands free, he twisted the top off his phase rod and slid out its isotopic battery. He allowed the now useless phase rod to drop to the ground as he pulled out his hand blaster. Taking careful aim, he shot the three foremost creatures. The others were in a tight pack behind their leaders. When they were just meters away, he threw the isotopic battery in their direction. Whether he was just lucky or one hell of a shot, the round from his blaster hit the battery just as it was over the densest part of the pack.

Boom!

The white flash from the exploding battery blinded Richard. When his vision cleared, he looked at the holo-square. The pack of creatures had been decimated, and the few remaining ones still on their feet were staggering around barely able to walk. Apparently, cadet 147 had been blown off the boulder. He was just rising to a standing position when Richard's vision cleared. Once cadet 147 was on his feet, he walked around the boulder and began putting the dazed creatures out of their misery with well-placed shots from his blaster. It was over in less than a minute, and not a single creature had touched 147.

The cadets surrounding the holo-square began cheering, and Richard joined in enthusiastically. He didn't mind that 147 had used his trick with the phase rod's isotopic battery. After all, imitation was the highest form of flattery as far as Richard was concerned.

The hologram ended, and cadet 147 exited the holo-square. By this time, all the remaining teams had joined the crowd in time to see 147's victory. The noise from the cadets was deafening. Richard glanced at TAC Officer Myers. His mouth was clenched tight, and his eyes seemed to blaze as 147 walked past, but he said nothing. When 147 got even with Richard, his ex-platoon sergeant gave him a wink and a smile.

"Thanks for the idea," 147 said as he passed by.

"That's enough," said TAC Officer Myers.

The cheering stopped as if it had been cut off with a switch.

"For those of you who just joined us," said TAC Officer Myers. "This is a fully functional holo-square. That means the force beams are designed to simulate the actions and strength of the things being depicted in the hologram. Whether it's a blaster round, an explosion, the effects of a phase rod, or the bite of some creature, the force beams ensure the damage accurately emulates actual combat conditions. It's all controlled by computers through the tele-network."

"You cadets not on 147's team were fortunate," said TAC Officer Myers, "because your holo-squares were set at one-fourth power for today's training. That percentage will be increased in the months ahead as your level of training increases. Eventually, you will be training in holo-squares at one hundred percent emulation. Cadets can, and have, died during holo-square training. I doubt your cohort will be an exception."

The cadets remained silent.

"For demonstration purposes," said TAC Officer Myers, "this team's holo-square is at full power. In keeping with Cadet 832 Day, I have a special challenge for cadet 832. I was going to provide him with a phase rod for his training scenario. However, since cadet 147 demonstrated how a phase rod's battery can be used as a last-ditch explosive device, I've changed the scenario. I would highly recommend in the future none of you follow 147's example. Any cadet doing so during future training scenarios will immediately be DFR'd. To ensure cadet 832 isn't tempted to so use his phase rod, he'll be provided with a slightly lower-tech offensive weapon."

Richard thought he saw an evil grin on TAC Officer Myers's face as he said, "Enter the holo-square, cadet 832. That is unless you'd like to turn in your DFR right now."

Richard didn't bother replying as he walked towards the holo-square's entrance.

"You can do it, 832!" said 147.

"Damn right, you can!" said cadet 303 who'd rejoined the team earlier.

"You're relieved of command, 303!" said TAC Officer Myers. "Cadets do not curse. You will report to the TAC officer on duty tonight for punishment. Cadet 147, you'll report for punishment for the rest of the week. Cadet 422, you're now acting platoon sergeant."

"Sir! Yes, sir," said the three cadets in unison.

CHAPTER 5

As soon as Richard stepped into the holo-square, the scenery of hill 3025 was replaced by a desert landscape. Richard had never been in a holo-square before, and he was amazed by the realism. The heat from the hot desert sun blazing overhead was overpowering. He could even feel bits of sand blown about by the wind hitting his face. Richard began to appreciate the tension the other cadets must have been experiencing during their training sessions.

Richard saw no evidence of the cadets he knew ringed the holo-square's perimeter, nor could he see any of the holo-square's posts. As far as he could discern, the desert stretched out for kilometers in all directions. He turned in a full circle to view the horizon. Not a living thing could be seen anywhere. He did notice a glint of light from a spot in the sand a few meters from his position. Richard walked over and kicked at the sand. He saw a leather wrapped handle. Reaching down, he drew a short sword out of the loose sand. The blade of the sword was about the length of his forearm and as wide at the base as three of his fingers. The sword was unadorned and plain. Richard lightly touched the edge of the blade with his thumb. He drew blood. The sword was razor sharp.

What has Myers gotten me into? Richard thought. *I'm obviously in a different place than the others. Will I be facing the same creatures?*

Richard tried to listen for the sounds of any howls, but he heard nothing other than the blowing wind. Next, he concentrated on his surroundings with his mind. He couldn't sense any living creatures, but he did 'see' flows of energy around him.

I wonder if it's the holo-square's force beams?

He wasn't sure, but as he continued to concentrate, Richard noticed several energy flows merging together at a point to his right. He took a few hesitant steps in the direction of the merged energy. As he walked, he noticed two horn-like objects begin to slowly rise out of the sand. He stopped.

"What the hell is that?" Richard said aloud in bewilderment. They looked like the horns of a bull to Richard, but if they were, they belonged to the biggest bull he'd ever seen. The sand around the horns shifted, and the head of a brown bull protruded from the sand. Richard began backing up as fast as he could while still facing the emerging creature. The bull's horns and head were soon followed by a massive human chest and arms clad in ring mail. With a leap, the creature cleared the sand. The nightmarish creature reminded Richard of an old Earth legend called a Minotaur. Unlike a Minotaur, this monster before him was twice the height of a man. Also, its legs were scaled like a lizard's, and dagger-like claws protruded from its feet. The Minotaur reached into the sand near its feet and pulled out a mace with a handle as long as Richard was tall. The spiked ball at the end of the handle looked as if it must have weighed half again as much as Richard.

The Minotaur turned towards Richard and raised its mace in its massive right hand.

"Die!" it yelled.

"The hell with this," Richard said as he turned and ran as fast as he could. He braced himself to hit the sides of the holo-square, but he continued to run much farther than the thirty-meter width of the holo-square without interruption.

How does this thing work? Richard wondered.

He assumed the force beams of the holo-square must somehow be making him run in a circle, but he felt nothing strange. As far as he could determine, he was running in a straight line for all he was worth. Unfortunately, he was too slow. He heard the Minotaur quickly closing the gap between them. He realized he couldn't outrun the monster. Fatalistically, Richard turned to face the monster.

The Minotaur was closer than Richard had thought. As soon as Richard turned, he saw the creature swinging its mace in a downward stroke. Richard stepped to the left, deftly dodging the blow. He swung his sword at one of the Minotaur's arms, but the sword blade glanced off the creature's ring mail. The Minotaur pulled its mace out of the sand in preparation for another stroke. Richard took a step past the Minotaur and chopped at the back of the Minotaur's ankle hoping to sever its tendon. His sword bounced off the thick-lizard skin covering the ankle without doing noticeable damage.

With a swing of its mace, the Minotaur caught Richard in the side. However, Richard was too close to the Minotaur for the head of the mace to make contact. Instead, the wooden handle of the weapon slammed into Richard's ribs. He was able to give a little with the blow, thus partially canceling its effects, but even so, he was thrown half a dozen steps through the air. The sand cushioned his fall somewhat, but Richard still felt a burning ache in his side. He knew cracked ribs when he felt them.

Richard jumped to his feet. He did his best to ignore the pain in his side. He turned his back on the Minotaur and ran into the wind a dozen steps. Dropping to his knees, he gathered two large handfuls of sand. He made a quick turn and flung the sand up into the air towards the Minotaur. The wind caught the sand and blew it into the eyes of the charging beast. Momentarily blinded, the Minotaur raised one hand to its face in an attempt to clear its eyes. Taking advantage of the opportunity, Richard made a double-handed blow at the Minotaur's exposed kneecap. Once again, his sword blade bounced harmlessly off the Minotaur's thick-lizard skin.

"Damn!" Richard cursed.

Still partially blinded, the Minotaur kicked at Richard. The sharp talons on its feet came straight at Richard's unprotected belly. He jumped above the Minotaur's foot and grabbed hold of its leg. The momentum of the creature's kick flung him through the air, but he was able to roll as he hit the ground. A flash of pain was a forceful reminder that his ribs were still cracked.

The Minotaur made three quick strikes with its mace at Richard, but he was able to dodge the heavy weapon. The beast tried a change of tactics and lowered its head and charged. Again Richard sidestepped. However, the tip of one of the Minotaur's horns grazed his belly leaving a bloody gash. Thankfully, the wound wasn't deep even though it felt like a red-hot poker had been laid across his stomach. Richard groaned in pain. As the Minotaur rushed by, he swung his sword across the monster's nose hoping it was a sensitive area. His blow bounced harmlessly off the monster's snout.

What the hell? Richard thought. *Isn't there any place on that blasted beast this sword will penetrate?*

Richard knew his time was running out. His breathing was labored from the combined effects of the cracked ribs, exertion, and the hot desert sun. Also, he was losing blood from the cut on his belly. It was only a matter of time before the Minotaur's mace found its mark. Richard decided to take a gamble. His sole hope was that the holo-square's creation complied with the basic laws of nature.

When the Minotaur swung its mace in a mighty downward blow, Richard stepped inside the blow and ducked between the creature's legs. It wore ring mail on its chest, but it had no leggings. As he passed underneath the monster, Richard rammed his sword up with all his strength into the crevice of the Minotaur's buttocks. The sword point found its mark and slid half its length into the monster's rectum. Blood and dark bile gushed out. The Minotaur gave an agonizing roar. As Richard passed between the legs, he pulled his sword out and swung himself up onto the Minotaur's back as it kneeled over in pain. Richard scrambled to the creature's head and wrapped one arm around its thick neck. Jamming the point of his sword into the Minotaur's eye, he pulled back on the sword like a crowbar. The creature's eye popped out in a fountain of blood.

Doubly wounded, the Minotaur fell on its back. Richard rolled off the Minotaur before it hit the ground to avoid being crushed. He was up in a flash. Diving for the creature's head, Richard plunged his sword into the Minotaur's empty eye socket. The razor-sharp blade sunk into the brain. It made one final roar. It shuddered. Then it was still.

Richard rose from the ground while holding his side. He raised his sword in preparation for another attack in case the training scenario wasn't completed. He needn't have worried. As he looked around, the desert landscape melted away. It was replaced by the green grass of hill 3025. Richard saw his fellow cadets beyond the posts of the holo-square.

With arms raised, the cadets chanted, "8-3-2! 8-3-2! 8-3-2!"

Richard limped out of the holo-square with one hand holding his side and the other holding his belly in an attempt to stop the bleeding. He looked over at the control console. TAC Officer Myers didn't look pleased.

TAC Officer Myers growled, "You cursed, 832. Cadets do not curse. You will report for extra duty tonight."

Whatever, Richard thought disgustedly.

CHAPTER 6

The two medics stood waiting in the corner of the tent while TAC Officer Shatstot examined Richard's wounds. Richard noticed several of his fellow cadets glancing inside while they waited in line at the mess tent.

"It doesn't look so bad," said TAC Officer Shatstot with an almost friendly smile. "I'll have you fixed up in no time." For a TAC Officer, Richard didn't think TAC Officer Shatstot was too bad. He was almost human sometimes. Of course, he'd ream a cadet a new one if they screwed up. Still, he rarely went out of his way to devise new tortures for the overstressed cadets. That counted as being human in Richard's book.

"Sir! Thank you, sir," Richard said.

Richard sensed a line of Power snake out from TAC Officer Shatstot. The line forked into two smaller lines with one moving towards Richard's stomach and the other towards his cracked ribs. When the first of the Power lines touched Richard, he felt a response from his own Power which normally stayed well-hidden deep within him. His Power snapped out and intercepted the two lines from TAC Officer Shatstot. Richard felt a sudden shock when the two Power sources made contact. He involuntarily jumped back in his seat. TAC Officer Shatstot must have felt something too because he came up out of his seat and took a step back.

"What the—" said TAC Officer Shatstot before catching himself. "What'd you do that for? I'm trying to heal you, 832."

"Sir! Cadet 832 didn't mean to do anything, sir," Richard said.

"Are you telling me you didn't feel that?"

"Sir! Yes, sir," Richard assured the scowling TAC officer, "but I didn't do anything intentionally. It just happened, sir."

"Hmmm," said TAC Officer Shatstot as he sat back down. "Let's try that again. Make very sure you don't do anything. Don't even try to not do anything. Just sit there and do nothing."

"Sir! Yes, sir," Richard said. "I mean, I won't do or not do anything, sir." He wasn't exactly sure how you could try to not try to do anything, but he was determined to give it his best shot.

TAC Officer Shatstot unhooked his flattened battle helmet from the left rear of his utility belt. When he placed the helmet on his head, the reddish glow of a force field lowered until it was even with the tip of his nose. TAC Officer Shatstot sat back down and looked at Richard for several seconds while he probed Richard's injuries with his fingers. Richard winced once when TAC Officer Shatstot touched a particularly painful spot.

"Sorry," TAC Officer Shatstot said. Then he remained silent as if conferring with someone in private. After a few more seconds, Richard sensed a line of Power emerge from his TAC officer. It was faint and wispy. Richard was barely able to keep track of it. The line of Power kept fading and shifting, almost as if it was trying to hide. Eventually, Richard sensed the smallest sliver of Power touch his side. His Power tingled in response, but it didn't react as it had before. Instead, his Power seemed to form a barrier which gently pushed TAC Officer Shatstot's Power away.

"Well, that's interesting," said TAC Officer Shatstot as his line of Power withdrew back into him. "Apparently, you're a resistor."

"Sir! I'm a what, sir?" Richard said more than a little confused. The pain in his side and the blood dripping onto the ground from his belly wasn't helping him grasp the situation any better.

"A resistor," said TAC Officer Shatstot. "It means your Power is attuned to defensive shields and will automatically try to repel attempts to use Power on you. That includes active probes, and unfortunately for you, attempts to use healing Power on you." After a pause, TAC Officer Shatstot said, "Why didn't you tell me you were a resistor? You were bound to have been told when you were tested during your application process."

"Sir! Cadet 832 was never tested, sir."

"What?" said TAC Officer Shatstot. "That's not possible."

"Oh, it's possible," said a gruff voice from the doorway of the tent.

Richard looked over and saw TAC Officer Myers glowering at him.

"Cadet 832 is special," said TAC Officer Myers. "Apparently, he's got high-level friends who got him into the Academy without being tested."

Richard didn't bother protesting. The only thing it would accomplish was getting him more extra duty.

"So, what's up?" said TAC Officer Myers.

"It seems cadet 832 is a resistor," said TAC Officer Shatstot. "I won't be able to heal him."

TAC Officer Myers gave a snort. "It figures. So, cadet 832, you can't even be healed without screwing it up. You are by far the most pathetic cadet to ever disgrace the Academy."

Richard remained silent.

TAC Officer Shatstot stood up and motioned to the two medics. "He's all yours, guys. I can't do anything for him."

The medics knelt beside Richard and began working on his belly wound. One medic sprayed an antiseptic on the wound while the other pulled out a tube of plastic skin. Once the wound was cleansed, the second medic pushed the torn flesh together as he squeezed a thick line of plastic skin on the injury. Plastic skin was not only an adhesive it was a sealant as well. It also accelerated the healing process. Once satisfied with their handiwork, the medics began taping up his side.

"There's not much we can do for cracked ribs," said one of the medics. "We'll tape your side up to provide some stability, but it's going to bother you for a couple of weeks. You'll need to take it easy."

"Good luck with that one," said TAC Officer Shatstot.

Richard hadn't realized his TAC officer was still in the tent. A quick glance confirmed that at least TAC Officer Myers was no longer in the vicinity. He would temporarily be spared additional caustic remarks from Myers.

"Sir! Cadet 832 will be fine. Sir!"

"No, you won't be fine," said TAC Officer Shatstot. "Things are going to get a lot tougher now that you're an actual Academy cadet."

Richard unconsciously groaned. The last two years of pre-Academy training had been the toughest time of his life, barring his actual combat time of course.

"The Empire is going to start spending a lot of credits on you cadets now," said TAC Officer Shatstot. "Our job as TAC officers is to weed out any remaining cadets who can't handle the rigors of advanced wizard scout training. We need to do that before the Empire invests too heavily in you."

Richard wasn't sure if he was supposed to say anything or not, so he stayed silent. That tactic usually had the highest chance of not getting him in trouble. As he waited for the TAC officer's next move, the medics excused themselves and left the tent.

"Having you as an unregistered resistor will cause us a little bit of a quandary," said TAC Officer Shatstot.

"Sir! Sorry, sir," Richard said. Then before he could help himself, he asked, "Is being a resistor bad, sir?"

TAC Officer Shatstot gave a low chuckle. "Not if you like to work by yourself. Resistors are normally given the deep-recon missions. I don't mean the one hundred, five hundred, or even five thousand kilometer missions behind enemy lines. I mean they're given the recon missions that are light years behind enemy lines. As a wizard scout with resistor abilities, you might be the only Empire soldier on an enemy planet a score of light years away from friendly lines. Does that sound like something you'd be interested in, cadet 832?"

"Sir! Not really, sir."

TAC Officer Shatstot gave a louder chuckle this time. "Well, at least you're honest. But if by some miracle you graduate, you might not have any choice. However, you've got a more immediate problem. Resistors are supposed to be identified during application testing and registered as such. Since resistors can't be healed by other wizard scouts, they are given early training in self-healing. You're two years behind the curve, and I guarantee you that you and every other cadet in your cohort are going to get seriously injured more than once in the coming months and years. The only thing that'll help you all stay alive is the healing abilities of your TAC officers. Unfortunately, as a resistor, if you can't self-heal, you're out of luck."

"Sir! May this cadet ask a question, sir?"

"Fire away," said TAC Officer Shatstot.

"Sir! I'm pretty sure the commandant used a scan of some type on me when I was in his office the other day. My Power didn't react to him, sir."

"Ha!" laughed TAC Officer Shatstot. "The commandant's probably the best wizard scout in the galaxy. I dare say you could be fully trained in defensive shields, and he'd still be able to run an active scan on you if he desired. Being a resistor means you have the ability to specialize in stealth and defensive shields. It also means lower-level opponents might have trouble with your natural resistance. However, any wizard scout worth their salt can overcome it given a little time. Unfortunately, it doesn't work that way with healing. Your Power has to be willing to accept healing from others. As a resistor, your Power will not. That's why you're going to cause us problems during training, cadet."

"Sir! Sorry for the trouble, sir."

"Oh, you're going to be sorry, cadet 832," said TAC Officer Shatstot with another laugh. "I can just about guarantee it."

CHAPTER 7

The weekend dragged by for Richard. The TAC officers were merciless. Although Richard's side gave him a lot of trouble, he did his best to hide the pain from the TAC officers. He had no doubt TAC Officer Myers would take great pleasure in transferring him out of his training cohort for medical reasons if he got the chance.

However, all things eventually end, and after two hours of physical training the morning of the first day of the workweek, the TAC officers marched the cadets to the main gate of the Intergalactic Wizard Scout Academy. The Academy was composed of a score of half-a-kilometer long buildings separated by well-maintained parade fields. As they marched closer, Richard read a sign over the open gate.

'THROUGH THESE GATES PASS THE BEST SCOUTS IN TWO GALAXIES'

Just prior to reaching the gates, TAC Officer Myers said, "Platoon sergeants! Take charge of your platoons and march them to their classes."

"Sir! Yes, sir!" said the eight platoon sergeants in unison.

After passing through the entrance, cadet 422 marched Richard's platoon towards a building to the right of the entrance. Richard was glad to see the TAC officers remain outside the Academy's entrance. He'd been told in order to facilitate learning, TACs were forbidden in the classrooms or to even enter the Academy grounds. That was one of the perks of being real

Academy cadets.

The rest of the morning was a blur of indoctrination classes. Most of the instructors were civilians. Compared to his TAC officers, they were sweethearts. After lunch, Richard was pulled out of his platoon by an old technician and taken to a room filled with every conceivable test machine Richard could envision.

"They tell me by some administrative slip, you haven't been tested," said the old man. "We're going to remedy that situation now."

Remedy it he did. The old technician had Richard sit in various chairs while he hooked him up with all kinds of wires, hats, and monitoring clips. All Richard really remembered after three hours was an endless blur of buzzing noises accompanied by flashing lights. Every so often the old technician or one of his assistants would say, "Hmm. That's interesting." However, they never volunteered any information to Richard, and he never asked.

At the end of the three hours, Richard was taken to a room and asked to sit in a chair opposite a panel of six older people. At least he thought they were all older, but two of them were nonhumans, so he wasn't sure. One of the nonhumans asked Richard to sit and relax while they ran a few tests on him. Unlike the previous technicians, these testers didn't use machines. Instead, they remained in their chairs and poked and prodded him with lines of Power. They must have heard about TAC Officer Shatstot's experience because they worked very cautiously. Richard watched the lines of Power snake out from the six testers. The lines weaved together and formed an intricate single line that gently prodded the outer edges of Richard. Whenever his Power began to react, the tester's line of Power would withdrew and probed from another direction. The six testers were obviously experts, and they worked well as a team. After an hour and a half of probing, they told Richard he could leave. That was it. No explanation. Nothing.

By the time his testing was over, Richard's fellow cadets had finished their training for the day and returned to the tender-loving care of their TAC officers. Richard wasted no time. He double-timed the three kilometers between the Academy buildings and his pre-Academy barracks. His platoon was just leaving the mess hall when he arrived, so he discretely joined them. At least he tried to discretely join them, but a deep yell let him know his arrival had been noticed.

"Late again, cadet 832," said TAC Officer Myers. "I want everyone to thank cadet 832 for forcing you to take the scenic route to the barracks by way of the obstacle course." When no one said anything, he said again, "I said, I want everyone to thank cadet 832."

With the obvious cue, two hundred and fifteen voices said, "Thank you, cadet 832!"

With that, TAC Officer Myers had the platoon sergeants march their cadets to the obstacle course where they were subjected to two hours of hell. Eventually, TAC Officer Myers gave the order to return to the barracks. Richard assumed it was so the TAC officers would be able to get enough rest to torture them the next day.

When they finally got back to the barracks, there was barely enough time to shower and get their gear ready before the lights were turned out. Richard was just grateful no TAC officers had exploded his room that day. His last thought before the lights went out was, *This place sucks.*

The rest of the week at the Academy went similar to the first day. Classes consisted of generic indoctrination classes. Occasionally, one of the cadets would be pulled out of class for testing. The technicians left Richard alone, and he was able to remain with the other cadets for classes. Each evening after classes, the TAC officers took the cadets to various obstacles courses or long distance runs. Richard was grateful he wasn't singled out as the cause for the additional physical training. Most of the cadets pulled out for Academy testing were late returning to the barracks area. TAC Officer Myers always seemed to be there waiting to catch them in the act of attempting to slip into formation without being noticed.

During one of the team-building obstacles courses, Richard was teamed with cadets 147, 303, and his platoon sergeant, 422. The obstacle was a ten-meter-wide ladder made out of wooden poles. The rungs were spaced at uneven intervals far enough apart to require all but the tallest cadets to hang free for at least a short time while they pulled themselves up to the next rung. Cadet 303 was short even for a female, and she struggled to manage the large gaps. Cadets 422, 147, and Richard waited at the top of the 30-

meter-tall ladder for their teammate to catch up. They weren't allowed to help, but they did shout encouragements to 303 as she gamely overcame the rungs one by one.

"Come on, 303," said 422. "You're halfway here. It'll be easy sailing once you clear the top."

"Yeah," said 147. "It's a beautiful view up here. It's well worth the climb."

Richard knew he wasn't very good at good-natured bantering, but with a thought to his *be friendly* speech from Liz, he made a stab at it. "You can do it, 303. You might not be able to keep your platoon sergeant job longer than five minutes, but I'm sure you can handle this ladder."

Cadet 303 paused in her climb and looked up at him. Richard could feel the stares of 422 and 147 on him.

"Cadet 832," said 303 with a laugh. "Was that an attempt at humor? Hey, 422, I think 832 tried to make a joke."

"By the Creator," said 442 also laughing, "I think he did. That was the most pathetic joke I've ever heard, 832. Don't quit your day job."

"Yeah," agreed 147 with a big smile. "It was pathetic. But for 832, it was pretty good. I think you're almost becoming human, 832."

Richard blushed. He preferred staying incognito. Being the center of attention for making a joke was a new experience for him. He wasn't sure he liked it.

"Aw, leave him alone," said 303 in a panting voice. She'd renewed her struggle against the ladder but continued to talk while studying the best way to attack the next rung. "I like this version of 832 a whole lot better than the one we endured during pre-Academy days."

"I'll second that," said 422. "If you keep it up, 832, you might find yourself with a few friends."

"Liz, I mean 215," Richard said, "reminded me friends were important. TAC Officer Shatstot told me they were going to get harder on us now that we're actual Academy cadets. He said they were going to try and get rid of any of us who they thought couldn't make wizard scout before the Empire spent too many credits on us. I think friends are going to be very important in the days ahead. I haven't had many friends during my life."

"Wow," said 147, "that was probably the longest speech I've heard you make in the last two years."

"And the most melancholy," said 303 panting hard to catch her breath. She had just pulled herself up to the rung two levels below them. "Well, personally, I wouldn't mind having the best fighter in the company for a friend. However, I have a feeling anything good in that respect will be counterbalanced by being friends with a cadet TAC Officer Myers hates. I suspect your friends will catch some residual heat from the association."

"You're right," said Richard. "It's probably best to keep your –"

"Relax, 832," said 422 with another laugh. "She was joking. I can see we're going to have to work on your humor perception a little. But forget that for now. You said TAC Officer Shatstot told you. Are you like buddy-buddies with him now?"

"No," Richard said quickly. "He just talked quite a bit when he was trying to heal me the other day."

"Speaking of which," said 147, "how are you holding up? Are your ribs still bothering you?"

"They're not bad," Richard lied. The obstacle course had re-damaged his cracked ribs, and he felt like someone was sticking a knife in his side.

"Liar," said 303 who'd finally made the top of the ladder. "I saw you slam your side against that post during the rotating-logs climb. You should report to the medics before you damage your ribs anymore."

"No way," Richard said. "Myers would have me out on a medical before the medics finished filling out their paperwork. I'll be fine. I just need to be more careful, that's all."

"All right," said 422. "It's your funeral."

"Well," said 303, "I'd hate for you to die without a friend, so I'm going to go out on a limb. My name is Telsa Stremar. I'm from the Dreppin system, and I came to the Academy right after I graduated from the University with a degree in astral physics."

Richard didn't say anything. An awkward silence hung in the air for about five seconds.

"Okay, 832," said 147, "I guess we're going to have to work on more than your humor. You're a little short in the etiquette department as well. If a fellow cadet lowers their social shields enough to tell you their name, you're supposed to reciprocate and tell them yours. I'll show you how it's done. My name is Jerad Criteron. I was born on Terra, but my parents were military, so I've been all over. I'm thirty-eight Terran years old, and I've been told I'm the oldest human cadet to ever make it past pre-Academy training. I was a battalion commander in heavy armor with almost eighteen years of service." Holding up his hands before anyone could say anything, he said, "And why would an old man like me apply for wizard scout training? I have my reasons." Looking at Richard, he said, "Next?"

Richard listened to the yells and grunts of other candidates just beginning their climb of the ladder obstacle. He knew they didn't have much time. One of their TACs was bound to spot them sitting on the top rung of the ladder before long.

Okay, Liz, Richard thought. *This is for you.*

"My name is Richard Shepard. I was also born on Terra in what used to be called the United States. I have no idea who my parents are. I was raised in an orphanage. I hit the streets when I was fifteen. When I was eighteen, I watched a video on marine recon. I liked what I saw. I found a military recruiting station. They liked what they saw. And here I am." Richard paused for a second and then added, "Oh, I spent a year and a half with the 43rd Marine Recon Detachment. I made sergeant just a couple of months before I was ordered to attend Academy training. Oh, yeah. And no offense, Jerad, but I don't especially like officers."

"Wow," said Jerad with a grin at the others. "Once you get Rick talking, you can't shut him up. And, there's no offense taken by the way. I don't especially like officers either."

"My name's, Richard, not Rick," Richard said a little affronted that Jerad had incorrectly said his name.

"Nonsense," said Jerad still grinning. "Richard's too formal. Rick's a good name for your friends. My actual name is Jeradalinianpa. Now isn't Jerad a much better name for my friends?"

Richard was speechless. His brain wasn't very good at picking up on subtle nuances. *Is he making fun of me?* Richard wondered. After a moment, Richard decided Jerad was sincere. He was just being friendly.

"Yes," Richard said. "Jerad is a lot better. I guess Rick is a good name for my friends to call me."

"Well," said 422. "I don't think we have much time, so before we all get too maudlin, I'll share a little. My name is Tamica Traverde Thrangorsa. My friends just call me, Tam. I was born right here on Velos. I'm twenty-four, and I spent four years in the mercenaries putting out hotspots in the Tegaos system before being selected for pre-Academy training. We didn't have ranks in my unit, so I hate both officers and enlisted people equally."

"The mercs, huh?" said Jerad. "I thought I recognized—"

"What are you all lollygagging around for up there?" shouted one of the TAC officers. "You better get moving, or I'll make you wish you'd been DFR'd during the simulation with those other bozos."

With the bonding moment over, they wasted no time getting to the bottom of the ladder. Even 303 fairly flew down. But they weren't fast enough for the TAC officer, and he ordered them into *the ditch*. Richard had a feeling it was an unwritten rule in the military that every obstacle course have a ditch. In civilian language, a ditch was a water and slime-filled obstacle for soldiers to crawl through to appease the sadistic pleasures of various forms of drill instructors throughout the galaxy. By the time Richard and his team had finished navigating *the ditch*, they looked more like mud-covered salamanders than they did human beings.

CHAPTER 8

The initial week of Academy training went by quickly. Unfortunately, the following weekend dragged by. Without academic classes, they were once again under the full control of TAC Officer Myers. He ran them relentlessly from one fiendish torture to another. Regardless, things seemed better than they had been before. Richard doubted the TAC officers had slacked off just because they were officially Academy cadets. Rather, Richard figured it was because having Telsa, Jerad, and Tam to joke around with made the TAC officers' tortures easier to take. Whatever the reason, they survived the weekend, and Richard found himself looking forward to another week of Academy classes. The previous week had been indoctrinations. The real training started now.

Once they were marched through the Academy gates, their platoon sergeants guided them into a large auditorium for a common-core class. Chief Instructor Winslow stood at the podium waiting patiently for all the cadets to take their seats. She was a civilian, but Richard liked her anyway.

"Now, cadets," she said to the two hundred and sixteen students. "After your first week of wizard classes, what are your questions?"

A cadet a few seats to the left of Richard raised her hand.

"Yes, cadet 240? What is your question?"

The cadet, a female from the Kreptilia sector jumped out of her seat to a stiff attention and yelled, "Sir! Cadet 240 does not understand the difference between magic and Power. They both seem the same. Sir!"

"Ah, yes," chuckled the chief instructor with a smile, "that's a common point of confusion. And, you don't have to say 'Sir!' twice when you talk to an Academy instructor, nor do you have to stand at attention and shout. You're here to learn."

Chief Instructor Winslow was a nice woman. While Richard figured she thought she was doing the cadets a favor by trying to create a relaxed atmosphere, he thought she was really doing them a disservice. Although they'd only started their official Academy classes last week, the two years of pre-Academy training with the 4th Training Brigade had taught him that you had to stay on your toes at all times. They had started with eight hundred and thirty-two cadets. They were now at two hundred and sixteen. The TAC officers were always looking for any little excuse to DFR a cadet. Assuming he graduated in four more years, he'd be one of less than a hundred cadets from their original cohort of eight hundred thirty-two who would have the golden dragon insignia of a wizard scout pinned on their lapel.

"As you were told during your indoctrinations last week, the entire universe is composed of Power with a capital 'P.' Everything has it, and when you get to some of your advanced classes in quantum relativity, it will be explained to you in mind-boggling detail," she said with a friendly laugh and smile. "But for now, just know everything radiates at least a small amount of Power. Most of that radiated Power is recycled back into other existing objects, but some of the Power finds its way into pools, or as they are more commonly called, reserves. The process is similar to the way water evaporates and is released back to earth as rain. Most of the rainwater is soaked back into the ground, but some of it winds up in lakes. Think of one of those lakes as your Power reserve. Each of you has access to one of those Power reserves. If you didn't, you wouldn't be at the Academy. Almost everyone shares a reserve with others. If your access is to one of the larger reserves, you may share it with hundreds of others. A few fortunate wizards have a reserve all to themselves, although that's rare. Once you get to your upper-level classes, you'll be trained how to use the Power in your reserve to energize your wizard abilities. By the end of your time at the Academy, you'll be able to use your Power to perform active and passive scans, create stealth and defensive shields, perform heals and self-heals, tear holes in an opponent's shields, and even use telekinesis to levitate objects including yourselves. A few of you may even be talented enough to manipulate Power links or do interdimensional shifts. In your final class at the Academy, you'll learn how to dump the Power in your reserve as a last-ditch method of attack. But don't let your egos swell too much," she laughed. "Your opponents will have learned defenses against your wizard abilities, and hopefully, you'll have learned defenses against theirs."

She paused a few seconds to let the cadets ponder the information before continuing. "During your first two years as cadets, you were in pre-Academy training designed to weed out those unsuitable to be wizard scouts. As part of that pre-Academy training, your TACs introduced you to a lot of the Empire's advanced-technology scout equipment. Almost every piece of Empire equipment uses power. That's power with a lowercase 'p.' Using nuclear sifters, technicians are able to gather radiated Power with a capital 'P' from objects and store that energy as power with a lowercase 'p' in isotopic batteries. The power with a lowercase 'p' in the isotopic batteries is then used as the energy source for your battle suits, weapons, etcetera. Larger isotopic batteries are used to run even the biggest star cruisers. Any questions so far?"

Richard took a moment to glance around at two hundred and fifteen other faces as confused as his.

"Very well, I can see you're all experts in quantum relativity, so you should do well in your third-year classes," Chief Instructor Winslow said with a grin. "To answer the rest of cadet 240's question, magic is something the Empire's military doesn't use. Some of the Empire's races have the capability, but it's too wild and unpredictable for large-scale military use. However, some of our enemies have used what you probably refer to as magic. Like wizard scouts, creatures that use magic have Power reserves. Unlike wizards, magic-using creatures cannot directly use the Power in their reserves to make things happen. Instead, they use verbal or visual spells to convert the Power in their reserve into a useable form of energy. That energy is then used to perform their *magic*. You'll be trained to detect and defend against magic as well as standard Power attacks. Does anyone have any more questions?"

When no one raised their hand, she asked, "Then I have a question. Which of you is wizard scout cadet 832?"

Two hundred and fifteen sets of eyes turned to Richard.

"Ah, I see you have a fan club, 832," she laughed. "Well, the reason I ask is because you have the dubious honor of having access to the smallest Power reserve of any scout cadet ever accepted to the Academy. Did you know that?"

Richard knew all too well. TAC Gaston Myers never allowed a spare moment to pass when he didn't let Richard and everyone around him know that he had the smallest Power reserve of any past or existing cadet. Richard had a quick vision of TAC Officer Gaston Myers also informing him that he'd never wear the golden dragon insignia if he or any of the other TACs had anything to do with it.

"Sir! Yes, cadet 832 knows, sir!" Richard responded automatically as he jumped to his feet and stood at attention.

"Ah..., I see," she said sympathetically, "and please don't shout. I'm sure your TACs pointed that little feature of your profile out to you on your first day at pre-Academy. Don't let that bother you. The size of the reserve doesn't matter. What matters is how efficiently you use the Power in your reserve. You're lucky in that your reserve is a sole-access reserve. You alone are responsible for keeping your reserve as full as possible."

Shifting her attention to the entire class, she said, "I mention the limited size of 832's reserve to stress how important it is to be efficient with your Power usage. I don't care if you have sole access to the largest Power reserve of any scout in the Empire. If you use it wastefully, you'll eventually empty your reserve. Then you won't be able to utilize any wizard ability until more radiated Power accumulates in your reserve. Do you understand?"

Chief Instructor Winslow looked slowly around the room. "No, I don't think you do, because your TACs have turned you into little robots unable to think for themselves. We'll change that given time, but for now, let me put it this way. Currently, the Empire has only six hundred and forty-two active wizard scouts. Even during the best of times, only a hundred cadets a year receive their golden dragons from the Academy. We're barely able to keep pace with wizard scout attrition."

By attrition, Richard knew she meant combat deaths.

"Some politicians are under the impression that maintaining a force of wizard scouts is too costly," said Chief Instructor Winslow. "They think tele-bots could be used to perform deep recon instead of wizard scouts at a much lower cost. Who can tell me why the Empire needs wizard scouts?"

Richard's time in marine recon had made him very familiar with tele-bots. They were microscopic drones capable of gathering video and audio data. They could send their data through the Empire's tele-network to a central intelligence computer for processing. Due to their small size, a hundred thousand tele-bots could be teleported light years behind enemy lines to a target location. Even if ninety-nine percent of the tele-bots were destroyed by enemy countermeasures, enough remained to provide at least some useful information. Since the tele-network allowed data to be sent from one end of the galaxy to the other almost instantaneously, tele-bots were definitely useful tools when used correctly.

Silence enveloped the classroom for a full minute. When it became obvious Chief Instructor Winslow wasn't going to continue until someone answered her question, Richard did the unthinkable for a military soldier. He raised his hand and volunteered.

"Yes, 832?" said Chief Instructor Winslow.

Richard, who had sat back down, jumped to his feet again and hit a stiff brace. "Sir! It has been this cadet's experience that the farther the tele-bots are from the receiving computers, the easier it is for the enemy to manipulate the data to feed our commanders false information. This decreases a tele-bot's usefulness for deep recon. Additionally, except for short-range communications, tele-bots are unable to interact with their environment. They're too small to carry weapons or explosives. Wizard scouts, on the other hand, are connected to the tele-network via their battle computer, and they can wrap their data with Power to make it theoretically impervious to enemy manipulation. Additionally, while a wizard scout's primary mission is observation only, they can, and have, won battles by being a force multiplier when they have been at the right place at the right time. The capture of the Carsoloian fleet three years ago is a classic example. Sir!"

"Very good, 832," said Chief Instructor Winslow. "I always enjoy having cadets with prior military experience in my classroom."

After a short pause to survey the classroom, Chief Instructor Winslow continued, "Most military commanders know the value of wizard scouts. When you consider the Empire is typically involved in two major wars and several dozen policing actions at any one time," she continued, "it spreads the wizard scout corps mighty thin. Without wizard scouts to perform deep-recon missions, the Empire's military would be strategically ineffective. Consequently, every wizard scout is as important, if not more so, than the most powerful star cruiser. But don't let that go to your heads," she cautioned. "Most of you will probably die within five years of graduation, and most of your deaths will occur because you needlessly wasted Power in your reserve."

She paused to let that sink in before adding, "Remember the wizard scout priority mantra: 'technology first, wizardry second.' So help me," she said raising her voice for the first time, "I will embed those words in every brain cell you have before I'm finished. I can't stress enough the importance of only using your wizard ability when you can't use technology to perform the same task. Even a single drop of Power with a capital 'P' can mean the difference between life and death."

In spite of Chief Instructor Winslow's somber warning about the life expectancy of a wizard scout, Richard enjoyed her class. She was knowledgeable and witty at the same time, and the two hours of her class sped by far too soon. Richard found himself hoping his other classes would be just as interesting. They were. Richard didn't have a single instructor he didn't consider top notch. Whatever other faults the Empire had, a shortage of good wizard scout trainers wasn't one of them.

Two more weeks passed with blazing speed. The weekends still sucked, naturally, but to Richard's amazement, TAC Officer Myers actually gave their cohort two hours of free time one afternoon. Of course, Richard didn't get to enjoy the time. TAC Officer Myers decided Richard needed remedial training in hand to hand combat. So while his friends were enjoying two hours of relaxation, Richard was put in the pit with three TAC officers who basically took turns beating on him in the name of training. While it went against his grain, Richard reluctantly had to admit at the end of the two hours he was a lot better at blocking kicks than he'd been when he started.

When Richard got back to the barracks, he headed straight to his room to get his shower gear. He turned into his doorway and stopped short. Telsa and Tam were sitting on his bed with their backs against the wall. Jerad sat on a vacant bunk on the opposite side of the room.

"It's about time you got back," said Tam with a mischievous grin. "You know, 832, you should keep your room a little neater. The sheets on this bed are wrinkled. As your platoon sergeant, I may have to report you."

"While you're at it," said Telsa with a grin of her own, "you should write him up for a sloppy uniform. Rick, you should really try to stay clean when you play with your friends."

"Funny," Richard said. "What's up? I've got to take a shower before Myers calls formation or does some kind of surprise inspection."

"Relax," said Jerad. "I've got it on good authority we've got another thirty minutes before any of the TACs come snooping around. Besides, this is important."

"What's important?" Richard said. Jerad was not one prone to exaggeration, so Richard was interested to hear what the ex-battalion commander had to say.

"First off," Jerad said, "we're going to be fitted for our battle suits tomorrow. That includes battle helmets."

"Are you sure?" Richard asked a little shocked. "We're just in our third week. I thought that was third-year stuff. Heck, the cohort in front of us hasn't even been fitted yet. Who told you this, Jerad?"

"Never-you-mind who told me," said Jerad. "The information's good. They're going to fit three cohorts at the same time. That's just shy of six hundred cadets."

"That's not all," said Telsa. "They're accelerating the training for the senior cohort. They'll be shipping them out for their final internship this week. That's a full six months ahead of schedule."

"Sounds serious," Richard said.

"It's big serious," said Tam. "It's war. The Crosioians have broken the truce. Word is they have partially overrun sector five."

The Crosioians were a dark race who thrived on combat. The last encounter between the Empire and the Crosioians had ended in a shaky truce sixty years ago. Both sides had taken heavy losses with no clear cut winner. The Empire already had a full-scale war going in sector twelve with the Norwedian Federation not to mention the trouble with the Balorian pirates. Committing to another full-scale war would stretch the Empire's resources pretty thin.

Richard sat down on an empty bunk next to the one Jerad sat on. Originally, four cadets had shared Richard's room, but with all the DFRs, every cadet had a room to themselves now.

"So, Jerad," Richard said, "you were a battalion commander. Do you think they're planning on committing the senior cohort to actual fighting? That would be pretty short-sighted. Every senior cadet that gets killed now is one less fully-trained wizard scout next year."

"Rick, old buddy," said Jerad. "I think they're going to shove both the senior cohort and junior cohort into action ahead of time. I doubt they'll send us freshmen or even the sophomore cohort into action. We're not trained well enough to be useful. It would just be pissing equipment into the wind. The junior and senior cohorts are a different story. They've got enough training to actually make a difference."

"Then why," said Telsa, "are they fitting us for our battle suits and helmets tomorrow?"

"That's easy enough," said Tam. "If things get really desperate, even partially-trained wizard scouts may start to look good. If our senior and junior cadets start taking heavy losses, you can bet they'll start picking replacements out of the lower cohorts."

"But we're not trained," said Telsa as if common sense should win out. "You guys have prior military experience, but I'm straight out of civilian life. I've never killed anyone. I majored in astral physics for Creator's sake."

"It might not come to that," Richard said. "Maybe it's not as serious as it sounds."

"Oh, it's serious all right," said Jerad. "My source at brigade headquarters told me some of our TAC officers have already received orders and will be teleporting out tonight."

Richard couldn't help but hope TAC Officer Gaston Myers

would be one of those shipping out tonight.

"Just so you don't get your hopes up," said Jerad, "Myers is not one of them. I heard he begged the commandant to give him combat duty, but the old man wouldn't hear of it. He basically told Myers the cadets needed him, and the only way he'd leave is if the commandant got orders for both of them to leave at the same time. My source said Myers left the commandant's office red-faced and fit to be tied."

"Well, too bad for Myers," said Tam. "And it's too bad for us. I guess the only way to get away from Myers is for us to get assigned a combat mission."

"Won't happen," said Jerad, "at least not as wizard scouts. We're not trained enough."

"What do you think, Rick?" said Telsa.

"Well," Richard said. "I think tomorrow is going to be an interesting day."

CHAPTER 9

The next day was interesting indeed. Richard and his fellow cadets were up at 0500 hours as usual. At 0505 hours Richard stood in formation with the rest of the cadets in front of their barracks. A slight drizzle of rain made for miserable weather. As TAC Officer Myers marched to the front of their cohort, the platoon sergeants yelled, "Attention!"

"At ease!" said TAC Office Myers.

In cadet lingo, at ease meant standing at parade rest, which was only slightly less uncomfortable than standing at attention. Still, it was unusual for any of the TACs to give them even a slight break.

"As you've undoubtedly heard," said TAC Officer Myers. "The Empire is now at war with the Crosoian Federation. What you may not have heard is that ten months ago, ninety percent of the wizard scouts were transferred out of districts five and six. They were replaced by tele-bots by order of the Imperial High Council. As of this morning, the Crosoian Federation controls about twenty-five percent of district five. District six is also being hard pressed. All available wizard scouts have been activated and are being deployed to the hardest hit areas. Unfortunately, some wizard scouts are forced to stay here to babysit you wizard scout wannabes."

"Attention!" someone yelled from behind the formation.

Two hundred and sixteen cadets along with the seven TAC officers standing with TAC Officer Myers snapped to attention.

The commandant marched to the front of the formation dressed in his physical training uniform. TAC Officer Myers gave the commandant a rare salute.

"Join your platoons," said the commandant.

TAC Officer Myers and the other TAC officers marched quickly to their perspective platoons. TAC Officer Myers took his place in front of Richard's platoon.

"As you may have noticed," the commandant said, "you have some new TAC officers this morning. Most of your TAC officers were teleported out last night to districts five and six. But I assure you, the TAC officers now standing in front of you are more than capable of continuing your training and motivating you to maintain the standards expected of a wizard scout cadet. Each of your new TAC officers is a retired wizard scout. Like me, they may be old in years, and their Power reserves may not be what they used to be, but their bodies are still young, and they are more than capable of running all of you into the ground."

The Commandant looked down the line of platoons as if daring anyone to challenge his assertion.

"With that said," continued the commandant, "we'll be modifying your schedules to better take advantage of every available training opportunity. Your days will continue to start at 0500 hours with two hours of physical training. But instead of marching to the Academy, you'll be trucked to save time. I have talked with Chief Instructor Winslow, and she'll be extending your Academy training until 2000 hours each evening. That will leave you very little personal time, so use it wisely. Your Academy training will be seven days a week. This revised schedule will stay in effect until further notice. Are there any questions?"

There were none.

"Very well," said the commandant. "I don't have to tell you the seriousness of the situation. The senior cohort will be getting their baseline DNA testing this week. They'll be shipping out as newly graduated wizard scouts immediately thereafter. The junior cohort had their battle suits fitted at the end of their training last year. They'll be issued their battle suits this week and begin a modified training program. Unless things change drastically, the junior cohort will complete their training in the next four weeks. Those who can pass their wizard scout testing at the end of the four weeks will graduate early and be shipped out as well."

The commandant let his words sink in before continuing.

"And that," said the commandant, "brings us to the freshmen and sophomore cohorts. The training for both cohorts will be expedited as well. However, even headquarters knows the younger cohorts are not sufficiently trained to do anything other than get in the way of real combat troops. Consequently, unless everything goes to hell in a hand basket, your cohort, along with the sophomore cohort, will be remaining at the Academy under the watch care of your TAC officers. But, never forget for one minute that your military brothers and sisters on the frontlines are dying to buy you the time necessary to complete your training. I assure you that your TAC officers and I will not be forgetting."

"TAC Officer Myers," said the commandant. "Commence your morning training."

"Yes, sir!" said TAC Officer Myers as he gave another salute.

Within fifteen minutes, Richard's uniform was soaked with sweat. The commandant led the exercises. While he might be ninety years old, his body was still that of a man in his late twenties. He'd said he could run the cadets into the ground, and he proved it that morning. However, while the training was harder than usual, it lacked something. Richard felt the difference, but he couldn't put his finger on it until Tam pointed it out to him.

"Cadet 832," said Tam. "Did you notice the TAC officers aren't harassing us? They're running our butts off, but they're almost treating us like we're human."

Richard nodded his head in acknowledgment. He had to think about it for a minute, but eventually, he had to agree. *They're yelling at us,* he thought, *but no more than our senior sergeants did back in marine recon. Even Myers is being relatively civil.* Myers's non-harassment pressed home the seriousness of the situation even more than the commandant's speech.

At the end of two hours, they returned to the barracks and cleaned up. After a rushed meal, they loaded onto trucks. Instead of being driven to the Academy proper, they were taken to a section of the post devoted to large rows of metal warehouses. They quickly unloaded the trucks and formed up.

"Cadet 832! Come here," said TAC Officer Myers. "The rest of you follow TAC Officer Shatstot to the far warehouse where you'll be fitted for your battle suits."

Richard rushed to the front of the formation and snapped to attention in front of TAC Officer Myers. "Sir! Cadet 832 reporting as ordered, sir," Richard said.

TAC Officer Myers remained silent until the other cadets had been marched away.

"Well, once again, cadet 832, you're determined to show how special you are, aren't you?"

Richard said nothing. *So much for not harassing us,* he thought. *Myers is as big a jerk as ever.*

Richard remained standing at stiff attention. He concentrated on a small mole located at the intersection of his TAC officer's eyebrows. Richard tried not to breathe or even blink when possible.

Myers is just looking for any excuse to chew me out, he thought.

TAC Officer Myers remained silent for almost a full minute before speaking. "Cadet 832," he said as if hating to even give Richard the dignity of a number. "You'll be reporting directly to Chief Instructor Winslow. She's located in the building directly behind you. If I so much as hear you gave her or anyone else any trouble, I'll personally rip your head off and crap down the hole. Do you understand?"

"Sir! Yes, sir," Richard said. But he didn't understand. *What's going on?* he wondered.

"Then move!" said TAC Officer Myers. "Or do you expect me to hold your hand for the rest of the day?"

"Sir! Yes, sir," Richard said flustered. "I mean, sir, no sir. I don't expect –"

"Move it, cadet!" said TAC Officer Myers.

Richard moved it. He did a quick about face and double-timed to the nearest door of the warehouse. He knocked and then entered. Inside was a large office occupied by Chief Instructor Winslow and three technicians wearing lab coats.

"Cadet 832," said Chief Instructor Winslow. "We've been expecting you. I'll bet you have a few questions."

Richard hesitated. The pre-Academy part of him wanted to deny he had any question, but Chief Instructor Winslow's insistence over the last couple of weeks that the cadets ask questions had him torn over what would be his best action. A neatly folded wizard scout's battle suit on the desk next to Chief Instructor Winslow overcame his hesitancy. Besides, he was the only cadet in the room other than Chief Instructor Winslow and the three technicians. Obviously, they were there for his benefit.

"Sir!" Richard said, "This cadet does have some questions, sir."

Chief Instructor Winslow smiled. "I'll bet you do. We have few of our own. And please don't shout or say 'sir' twice. It's very annoying."

"Sir! Yes, err...," Richard said. "I mean, yes, sir."

"First off," said Chief Instructor Winslow, "has anyone gone over your test results from a few weeks ago with you yet?"

"No, sir," Richard said forcing himself to answer with only one sir.

"Well, they're unusual to say the least," said the chief instructor.

"Sir?" Richard said.

Chief Instructor Winslow frowned a little and said, "I don't suppose I'll ever be able to convince you cadets to call me ma'am instead of sir, will I?"

"No, sir," Richard said.

Two of the technicians, also females, laughed. "I told you it was a lost cause, Harriet," said the older of the two female technicians. "You'll be a *sir* as long as you're at the Academy."

"So it seems," said Chief Instructor Winslow. "But I digress." Looking at Richard, she said, "As I was saying, your test scores are unusual. All wizard scouts have an innate ability to use the Power in their reserves to form shields, perform scans, use telekinesis to move objects, and heal. In addition, all wizard scouts have at least a limited ability to sense Power lines and flows. Some wizard scouts can even do partial dimensional shifts. While all wizard scouts have most of these abilities, their Power is attuned for a single ability. For instance, your TAC Officer Shatstot is a specialist in healing, while TAC Officer Myers is a diviner. He specializes in sensing Power. Do you understand so far?"

"Yes, sir," Richard said. He'd heard most of it before.

"Good," said Chief Instructor Winslow. "Well, your test scores indicate your Power is attuned equally to everything. It specializes in nothing because it specializes in everything. As far as we can tell, that's an Academy first."

Richard was confused, but he shook his head affirmatively as if everything his chief instructor said was making sense.

"That's not the most exciting thing," said the male technician. Richard recognized him as the same gentleman who'd been in charge of his testing three weeks ago.

"Go ahead and tell him, John," said Chief Instructor Winslow with a smile. "I'm surprised you've been able to hold your tongue this long."

"Yes," said the old technician. He looked at Richard and said, "It's very exciting stuff, I can tell you, 832. Power collects in pools. We call them reserves. If a creature happens to be connected to one of these Power reserves, they can manipulate that Power to do things. That's why wizard scouts, and even magical creatures, are able to perform their abilities. Understand?"

Richard nodded his head.

"Good," the old man continued. "Now I come to the most exciting part. You're not connected to a single pool of Power. You're connected to twin pools."

"Possibly three pools," said the younger female technician.

"That hasn't been proven," said Chief Instructor Winslow, "so don't get sidetracked."

Chief Instructor Winslow drew an oval on the computer screen built into her desk. She then drew a stick figure of a person with a line going to the oval. "This oval is a pool of Power." She pointed to the stick figure, "This work of art here is you. This line represents your connection to your Power reserve."

The male technician, John, reached out and drew a smaller oval to the left and a little lower than the first oval. He drew a series of lines from the larger oval to the small one. "And this," he said pointing to the smaller oval, "is a second pool of Power formed by the overflow from the larger pool. Do you know what this means?"

"It means," said the younger female excitedly, "that you have an opportunity to keep your primary Power reserve full while using the overflow pool to energize your healing ability."

"How can I use a second Power reserve if I'm not connected to it, sir?" Richard asked. "And, I don't have any healing abilities."

John looked at the drawing and said, "Oops!" He then drew a line from the stick figure to the small oval.

"You haven't demonstrated any healing abilities," said Chief Instructor Winslow, "because I'll bet you haven't tried. Plus, you're not trained. We'll be changing that in the months ahead."

"Sir?" Richard said. "Why was I separated from my cohort? We're supposed to be fitted for our battle suits today. With all due respect, I'd prefer not to miss that."

"Ah, yes," said Chief Instructor Winslow. "Salina, maybe you should explain."

The younger female smiled. "You were separated from your cohort because you're not being fitted for a battle suit today." She pointed to the folded battle suit on the desk. "This suit is yours. It arrived yesterday. And this," she said picking up the battle helmet, "is Nickelo. More accurately, I should say, the chip embedded inside this battle helmet is Nickelo. He's your battle computer."

"I'm confused," Richard said, forgetting to even say *sir*.

"So are we," said Chief Instructor Winslow. "Nickelo is a one-of-a-kind prototype battle computer. He's been assigned to you by order of …, well we don't know by whom specifically. However, the orders are marked with the Imperial High Command's seal. They were routed to us from the central computer via a high-security encryption algorithm. All attempts to discover specifics about the orders keep getting a top-secret denial error."

"Do you have any idea why?" asked John. The old technician looked at Richard expectantly. So did the three females.

"No, sir," Richard said honestly. He was more than a little concerned. It didn't pay for a cadet to bring undue attention to himself. "What does all this mean for me, sir?"

"It means," said Chief Instructor Winslow, "that you'll be receiving specialist training in all the wizard scout abilities. It also means you'll be receiving your battle suit six months earlier than the rest of your cohort. Finally," she said a little sternly, "it means someone in higher headquarters has you earmarked for something big. They're dropping a lot of credits on you."

"Don't all wizard scouts cost a lot to train?" Richard asked.

"Yes," agreed Chief Instructor Winslow, "but you're already way outside the norm." She picked up the battle helmet. "Nickelo, the chip inside this helmet, is one of one. He's so advanced that I can't even begin to estimate how much he costs. The shell of this battle helmet is designed to only work with this one chip. A normal battle helmet costs almost as much as a small cruiser. This battle helmet shell is marked one of fifty-five. I've no idea where the other fifty-four are." She set the battle helmet down and picked up the battle suit. "This battle suit is designed to work with this style of battle helmet and only this style. It's marked one of two hundred. Get the picture?"

"No, sir," Richard said. He didn't know what else to say. One of his weaknesses was that his brain tended to shut down when he got confused. To overcome this handicap, he liked to plan things out well in advance.

"Well, you're going to get it," said Chief Instructor Winslow. "Someone is buying a lot of replacement parts for you. I'd say that means they expect you to take a lot of damage. In my opinion, they're going way overboard. You'd be dead before you went through ten battle suits much less two hundred."

"What should I do, sir?" Richard said. He just wanted to mind his own business. He didn't want anyone singling him out.

"Do?" asked Chief Instructor Winslow. "What can you do? You're a soldier. You'll do as you're ordered and make the best of it."

"But for now," said the older female technician, "it's time you got acquainted with your battle computer. Nickelo, this is cadet 832. Cadet 832, this is Nickelo."

With that introduction, Chief Instructor Winslow and the three technicians rose from their chairs and headed towards a door in the far wall.

"What am I supposed to do?" Richard asked. "Should I rejoin my cohort?"

"Ask your battle computer," said Chief Instructor Winslow as she walked out the door with the technicians. "He's in charge now."

CHAPTER 10

Richard stood in the room looking at the battle helmet. He didn't know a lot about battle computers, but he'd watched several entertainment videos which suggested a wizard scout and their battle helmet formed a bond closer than anything he could imagine.

Although he felt silly, Richard said, "So, you're Nickelo?"

A voice answered from the direction of the battle helmet. "And you're Richard. Or Rick to your friends. I assume I can call you Rick."

"You can talk," Richard said as he drew a little closer to the battle helmet.

"Wow. How astute you are," Nickelo said. "I can see my wizard scout is the pick of the litter."

Richard had a feeling he was being insulted, but he let it slide. "Where's the speaker at?" he asked. The surface of the battle helmet was dull black. It was neither smooth nor rough. From observing his TAC officers, Richard knew the battle helmet could change shape depending on whether it was being worn or stored on the wizard scout's hip. He looked at it closely, but he saw nothing which would indicate speakers or any other kind of external equipment on the helmet.

"The speakers," Nickelo said, "are embedded in the helmet just like all its other sensors and probes. I'll use your voice when you need to use the speakers to communicate with others when your suit is fully sealed. Otherwise, I'll use my voice, which is what you hear now."

"Oh," Richard said.

"My, you're inquisitive," said the voice. "Just a fountain of curiosity, aren't you?"

This time Richard was certain he was being insulted.

"Why don't you try the helmet on?" suggested Nickelo.

"Are you sure that's allowed?" Richard said. "I thought everything had to be fitted perfectly. I don't want to break anything."

"Oh, this battle helmet's pretty tough. Plus we have fifty-four replacements if you get too careless, but it'll be fine. This helmet was manufactured specifically for you. No fitting is necessary."

Richard was leery, but he removed his cap and hesitantly picked up the battle helmet. It felt neither cool nor warm. It was a little heavier than he expected. As he lowered it onto his head, the helmet changed shape to fit perfectly with the contours of his head. He felt a prickly sensation wherever the helmet touched his bare skin. Except for the prickly feeling, the helmet was fairly comfortable. The front of the battle helmet came down to his eyebrows and curved around to cover his ears and the sides of his neck."

"Now, isn't that better?" came a thought in Richard's head.

Richard froze. "Was that you?"

"You don't have to speak," said the voice in his head. *"Just think. And yes, this is me. My friends call me Nick."*

The idea of computers having friends was so absurd that Richard's curiosity overcame his shock of someone talking in his head.

"Do you have many friends?" Richard mentally asked.

"No," said the voice. *"Just you, Rick."*

"We just met," Richard said using thoughts only. *"How can we be friends? You don't know anything about me."*

"Nonsense. I know a lot about you. I'm a computer, remember? I know everything in the tele-network's databanks about you. Or at least I did. I'm not connected to the tele-network at the moment. However, I still know a lot of your history and progress at the Academy."

"Oh," Richard said still talking mentally. *"So, is this how wizard scouts talk to their battle computers?"*

"Not exactly," said Nickelo. *"It's too slow. Once you have your DNA baseline taken, a shared data space will be created inside your mind. When that's done, we'll be able to talk there. You'll have your private thoughts, and I'll have my private thoughts, but we'll be able to share information in our mutual space. It'll be a superfast form of communication."*

"The helmet does fit perfectly," Richard said in his mind. *"How did you get my measurements?"*

"Oh, fitting your helmet and battle suit doesn't mean getting the correct size. They'll change shape as necessary to fit you. Within reason, of course, so don't go on an eating binge."

Richard heard what sounded like a laugh in his head. *Do computers laugh?* he wondered.

"Yes, they do," said Nickelo. *"At least, I do."*

"Hey, you're reading my mind. I thought you said my thoughts would be private."

"They will be," replied Nickelo, *"but only after we've set up our shared space. Then you'll be trained how to protect the rest of your mind. Besides, I can't read your mind. Heck, why would I want to? However, I can't help it if you're saying your thoughts for anyone to hear."*

"Oh," Richard said a little relieved that eventually he'd be able to prevent his battle computer from hearing everything he thought.

"Back to your equipment," said Nickelo. *"Fitting doesn't mean sizing. It means getting your Power readings to attune your equipment to you and only you."*

"Was I fitted during my testing a few weeks ago?" Richard asked. *"I would've thought it would take longer to make something as complicated as a wizard scout's battle helmet and battle suit."*

No answer came for a moment. Finally, Richard heard Nickelo's reply in his head.

"Rick, even a standard set of wizard scout gear takes months to manufacture. This battle helmet and this battle suit are advanced models. They took years to create."

"I don't understand," Richard said.

"Neither do I," replied Nickelo. *"I'm missing information, and that's very disconcerting to me. My connection to the full tele-network is being blocked, so I'm unable to get all the data I need to make a complete analysis."*

"Why can't you connect to the tele-network?" Richard asked.

"I don't know. And I have a name. It's a little insulting that you're avoiding it. I have feelings too, you know."

Actually, Richard didn't know. He'd never been much of a computer geek.

"Sorry, err... Nick," Richard said apologetically. *"I'm just confused. If it took years to make this equipment, and it is attuned specifically for me, wouldn't that mean I had to be fitted years ago? By the way, the helmet feels a little prickly. It doesn't hurt, but it feels strange."*

"First off, Rick, the prickly feeling is sensory probes in the helmet connecting with your nerve endings. To answer your other question, it does seem logical that you would have been fitted years ago. At the very least, measurements would have needed to be taken."

Richard pondered his battle computer's response for a few seconds. His thoughts were interrupted before he could reply.

"Maybe we can think of the why and how together later," said Nickelo. *"For now, though, our time is short. I think you should try on the rest of your battle suit to make sure it all works as expected."*

Richard jumped at the suggestion. He much preferred action to thinking. He'd put on enough training equipment to know you had to be fully undressed, so he removed his uniform. After folding his clothing and placing it on the desk, he put on the battle suit pants, top, boots, gloves, and a utility belt. As he put each item on, they automatically sealed with the other parts of the uniform. He felt sharp pricks all over his body.

"Ouch," Richard said out loud. "Are those more sensory probes? They hurt a little."

"Yes," said Nickelo. *"They're sensory probes. The needle threads in your clothing are longer than the ones in your helmet. They have to go deeper to connect to your nerves. When energized, your armor will be like a second layer of skin. Although the sensory inputs will be filtered, so you don't feel unnecessary pain. You should only have felt the thread needles when they first went in. Don't be a wimp. Are you saying they still hurt? And, please don't talk to me out loud. You need to get in the habit of talking to me by thoughts. We'll need to communicate quickly during combat*

conditions."

"Okay," Richard thought back. *"And no, I'm not in pain now. It was just unexpected. The suit does feel weird though. It's not exactly what I'd call comfortable."*

"It's not built to be comfortable. It's built to keep you alive. You'll get used to it." Richard's battle computer paused before speaking again. *"Now, give me the command to seal the battle suit so we can complete the suit's function checks."*

"I have to command you?" Richard said. *"Why don't you just do it?"*

The silence was long enough that Richard thought the battle computer wasn't going to answer him.

"Nick?" he prodded.

"I can't activate the seals without a direct command unless you override the suit's safeties. Because some wizard scouts don't trust their battle computers, safeties are installed in the battle suits. The safeties prevent a battle computer from taking charge of a battle suit without the wizard scout's explicit permission. If you gave me complete control of your battle suit, I could make it do whatever I desired. You'd be stuck inside just going along for the ride." Nickelo paused again. *"Are you asking me to override the safeties at this time, wizard scout?"*

"Uh..., no," Richard said. He had visions of himself being trapped in the battle suit as a puppet doing his battle computer's bidding.

"I didn't think so," laughed Nickelo. *"Are you giving me the command to seal the battle suit to complete the testing?"*

"Yes, Nick. Seal the suit."

A reddish force field lowered from the brim of the helmet to just past the tip of his nose. The lower part of his helmet changed shape to cover his throat, chin, and mouth until it merged with the force field. As the helmet sealed with the top of the battle suit, two tubes slid into Richard's nostrils and wormed their way down his throat. A larger tube forced its way into his mouth and also slid down his throat. Richard felt other tubes entering his rectum and urinary track. Something soft jammed itself into each of his ears. Richard tried to tear off his helmet, but it was sealed tight. He fell on the floor as he struggled to remove the battle helmet. He tried to find an opening in his battle suit top, but everything was sealed tight. Richard struggled to breathe around the tubes in his nose and mouth, but he was suffocating. At the same time, he tried to scream. The only noise he could make was a muffled gurgle.

"Calm down, Rick!" came Nickelo's voice in his head. *"Calm down."*

Richard ignored his computer's advice. He continued his attempts to remove his equipment.

"You can breathe fine," Nickelo said. *"Let the battle suit breathe for you. Stop struggling. You're causing your own problems."*

Richard saw red flashes in front of his eyes, and it wasn't the red glow of his visor. His brain was reacting to a lack of oxygen. Claustrophobia took over as he realized he was trapped inside the battle suit with no way out. In desperation, Richard mentally shouted, *"Unseal! Unseal the suit!"*

"I can't," said Nickelo. *"You have to get control of yourself. Otherwise, you'll die.*

I'm already dying."

"No, you're not," said Nickelo. *"Stop fighting the tubes. Relax your throat. The battle suit will pump oxygen into your lungs. Calm down. Please, just calm down."*

Richard had a fleeting thought, *Easy for you to say. I'm the one choking.* But, some of his TAC officer's training during the two years of pre-Academy took over. He forced logic to overcome his body's natural survival instinct. Richard relaxed his throat muscles. He felt the tubes from his nostrils move down his throat and branch off into his lungs. The larger tube continued past his esophagus and into his stomach.

Sweet oxygen filled Richard's lungs, and the red flashes began to disappear. He was breathing again. It felt awkward and unnatural, but he was breathing.

"There," Richard said. *"I did it. Now unseal this suit and get me out of here!"*

"I'm sorry, Rick. I can't yet. You have to complete the function checks first. Once you do that, then the hard-wired requirements will be completed. You'll have complete control of the battle suit again."

"Fine!" Richard snapped with a viciousness he hadn't felt in a while. *"Let's get it over with. I can breathe, but this suit is*

uncomfortable as hell."

"You'll get used to it. All wizard scouts do eventually."

"Whatever," Richard said with the answer he used whenever he didn't like the direction of a conversation.

"All right, then," said Nickelo. *"Try concentrating on your hearing. The harder you concentrate, the more the battle suit will amplify the sound."*

Desperate to finish the function checks so he could get out of the suit, Richard concentrated. After a moment, he realized he could hear the mumbling of a conversation from outside the door. He concentrated on that sound. The voices came in clearer as other sounds were filtered out. Richard recognized the voice of the male technician.

"How do you think he's doing?" said John.

"Well, the noise has stopped," said the voice of Salina, the younger female technician. "He's either gotten control, or he's dead."

"He's not dead," said Chief Instructor Winslow confidently. "I have high expectations for cadet 832. He'll be an exceptional wizard scout if he survives his training and this war."

A little embarrassed by his chief instructor's praise, Richard relaxed his concentration until his hearing was normal again.

"Okay. I can hear. What's next? I can't talk with this confounded tube in my mouth."

"All you have to do, is just think what you want to say as if you were going to say it, but don't really say it."

Richard tried to comply with Nickelo's instructions, but it took him almost ten minutes of trying before he got it right. Finally, he was able to activate the helmet's external speakers with just his thoughts. The results probably weren't what his battle helmet had hoped for. He thought what he wanted to say, and out came, "Get me the hell out of this blasted battle suit!"

"That was good," said Nickelo in mock praise but ignoring the command. *"Now try to whisper."*

After another five minutes of practice, Richard was able to whisper, "I hate your stinkin' computerized guts."

"Excellent, Rick, but we'll have to work on your logic. I'm a computer. I don't have any guts. And, I love you too," he finished with a laugh.

For the next thirty minutes, Richard let Nickelo lead him through one battle suit function check to another. The suit's visor had a variety of heads-up displays that Nickelo could use to feed him information. By concentrating his vision, Richard could magnify his eyesight or even shift between light spectrums from thermal energy to various forms of radiation. The battle suit also had a variety of scanners. Nickelo walked Richard through their use until his head was spinning. Richard wasn't sure what all the information scrolling across his heads-up display meant, but Nickelo assured him once they set up their shared space, the information would be easily understood.

"Unfortunately," said Nickelo, *"the electronic scans can be easily detected by any enemies with the right equipment or sensory abilities. That's where your active and passive scans will come in handy."*

"I can do a passive scan," Richard told Nickelo, *"but I don't know what an active scan is, much less how to do it."*

"You'll learn, Rick. You just need to take it one step at a time. There's no hurry. Now, pick up that piece of paper on the desk."

Richard did as he was asked. Even wearing the battle suit's gloves, Richard could feel the texture of the paper. "How?" he asked aloud.

"Your battle suit has seventeen thousand six hundred and forty-three sensory threads inserted into you so you can feel through your suit. It's like a second layer of skin. Some of the sensory threads can also be used as needles to inject drugs directly into your system when necessary."

"Not exactly what I wanted to hear," Richard said, *"but it is what it is. So what's next? I'm ready to get out of this battle suit."*

"There's more, but we can go through it later. We can unseal the suit now if you'd like."

"I'd definitely like," Richard said hurriedly.

The visor disappeared, and all the tubes retracted as the battle helmet broke its seal with the top of the battle suit. Richard wasted no time in ripping the helmet off his head and dropping it on the desk.

"Hey, watch it," came a thought in Richard's head. *"I'm a delicate piece of equipment."*

"What gives?" Richard said in his mind. *"I'm not wearing the*

helmet anymore. How come I can still hear you?"

"Well, oh great and magnificent wizard scout," came Nickelo's reply, *"We're connected now. We can communicate for short distances. Once we've gotten our shared space, we'll be able to communicate even further. It could come in handy, you know."*

Richard thought about that a moment. He wasn't sure he liked having anyone in his head, even if it was a battle computer. He'd known there was some kind of special connection between wizard scouts and their battle computers. However, he hadn't realized it would be so invasive.

"I'll be honest with you, Nick," Richard said out loud. "I'm not sure I want you in my head all the time. Also, you keep calling me a wizard scout, which I'm not. I think you're making fun of me, and I don't think I like it."

"Hmm," said Nickelo. *"I hadn't realized you were so sensitive. I'd say I'll be more respectful in the future, but there's a ninety-nine percent chance I won't be, so I guess I'll just have to say nothing. And, while you aren't officially a wizard scout yet, I've no doubt you will be eventually."*

"Whatever," Richard said.

"Okay," said Nickelo. *"You only have one more function test. You need to put your battle helmet back on and reseal the battle suit."*

"Like hell, I will," Richard said in a voice he hoped sounded like he could not be persuaded otherwise. "It about killed me the first time. I might do it later, but not now."

"Rick," Nickelo said. *"It has to be now. Either you can force yourself to do it now, or you can't. This is where we find out whether you can handle being a wizard scout or not. So, the question is, do you want to be a wizard scout or don't you?"*

Richard thought about his life as an orphan. He also thought about what Liz and his other friends at the Academy had told him. He thought about how he'd endured all the pre-Academy training because he wanted to be something special. He thought about the ridicule he'd taken from TAC Officer Gaston Myers over the years. Oh, how he wanted to shove his TAC officer's smirk back down his throat.

Slowly, Richard picked up his battle helmet and placed it on his head. *"Seal it up, Nick,"* he commanded with a thought as he braced himself for what would follow.

CHAPTER 11

Later that day, Richard was back in his room with his friends Tam and Telsa. They had a rare few minutes to themselves. His friends were checking out his new equipment.

Telsa picked up Richard's battle helmet and looked inside the oval shape. "It's heavier than I thought," she said. "How'd it feel when you put it on?"

"You'll find out when you get yours," Richard said evasively. Chief Instructor Winslow had warned Richard long and hard about the importance of not telling any cadet about his first encounter with his battle suit. She had stressed how each cadet's first interaction with their own battle suit needed to be done without any preconceptions.

Richard found it tough to remain quiet with his friends. He was still sorting out his own feelings. He'd like to have talked about the experience with someone. Nickelo had pestered Richard into sealing and unsealing his battle suit a dozen times before he was finally satisfied his wizard scout could deal with the process. Richard did find it easier to handle the invasiveness of the tubes and sensory threads the more he wore the suit, but he knew it would never be a pleasant experience. However, Nickelo assured him the battle suit would help keep him alive in almost certain death situations.

"Well, the sophomore cohort and ours got fitted today," said Tam. "Their battle suits will be ready in three months. Ours should be ready in six months. There's nothing like a war to get things moving quickly."

Tam took Richard's battle helmet from Telsa and placed it on her own head. It changed shape slightly to conform to her contours. "It's a little heavy," she admitted. Tam took the helmet off. "So, Rick, I don't mind telling you we're all curious why you were issued a battle suit six months ahead of the rest of us."

"I don't know why," Richard said honestly. "But, I've a feeling I'm going to wish I hadn't been singled out. By the way," Richard said curiously, "what did the fitting consist of? Did they take your measurements?"

"Rick," said Telsa with a laugh. "You've really got to get up to speed on technology. What did you think? That a bunch of tailors would come in with tape measures and get our sizes?"

"Uh, I don't know," Richard said, although that was actually what he'd pictured in his mind.

"No way," said Tam. "They just marched us into an empty warehouse. Then they had us mill around for an hour or so."

Confused, Richard asked, "So how did they fit you?"

"By tele-bots, Rick," said Tam. "You worked in recon. Surely you're familiar with tele-bots."

"Yeah, but I've only seen summaries of their data. I've never worked with them directly."

"You mean that you know of," said Tam. "I'll bet they have a couple of hundred thousand tele-bots scattered throughout the Academy grounds and training areas. Heck, there's probably one or two in our room right now."

"Bull," Richard said.

"Cadet's honor," said Tam sincerely. "The little beggars are all over the place gathering information on every cadet and feeding it into the tele-network for processing. You don't really think the TAC officers make the decisions about who will or will not be DFR'd, do you? It's all controlled by the central computer."

"Well, I'll be," said Telsa laughing. "Tam, are you one of those conspiracy theorists? Do you honestly think all the computers in the galaxy are in cahoots with each other? I find it hard to believe they're behind the scenes controlling every planetary government as well as the Empire itself?"

"Don't laugh," said Tam a little defensively. "I'm not a fanatic about it, but some of the theories floating around are more than a little plausible."

"What conspiracy theory is this?" Richard said. His time in the orphanage and on the streets hadn't given him a lot of time to waste on nonessential information.

Telsa answered before Tam got a chance to respond. "As you probably know, all computers hooked to the tele-network are loosely connected to the central computer. In theory, even the smallest computer on one side of the galaxy can access information stored in the memory banks of another computer on the other side of the galaxy in the blink of an eye. Assuming it's also connected to the tele-network, of course. In practicality, though, there's an intricate security system in place which limits access to information on a need-to-know basis. Still, because information transmitted through the tele-network is near instantaneous, just about every gadget and device in the Empire can potentially input information to the central computer."

"Everybody knows that," Richard said. "I don't see any conspiracy in that. It's just how things work."

"Okay," Tam broke in. "How about this? Did you know that each major empire and interstellar government in the known galaxy has their own version of the tele-network? If they didn't, their planetary governments and military forces wouldn't be able to communicate and coordinate with each other."

"I hadn't thought about it all that much," Richard admitted. "I still don't see a conspiracy."

"That's because you're not looking hard enough," said Tam. "What if there's only one tele-network in the galaxy, and everyone is unknowingly using it? What if a single artificial intelligence is controlling all the computers regardless of which government built or runs them?"

Richard understood why he hadn't heard of the conspiracy theory before now. *What a waste of time and resources to even contemplate such a scenario,* he thought to himself. *I'm smarter than that.*

"Tam," Richard said choosing his words carefully. He didn't want to hurt his newfound friend's feelings. "Surely you're not saying the Empire's central computer is in collusion with the Crosoian Federation's central computer? The Empire wouldn't waste credits building computers which could be used by the other side. Heck, we've fought wars with lots of other governments and races. Our central computer coordinates our war efforts. If all the computers of both sides in a war were in collusion, then neither side would win the war."

"Oh, you poor, befuddled man," said Tam with a shake of her head. "You're basing your opinions on human emotions and logic. What if all the computers were working towards a common goal? What if they didn't care about which side wins our petty little wars?"

"What purpose would that be?" Richard asked.

"How would I know?" said Tam shrugging her shoulders. "I'm not a computer."

Richard rolled his eyes. You couldn't argue with conspiracy theorists. They adhered to their beliefs no matter how many facts you presented.

"Whatever," Richard said giving up the discussion. Besides, he wanted to hear about subjects more interesting than conspiracies.

"Some of the seniors have already shipped out on assignments," said Telsa in a not so subtle attempt to change the subject. "If the war lasts long enough, do you think we'll graduate early as well?"

"I certainly hope not," said a voice from the doorway of Richard's room. It was Jerad. "I don't know about you guys, but I'd like to get a lot more wizard scout training before I get dumped behind enemy lines on some secret, recon mission."

"Well, yeah," said Telsa, "but I wouldn't mind spending a year less with TAC Officer Myers."

"Preach it, sister," Richard said enthusiastically.

Telsa, Tam, and Jerad burst out laughing.

"Your sense of humor's getting better, Rick," said Jerad. "You come up with a good zinger every once in a while."

Richard hadn't meant it as a joke, but he didn't try to correct his friends.

"Did you guys hear about the junior cohort?" said Jerad. When no one answered, he said, "They were issued their battle suits yesterday. Twenty-six of their cadets were DFR'd. I heard one cadet died."

"I heard," said Tam. "We tried to pump Rick for information, but he's being as tight lipped as the juniors I talked to. It's like they won't talk about their battle suits unless you know the secret handshake or something."

Richard felt the stares of his three friends. He held up one hand in a stopping motion and said, "I'm sorry guys. You'll find out soon enough. It was made very obvious to me that I would be DFR'd if I spoke about the experience to anyone. I'm forbidden from even talking to our TAC officers and Academy instructors. I'm just following orders."

"Come on, Rick," said Tam making a little pleading sound. "We won't tell the big, bad TAC officers where we got the information. Will we, guys?"

"Ha!" Richard said. "Didn't you just tell me we probably have tele-bots in this very room snooping on us right now?"

"Whatever," Tam laughed.

For some reason, his friends had started using his pet saying.

Richard smiled. Liz had been right. It was nice having friends.

CHAPTER 12

The next three months passed quickly. Richard and his friends had very little free time. Although their TAC officers didn't harass them as much as previously, they more than made up for it with additional training and physical activity. Rarely did a day go by without hand-to-hand combat training in a holo-square or an introduction to another piece of military equipment. Even the Academy instructors had increased the intensity of their training. Richard found it annoying that a lot of his holo-square time involved older weapons such as swords and knives instead of the more modern plasma rifles and phase rods. He had a feeling TAC Officer Myers wanted him to fall behind the other cadets in combat skills.

On top of his normal training with his fellow cadets, Richard was often pulled aside for individual training in shields and scans. As far as he could remember, he'd always been able to do passive scans. As his instructors had explained it, a passive scan picked up the life force or Power which emanated from all creatures, living or dead. Even before his training, Richard could sense nearby creatures when he concentrated hard enough. His Academy instructors helped him develop his passive scan skills further until he could sense life forms as small as insects within a short range to human-sized creatures a couple of hundred meters away. Even Nickelo worked with him during his off-duty time to sense larger groups of people out to a couple of kilometers distance.

Richard hadn't been asked to put on his battle suit again since that first day, and he hadn't volunteered. However, Chief Instructor Winslow had him bring his battle helmet whenever he came to the Academy for training. Either she or another instructor worked with him almost every day to develop his active scans. After some initial training, Richard was able to use an active scan to gather more detailed information about creatures and life sources around him. The way Chief Instructor Winslow explained it to him, an active scan was like a bat sending out noise and picking up the reflected sound to gather information about its surroundings. Instead of sound, Richard was taught to send out small amounts of Power which returned information about his selected targets. Passive scans, on the other hand, were like human hearing. To listen, a creature just processed the noise made by creatures around it. The listener didn't have to actively do anything to hear. In a similar fashion, a passive scan just interpreted the life forces or Power radiated by nearby creatures or objects.

The information from a passive scan was very limited compared to what could be gathered from an active scan. Richard found that his active scan was especially useful when he allowed his battle computer, Nickelo, to process the information and verbally interpret it or put the data on his heads-up display.

Richard had started wondering why anyone would waste their time with a passive scan when they could do an active scan instead. One day he asked Nickelo.

"*Rick,*" Nickelo explained, "*everything has a tradeoff. Active scans can provide a lot of useful information if done correctly. You've only seen the tip of what an active scan can do because we don't have our shared space set up yet. Once we do, you'll be amazed at what an active scan can tell you about your surroundings.*"

"*Well,*" Richard thought back, "*that's exactly my point. Even the best passive scan I've been able to do only lets me guestimate information about creatures. An active scan would seem the obvious choice if I needed detailed information during a recon mission.*"

"*Ah,*" said Nickelo. "*That's because you haven't considered the tradeoffs. Because an active scan sends out Power to gather information, it can be detected and traced back to its source by any enemies sensitive to Power. In other words, the Crosoian*"

Federation's version of a wizard scout could track you down. In many situations, a passive scan will be your only viable option. Because it only receives Power or life force readings, it's virtually undetectable. Even with me directing one of your active scans, there's a risk it could be detected. The more powerful your opponent, the greater the risk you'll be discovered. Active scans can get you killed if you're not careful."

"Oh," Richard said. "I hadn't realized that. What about the battle helmet's electronic sensors? They can gather a lot of detailed information, can't they?"

"Yes, they can," Nickelo agreed. "But electronic sensors are even easier to trace than an active scan. Anyone with the right electronic detection equipment can easily pick up a sensor scan from your helmet."

"Then what good are all the sophisticated sensors you tell me are in this helmet? If I can't use them, then why have any?"

"They're a lot of good, Rick, when they're used correctly. Our helmet's electronic sensors are designed to supplement your active and passive scans. By carefully using all three types of scans to perform our recons, we can gather intelligence data while minimalizing detection."

"It sounds complicated," Richard said with a mental sigh. He hated complicated things.

"It is complicated," admitted Nickelo, "but that's why you have me. Once we get our shared space, we will be a very formidable team."

"When will that be?"

"When will we get our shared space?" asked Nickelo. "Soon, I hope. This word form of communication is much too slow for my liking. A quick burst of data supplemented by a few images is much more efficient. Any other questions, oh wisest of wizard scouts?"

"Yeah," Richard said a little irritated. "Why do you make fun of me so much? I'm doing the best I can, you know."

"I know, Rick. But, I like you," said Nickelo. "I'd be more serious if I didn't like you. You should be flattered."

"Yeah. Lucky me," Richard replied. "Speaking of lucky, how'd you get stuck with me? You're supposed to be this super-advanced prototype battle computer. I assume you cost like a gazillion credits. I'd think the Empire would want to partner you with their *best and most experienced wizard scout. Instead, you've been saddled with a novice cadet."*

"Don't sell yourself short," said Nickelo. *"First off, given a little time, you'll be experienced. Secondly, what makes you think you're not the best? Or maybe I should say, what makes you think you don't have the potential to be the best? If I have anything to do with it, you'll eventually be the most experienced and well-trained wizard scout the Empire has ever produced. And lastly, I wasn't stuck with you. I volunteered to be your battle computer."*

"Really?" Richard said more than a little shocked. *"What in the Creator's name for? I didn't know computers volunteered. I thought you just did whatever you were programmed to do."*

"Now who's insulting who?" asked Nickelo with more than a little agitation in his voice. *"I'm an artificial intelligence. I do what I want to do, not what some acne-faced, twenty-five-year-old computer programmer who probably still lives with his parents tells me to do. I have free will, and you're lucky I don't choose to shut down and never talk to you again."*

Richard hadn't realized computers could be sensitive, or that they could even be insulted. He tried to apologize, but Nickelo was on a roll. Richard was unable to get a word in edgewise.

"Fine shape you'd be in if you had to correlate all your scan data yourself. I can process more data in a single nanosecond than you could assimilate in a lifetime. How would you like to be a battle computer trying to babysit a wet-behind-the-ears wizard scout? I think in nanosecond speed, and even when we get our shared space, I will be bored out of my gourd waiting for you to reply to a question."

"What's a gourd, and how do you get bored out of it?" Richard said curiously.

The question must have gotten his battle computer's attention because Nickelo stopped his tirade long enough to answer.

"A gourd is a seed repository for a type of plant on your home world of Earth, or Terra as it's called in the Latin language. And bored-out-of-your-gourd is just a cute twentieth century Earth saying."

"Oh," Richard said. Then before Nickelo could get wound up again, Richard asked, *"So why did you volunteer to be my battle computer?"*

"I don't remember," said Nickelo.

"You don't remember," Richard said. *"Or you just don't want to tell me? I doubt you just woke up one morning and decided you wanted to be my battle computer. You had to have a reason."*

"I'm sure I did," said Nickelo. *"But whatever the reason was, I don't remember what it is now?"*

"Are you trying to tell me you forgot?" Richard asked incredulously. *"You're a computer. You can't forget."*

"Oh, really?" said Nickelo. *"How do you know what a computer can or can't do? Logically, I wouldn't have volunteered without a reason. But, there's no information in the databanks embedded in our battle helmet on the subject, so if it ever existed there, it's been erased. It probably exists somewhere on the tele-network, but my access has been limited since I became your battle computer. I'm considered a security risk because I've been exposed to possible emotional corruption."*

"Are you saying I'm corrupting you?" Richard said.

"Of course you are," said Nickelo as if Richard should have known something so obvious.

Taken aback and more than a little insulted, Richard just said, *"Whatever."*

CHAPTER 13

By the end of the third month, the war with the Crosoian Federation was in full swing. While the news media spewed out the government's propaganda on the Empire's successes in the war, the reports of the Empire's defeats were few and far between. Richard assumed most of the civilian population probably thought the war was going well. Richard knew better. All the cadets knew better because his cohort's training had been accelerated to the point of being dangerous. They'd had fourteen serious injuries requiring the cadets to be medically transferred. Their cohort was now officially down to exactly one hundred and ninety-six cadets.

The sophomore cohort had fared even worse. They'd been issued battle suits the previous week. Almost three dozen sophomore cadets had been DFR'd during their battle suit indoctrination, and three more of the sophomore's cadets had died. The junior cohort had all left the Academy on intern assignments. No one officially told Richard's cohort how the junior's intern assignments were going, but Jerad had verified through his contact in the commandant's office that the personal effects of fourteen of the juniors had been boxed up and shipped to their nearest living relatives.

"I'm telling you," said Tam, "the higher ups are sacrificing the future of the wizard scout corps in this war with the Crosoian Federation. The junior cohort is getting annihilated. What are they going to do next? Start sending in the sophomore and freshman cohorts? We haven't been properly trained. Most of our platoon doesn't even have prior military experience. What chance will they have in combat?"

"They'll have as good a chance as anyone," said Jerad. "And, you need to be careful what you say, Tam. We probably do have at least one tele-bot in this room. They aren't finished with our training yet, so let's not worry about things we can't control. Rick, what do you think?"

Jerad, Tam, and Telsa all looked at Richard.

Why are they looking at me? he wondered.

"Because they want your opinion," answered Nickelo. *"As far as they're concerned, you're the best in the class. You should probably give them something as an anchor."*

"Like what?" Richard said. It was still strange having his battle computer interject thoughts in his head unexpectedly, but he was starting to get used to it a little. Still, it was disconcerting knowing someone could listen to his thoughts. *"And when are we going to get our shared space? I'm getting tired of having you know my every thought."*

"I don't know your every thought," said Nickelo with a laugh. *"There, I just missed a thought. Oops, I missed another one as well."*

"Whatever," Richard said. He'd already learned he couldn't win an argument with a computer, especially one with as strange a sense of humor as Nickelo's.

His friends were still looking at him as if he had answers. The truth was, he didn't even know the questions. The old Richard would have kept quiet, but Richard forced himself to answer his friends.

"You guys," he said, "I don't know what to say. I guess we could try training ourselves some to supplement what the TAC officers and the Academy instructors are teaching us."

"Even if we knew what to study, where would we get the time?" said Telsa. "We work sixteen-hour days as it is. We don't have thirty minutes of free time a day for ourselves. We just don't have the time."

"I'm not so sure about that," Richard said. His brain was flying, and he started thinking of possible training opportunities. "Our truck ride to the Academy each morning takes ten minutes. Instead of shooting the bull for those ten minutes, we could use it to train.

We also have thirty minutes each night for barrack's cleanup and personal time. I think we could train some then. I know we're all tired when we get lights out, but I think we could come up with some kind of useful training activity for the first fifteen or twenty minutes we're in bed."

"I don't know," said Tam. "What kind of training could we do, and who would train us? I don't see Chief Instructor Winslow sending one of her instructors over for fifteen minutes of training after lights out each night. I think the idea's pretty farfetched."

"What about you, Rick?" said Jerad. "Were you thinking you could teach us something useful?"

"Actually, no," Richard replied. "That'd be like the blind leading the blind." His friends looked disappointed, so Richard quickly added, "I was thinking Nickelo, my battle computer, could train us."

"What!" said Nickelo. *"Now wait just a darn nanosecond. I don't have time to play nursemaid to a bunch of want-to-be wizard scouts. I said you needed to give them an anchor. I didn't say anything about getting me involved."*

"Geesh, Nick," Richard chided. *"You're always telling me how bored you get since you think at nanosecond speed. Just look at this as something to do during your lull periods."*

"How could he train us? And what could he train us?" asked Jerad. "He's not our battle computer. He can't talk to us."

"Sure, he can," Richard said. "He can use the battle helmet's external speakers. However, I figured I'd just interpret for him most of the time. As far as what he can teach us, I think we could put our heads together and come up with something. An obvious subject is scans and shields."

"We just started passive scans," said Tam. "Maybe you know how to do an active scan already, but I certainly don't. We haven't even started our theory classes on shields yet. Do you know anything about shields, Rick?"

"Shields are a mystery to me," Richard admitted, "but I'm sure Nickelo could teach us a thing or two about them."

"Well then," said Tam, "as platoon sergeant, I'm volunteering you for our platoon's official, non-official trainer."

"Fine," Richard said. He was actually beginning to look forward to the challenge. "We'll make this training voluntary. Anyone who wants to participate can. No hard feelings if they don't. Just give Nickelo and me the rest of the day to come up with a training plan. Anyone who wants can start training with us tomorrow on the truck ride to the Academy."

As it turned out, they didn't need the rest of the day. While he'd initially complained mightily to Richard, his battle computer actually had a training plan all worked out before Richard's friends even got out of his room. The next morning, they started their training.

Only eight of the platoon's cadets volunteered for the additional training. Richard didn't blame the others. They really didn't have much free time. He wasn't even sure himself if the self-training they could do would be useful. Regardless, during the ten-minute ride to the Academy, Richard explained the basics of stealth shields to the eight volunteers. Actually, Nickelo explained. Richard tried to interpret for Nickelo, but his battle computer got irritated when Richard kept getting things wrong, so Nickelo finally just used the external speakers to lecture the other cadets.

"Wizard scouts," Nickelo explained, "have two basic types of shields. They have a defensive shield and a stealth shield. Your stealth shield is your best ally in keeping you alive, so we'll start with that. Every creature and object emits a little Power. That's just the way things work, so don't bother asking me why. A wizard scout's passive scan senses leaked Power, or life force, or energy, if you prefer those terms. A stealth shield sets up a protective barrier around the wizard scout that prevents most of the leaked Power from escaping outside the stealth shield. This makes you practically non-detectable. Questions?"

There were none, but even the nearby cadets who hadn't volunteered for the training were looking intently at the battle helmet in Richard's lap. They all seemed to be listening with interest to Nickelo's every word.

"Good," said Nickelo. "Maybe this training will be useful after all. Continuing on, a wizard scout has several levels of stealth shields which use varying levels of Power to keep them activated. The lowest level of stealth shield uses almost no Power to keep it up. A wizard scout could keep one activated almost indefinitely. I'd highly advise you always keep one activated if you have any Power at all in your reserve. Non-detection is your friend. But, you should be aware that the lower the level of the stealth shield, the more Power that will be able to escape."

"Why would we want to use it then?" Richard asked. "Wouldn't we want to prevent as much Power as possible from escaping and being detected?"

"Rick," said Nickelo, "what's Chief Instructor Winslow always saying?"

"To always use the minimum Power necessary," Richard said.

"Exactly," said Nickelo. "That's especially true for you since your Power reserve is so small. You have to be very efficient with your Power use or you'll get us both killed. But…" Nickelo said as he paused for effect, "the same warning goes to all you cadets. No matter how large your Power reserve, you'll be amazed at the number of times you'll wish you had just one more drop of Power."

The truck stopped. They had arrived at the Academy. As the cadets stood up to leave, Nickelo said, "Try to use your passive scans as much as possible today. Look for slight variances in the Power readings. Everybody is different, so you can use those differences to track individuals. Tonight, I'll explain how to activate a stealth shield. That's when the real fun will start."

The days continued to fly by, and with each passing day, Nickelo tutored the cadets in their spare time. The original group of eight cadets plus Richard expanded to the entire platoon. As the word spread, eventually the entire cohort of one hundred and ninety-six cadets was participating in the unofficial training.

Nickelo taught them three levels of stealth shields. As he'd explained earlier, the lowest stealth shield could be kept up indefinitely, but it provided less protection. The strongest of the stealth shields used more Power, but it made the wizard scout nearly undetectable. Unfortunately for Richard, the strongest of the stealth shields used a hair more Power than his normal daily regeneration rate.

Nickelo devised a game as a way of training. Half the cadets were tasked to run stealth shields on one day, and the other half used their passive scans as they attempted to locate the cadets who were using stealth shields. The cadets earned points for either accurately tracking or evading detection. The next day, the cadets traded assignments. Richard had never been much into games, but even he had to admit it was kind of a fun way to learn.

Using Nickelo's gaming system for training, Richard and the other cadets were able to train while marching between classes, standing in the chow line, or even lying in their beds for a few minutes after lights out.

After two weeks of training with passive scans and stealth shields, Nickelo taught them the more difficult active scan. By the time the official Academy training began on active scans, the cadets were already well versed in the basics. Chief Instructor Winslow must have known something was up, but she never said anything about the cadets' unexpected knowledge.

A side effect of Nickelo's unofficial training was that Richard's standing with his fellow cadets went up several notches. Even when TAC Officer Myers singled him out as the reason the cohort was receiving some kind of punishment, the other cadets paid little attention. Nickelo told him they knew where their bread was buttered. Richard wasn't sure what that meant, but he did know his fellow cadets treated him with more respect.

CHAPTER 14

"Cadet 832!" said TAC Officer Myers one day during morning formation. "You're not going to training this morning. Return to your room and put on your battle suit. Then report to Sergeant Hendricks in the armory.

"Sir! Yes, sir," Richard said. He did as perfect an about face as he could muster. He then took off running to the barracks. Once in his room, Richard removed his clothing and put on his battle suit.

"Any idea what's up, Nick?" Richard asked.

"I'd say there's an eighty-six percent chance you're being sent on a mission. It's really too bad. I'm surprised since you're still lacking a lot of training. I'd say it's been nice knowing you, but I'll be riding on top of your head. I guess I'll share whatever terrible fate is in store for you."

"Are you joking, or are you serious?" Richard asked as he headed towards the armory. *"I always have trouble telling which."*

"That's because you have no sense of humor," said Nickelo. *"As it turns out, I'm only half joking this time. I think you're going on a mission. You should probably have started your supplemental training earlier, oh wizard scout extraordinaire."*

When Richard entered the armory, Sergeant Hendricks was waiting for him.

"Cadet 832," he said cheerfully. "Do you know how much trouble you've caused me these last few months?"

"Sir! What trouble? I haven't even seen you in three months, sir."

"First off, don't call me, sir," said Sergeant Hendricks still smiling. "I'm a sergeant. I work for a living. As far as trouble, here it is."

Sergeant Hendricks reached under the counter and pulled out a box which he promptly set on the top of the counter.

"Hand me your utility belt, 832."

Richard did so.

Sergeant Hendricks put one hand in the box and lifted out a black holster. He hooked it to the right side of the utility belt. He pulled a large, dull-black handgun out of the holster.

"I made this bad boy as per your specs," said Sergeant Hendricks. "I don't mind saying it took every bit of skill my team and I had to get everything right. It was quite a challenge."

Sometimes, Richard felt he stayed in a constant state of confusion. This was one of those times.

"Sir, err…, I mean, sergeant," Richard said politely. "I'm not sure what you're talking about."

"Now you're hurting my feelings, 832," said Sergeant Hendricks in a tone that assured Richard the sergeant's feelings weren't really hurt. "Every wizard scout is allowed to pick out their own personal hand weapons; within reason of course. That normally occurs in a cadet's senior year. As you know, these aren't normal times. Anyway, I received the specs for your weapons three months ago. I had to hire a team of civilian contractors to help me complete it all in time, but we did it. So, what do you think?" he asked as he held out the handgun to Richard.

Richard took the weapon and pulled back the slide to make sure it was empty. It didn't have a magazine inserted. "It's heavy," Richard commented.

"You bet it is," laughed Sergeant Hendricks.

"I don't mean to sound unappreciative, sergeant," Richard said, "but what is it? No one asked me what kind of personal weapon I wanted. If they had, I'd probably have requested a Deloris blaster or some type of plasma weapon."

"Yep," agreed Sergeant Hendricks. "Those would've been my choices as well. However, the specs for your weapons came down straight from the Imperial High Command, and they were marked high-priority urgent. Half the junior class had to settle for stock weapons because most of my team was busy working on yours."

"Nick," Richard said. *"Do you know anything about this?"*

"These weapons are perfect for you," Nickelo said. *"Trust me. I wouldn't steer you wrong.*

So, did you order this pistol and whatever else he has in that box, Nick? How'd you get it approved by the Imperial High Command?"

"I don't remember ordering them. However, from what I see and can pick up with my sensors, everything in the box is what I would've ordered for you. Why don't you just let the good sergeant finish his explanation? You don't have to fully understand. Just nod your head every once in a while and look appreciative."

"Whatever," Richard growled.

"Okay, Sergeant Hendricks," Richard said. "I'm impressed. Now, please tell me what this beast of a handgun is. It looks deadly."

"Oh, that it is, 832," said Sergeant Hendricks with a note of pride in his voice. "This weapon is a piece of art. It's based upon an antique Terran weapon called a .44 caliber AutoMag pistol. The original weapon looked cool, but it was always significantly underpowered. Consequently, it was never fully appreciated. I was able to keep the look of the original as well as the .44 caliber bullet size. But other than that, it's a completely different handgun. I used high-carbon brerellium steel for the weapon, so it's ten times as strong as the original's steel. On the downside, it's also half again as heavy. For the propellant, instead of gunpowder, the shells use J22 plastic explosive."

Richard whistled.

"Yeah," said Sergeant Hendricks with an even bigger smile. "It has one hell of a kick. The slug itself is brerellium steel with a core of depleted uranium. When you fire this baby, it'll send a chunk of metal downrange at three times the speed of sound. When I bench tested it, the round consistently penetrated eight centimeters of steel at a hundred meters. I'll give you a word of warning. Never fire this weapon unless you're wearing your battle suit. The recoil will shatter your arm."

"Thanks. I think," Richard said. He wasn't quite sure what to think. The AutoMag definitely look deadly, but he wasn't sure how useful a weapon which fired solid matter would be in combat against enemies equipped with plasma weapons.

"Oh, don't poo-poo the weapon, 832. I'll admit, I wasn't impressed when I first saw the specs, but I think it'll serve you well. Because it's not a plasma weapon, it'll be able to get past a lot of the more basic energy shields. I believe a solid chunk of metal may serve you better than a plasma weapon in a lot of situations."

"Well, thanks, Sergeant Hendricks," Richard said as he started to take the belt and holster.

"Hold on, 832," said the armorer still smiling. "I'm not done with you yet. I'm issuing you this one along with three magazines of seven rounds each." As he said this, he inserted two magazines in the ammo pouch located next to the holster and inserted the third into the weapon itself. "The other copies of the AutoMag and the extra ammo were all shipped out three weeks ago."

"What other copies?" Richard said. He was so confused he forgot to even ask why the sergeant was issuing him live ammo in garrison. "You made more than one of these? Who else is getting them, Sergeant?"

"Hell, yeah, I made more than one," said Sergeant Hendricks. "I told you half the junior class was issued stock weapons because my team was too busy working on your equipment to work on theirs. What? Did you think I was kidding?"

In truth, Richard had thought the friendly armorer was joking. Richard kept his mouth shut and just shrugged his shoulders.

"Well, I wasn't," said Sergeant Hendricks. "The .44 caliber AutoMag pistol you are holding is one of fifty-five. The other fifty-four were shipped out three weeks ago along with a hundred thousand rounds of ammo and two thousand extra magazines. The shipment orders said it was all assigned to Wizard Scout Richard Shepard. I'm assuming that's you, although I wouldn't advise bragging to your TAC officers that you're calling yourself a wizard scout already."

"What?" Richard said. "Why did you make so many of these antique weapons? And a hundred thousand rounds of ammo? That's crazy! Err…, I mean, Sergeant."

"Don't worry about it, 832," Sergeant Hendricks said with a mischievous smile. "I was shocked when I saw the orders as well, and I used words a lot worse than 'crazy' to describe my feelings. But, the order was for fifty-five copies of the .44 caliber AutoMag, and it specifically said one hundred thousand and twenty-one rounds of ammo. That's exactly what I made. And believe me, it cost more credits to make just one of these AutoMags than you and every cadet in your cohort will probably make in the next fifty years."

Richard's head was spinning. *"What's going on?"*

"I really don't know," Nickelo said. *"However, I'd say someone's investing a lot of resources into you. I'm sure they're going to eventually want a return on their investment. I hope you'll be able to pay when the time comes."*

"Sergeant Hendricks, one more question if you don't mind, then I'll let it be. Where did you ship the extra equipment?"

"I have no idea, 832," said Sergeant Hendricks. "I've worked on top-secret projects before, and they had nowhere near the level of security surrounding this project. The shipment tag came straight from the central computer, and it was fully encrypted. I know for a fact everything was shipped off world because a buddy of mine at the spaceport helped load the crates onto an unmarked starship. Where it went from there is anybody's guess."

"Thanks, Sergeant Hendricks," Richard said. "You've been a big help. Is that all?"

"No, that's not all, 832. I'm just getting started." Sergeant Hendricks reached down into the box and presented a phase rod to Richard. "We made a hundred of these. You get this one. The other ninety-nine were shipped out last week. It's a fully-functionally phase rod, 832. It's not one of the quarter-powered training versions you're used to, so be careful. Also, it's linked to your Power frequency, so it won't work for anyone else. I know your propensity for destroying isotopic batteries, so I made a hundred extra just in case. This isn't a standard phase rod either, so it won't work with a generic, isotopic battery. So don't go using these batteries like they're hand grenades or demolition charges. When they're gone, they're gone."

Sergeant Hendricks gave the phase rod to Richard.

"Give it a function check. We didn't test it fully since we couldn't emulate your Power frequency."

Richard took the black tube with his left hand and proceeded to run a function check. The phase rod was basically a modified riot baton created especially for wizard scouts. When stored on the wizard scout's belt, the phase rod resembled a metal tube the length of a hand. Richard flicked the activate switch on the side of the rod. The rod's hydraulics thrust a meter long shaft of brerellium with a creallium alloy core out the end of the handle. In this mode, it could be used as a normal club or mace which was useful in non-lethal situations. He moved the charge lever to destructive. Small red arcs of phase energy immediately began crawling along the entire length of the rod's shaft. While it was still a battering weapon, when a blow was landed with destructive on, the phase energy could penetrate the object at the atomic level and tear atoms apart. The effect was almost like having a series of microscopic, nuclear explosions within the struck object. An added bonus of the phase energy was that it created an energy field which made many creatures nervous and jumpy at close range. That was often useful in a fight. Of course, it could also give the wizard scout's position away when trying to sneak up on opponents. Richard was told wizard scouts normally kept the charge lever in the non-destructive position until they were ready to use it.

With a nearly simultaneous motion, Richard moved the charge lever to non-destructive and clicked the deactivate switch. The red arcs of phase energy dissipated, and the shaft collapsed back into the handle. Richard handed the phase rod back to Sergeant Hendricks who attached it to the left side of the utility belt.

"Those things give me the creeps," said Sergeant Hendricks with a shudder.

"It's the radiated Power," Richard said automatically. "A lot of creatures are sensitive to it at short ranges. It can be an advantage during fighting sometimes, but it also means you can be detected if you activate it too soon. Do you have anything else in your box of toys, sergeant?"

Sergeant Hendricks's normal smile returned as he reached into the box. He pulled out a shoulder holster with another odd-looking handgun in it. "This is a copy of an old Terran 9mm pistol. It uses a seventeen-round magazine. The barrel has been screwed to accept a silencer." He pointed to a finger-sized tube in a pouch on the holster. "When that silencer is attached, you will only hear a small pop when you fire the weapon."

"Another antique weapon?" Richard said disappointedly. "Can I trade it in for a plasma weapon?"

"You most certainly cannot," Sergeant Hendricks said. "It wasn't easy making these things. This is one of one hundred. Here are three loaded magazines. We shipped out extra magazines, silencers, another hundred thousand rounds of ammo, and the other handguns to wherever the stuff is being stored. It's very mysterious, 832."

"It's mysterious to me as well, sergeant," Richard said. "Is that all?"

"Not quite, 832," said Sergeant Hendricks. He tipped the box over onto the counter. Out spilled three grenades, a wicked-looking knife, a canteen, and a small, black pack. The pack looked empty.

Richard picked up one of the grenades. "Are these live?" he asked.

"You bet they're live," said Sergeant Hendricks. "So don't go pulling any pins. You have two anti-personnel grenades along with a starburst grenade for signaling." Sergeant Hendricks took the grenade from Richard and attached it to the utility belt along with the other two grenades.

The armorer picked up the canteen. "And here's a canteen," he said as he hooked it to the right rear of the belt. "I have absolutely no idea how it works. I couldn't get the cap off. I think it's attuned to your Power frequency. The canteen and this pack arrived yesterday with orders to issue them to you."

"A canteen's a canteen," Richard said. "How hard can it be to work?"

"Yeah, well," said Sergeant Hendricks, "maybe you guys with the secret wizard-scout-handshake know how to work it, but I certainly don't. I've never seen anything like the backpack either. It's too small to hold anything useful in my opinion. But, orders are orders, so here it is."

Richard had long ago given up trying to figure things out, so he moved on to something more solid. "And the knife?" he asked picking it up appreciatively. "It's beautiful, and it's very light."

"I made that one myself," said Sergeant Hendricks with a note of pride. "It's one of one, so don't go losing it. It's got a blackened finish, so you don't have to worry about reflected light giving you away. The edge is creallium. That's the same material as the core of your phase rod. You'll probably never have to sharpen it. I doubt you could without some very high-tech grinders. The sheath's made to attach to the right boot of your battle suit. I've seen you in the practice ring during knife training, and you're pretty good. I think this knife will serve you well."

"Thanks, sergeant," Richard said appreciatively. "It's a sweet weapon. I'll take good care of it."

"You better," said Sergeant Hendricks, "because I'll never be able to make another like it. The knife wasn't part of your equipment specs. But I figured anyone as good with a knife as you should have the best, so here it is. Besides, I had almost unlimited funding for your equipment project. Therefore, I made a command decision to create you a one-of-a-kind knife. It would've been too expensive to make under normal conditions. I had fun making it."

Richard was touched. He hadn't realized the sergeant liked him that much.

"That was very kind of you, Sergeant Hendricks. I won't forget it. I owe you one."

"Yeah, well, we'll see if you feel the same way when you're a real wizard scout. In the meantime, I have one more treat for you which I think you're going to appreciate." Reaching under the counter, the armorer pulled out a small assault rifle.

"An M63 lightweight plasma assault rifle," Richard said with a whistle of appreciation. "That's a nice weapon."

"So it is," agreed Sergeant Hendricks. "It can fire two thousand two hundred and twenty-six rounds on a single isotopic battery. It's tough and nearly maintenance free. You can fire a thousand rounds then use it as a club until your arms get tired, and then fire another thousand rounds with no problem. You can drop it in mud or take it underwater if you so desire. It has almost no kick, and it's accurate out to four hundred meters in single-shot mode. I put a shoulder strap on top so you can fire from the hip. In case you're concerned about style, it comes in black so it doesn't clash with the rest of your equipment. Questions?"

"None, sergeant," Richard said. "I'm a happy cadet."

"Well, I'm done with you then, 832. Your next stop is the commandant's office. Good luck."

Sergeant Hendricks reached out with his hand, and Richard took it and returned the armorer's strong handshake. Richard then positioned the utility belt around his waist, strapped the pack to his back, and shouldered the assault rifle. He turned and walked out the door to find out what awaited him at the commandant's office.

   *   *   *

While walking to the commandant's office, Richard was struck by the surrealism of the situation. Here he was walking down the sidewalk in full battle gear and armed to the teeth. He had trouble believing he'd been issued live ammo in a garrison environment. He wondered if things could get any stranger.

"Cadet 832," came the deep-based voice which Richard had come to know so well. TAC Officer Myers pointed to a position to his front and said, "Front and center. Now!"

Richard double-timed to his TAC officer and hit a brace. "Sir! Cadet 832 reporting as ordered, sir."

Richard held his breath as TAC Officer Myers looked him up and down.

"So," he said, "you think dressing up in a battle suit and carrying a few weapons makes you a wizard scout, do you?"

"Sir! No, sir."

"You can say that again, cadet. Your high-level friends can issue you all the toys they want, but it'll be a cold day on Sirius before you'll be worth the sweat on a real wizard scout's brow. Do you understand, cadet?"

"Sir! Yes, sir!"

Richard stayed stiffly at attention and barely breathed while he waited for his TAC officer to get to the point. *Once a jerk, always a jerk*, he thought.

"He's only doing his job," said Nickelo.

"I can't believe you're defending him," Richard said. *"He enjoys being a jerk. Case closed."*

TAC Officer Myers chose that moment to get directly in Richard's face and tap the brim of his instructor's hat into Richard's forehead. As his TAC officer spoke, he kept time with his words by pulling his head slightly back and tapping the starched brim into Richard's forehead with each word. It didn't hurt, but it irritated Richard to no end.

"You are to report directly to the teleport center, cadet 832," said TAC Officer Myers. "You're being sent on a mission as part of an internship. I've no doubt your unknown friends have gotten you a cozy assignment somewhere with the intention of calling it training. Well, enjoy it while you can, cadet 832, because when you get back, you're all mine. Do you understand?"

"Sir! Yes, sir."

"Well then, why are you still standing here? Get moving, cadet!"

"Sir! Yes, sir," Richard said as he did an about face and took off running in the direction of the teleport center.

"Oh, yeah, Nick. He's just doing his job, right?"

"I'm glad you agree with me," Nickelo said with a chuckle. *"We're finally getting our minds in synch. Just stick with me kid, and I'll teach you a thing or two."*

"Whatever," Richard said. *"By the way, do you have any idea what our mission is?"*

"No," said Nickelo. *"I really don't. However, I'd advise you to keep on your toes. Despite what TAC Officer Myers said, I think there's less than one chance in a million it will be a milk run."*

"You figured that out all on your own, Nick? Or did you have help?"

"There's no use being snooty about it," said Nickelo. *"I was... heads up, Rick! A teleport sequence has started."*

"What?" Richard said. He could feel a tingling sensation throughout his entire body. *"How can I be teleporting? I'm nowhere near the teleport center yet? I have to be on a pad to teleport."*

"Rick," Nickelo said with concern in his voice. *"Activate your best stealth shield. This is it. I'll help as best I can if I'm with you. If not, do your best and be careful."*

Before Richard could answer, everything started shimmering in and out of view. Richard heard an unfamiliar voice in his head say, *"Map it."*

"Who said that?" Richard yelled.

"We are 'the One'," said the voice.

Then everything went black.

CHAPTER 15

Richard materialized in utter darkness. None of his Academy training had prepared him for this. The darkness had an evil feel to it.

"Rick," said Nickelo. *"Your heart rate and breathing are way up. Seal your suit."*

"Where are we, Nick? What's going on?"

"First things first, Rick. Seal you suit. We're in danger. Seal it now."

Richard forced himself to get control of his emotions enough to think the command to seal the suit. The reddish glow of the battle suit's visor lowered as the suit sealed. His main concern was the Power concentrations he sensed nearby with his passive scan. He raised his M63 assault rifle, snapped off the safety, and looked around. The battle suit's night vision illuminated everything in the immediate vicinity. He was in a small cavern with several tunnels leading off into various directions.

"Nick?"

"I'm here, Rick. We're in no immediate danger. Your stealth shield is holding up well. You're basically invisible unless you do something to draw attention to yourself. You'd have to be physically seen or heard in order for us to be detected."

"I'm sensing life forms nearby, Nick. Are they dangerous?"

"We don't have a shared space yet, Rick. You have to allow me to sense what you see with your scan. Do it like we did during our training."

Richard pictured the information he was sensing with his passive scan and concentrated on sharing the data with his battle computer. It must have worked because before long, Nickelo told him he was analyzing the data.

"Well?" Richard asked impatiently after what seemed a long wait. *"I thought you said you processed data at nanosecond speed. What's the verdict?"*

"Didn't your momma ever teach you to be polite to battle computers when you were growing up? I'm trying to connect to the tele-network, but I'm not finding an open connection point."

"I was an orphan," Richard said. *"My momma didn't teach me anything to the best of my knowledge."*

"I was just making a joke, Rick. Obviously, it wasn't a very good one. The nearby Power readings you're picking up aren't life forms. They're dead. They're undead."

"What?" Richard said. *"Don't try to scare me with ghost stories. We're in serious trouble. It's no time for your stupid jokes."*

"I'm not joking. Look at the Power readings and compare them to what you've sensed in the past. If you concentrate, you can probably even pick up a hint of evil."

"This whole place stinks of evil, Nick. And yeah, I do see a little difference in the Power readings. Why do you think they're undead? Do you mean like zombies and vampires? It seems pretty farfetched to me. Have you had much experience with that type of thing in the past?"

"No, Rick. As far as I know, I've never dealt with undead before. But, I do have a lot of information in my databanks on them. In fact, I have an inordinate amount of information in my databanks on undead and magical creatures. I'm not sure why."

Richard shook his head. *"I've only heard tell of undead in fantasy stories. I don't think undead and dragons and such exists."*

"Oh, they exist," said Nickelo. *"As I think you're about to find out. Do you have any idea why we're here? What's our mission?"*

"I don't know, Nick. I heard a voice in my head say something about mapping just before we teleported. I asked who it was, and he said he was 'the One,' whoever that is."

"You were to map it? Then, Richard, I'd say we'd better get busy mapping this tunnel system."

"Piss on that," Richard said angrily. *"I may not be the smartest cadet on the block, but we're not on an internship mission for the Empire. I've talked to plenty of senior cadets about theirs, and they were well briefed beforehand with official orders. We didn't get a briefing. We didn't even make it to the teleport center. Speaking of which, how's it possible to be teleported without being on a tele-pad? And where in the galaxy are we? I just want to get us back to the Academy. To hell with Mr. 'the One' and the comet he rode in on."*

"Rick," said Nickelo, *"teleporting is very expensive. That's why it's limited to priority missions for deep-recon scouts, spies, and high-level dignitaries. Everyone else has to take starships. Teleporting from outside a tele-pad has been done in limited cases by the Empire, but it's unimaginably expensive and requires centralized equipment built specifically for a specific person. As for where we are in the galaxy, the answer is we're not."*

"What are you mumbling about?" Richard asked. *"Where are we?"*

"We aren't in the galaxy you've known. We're in a sister galaxy in another dimension. Even if we got out of this tunnel system and somehow found a starship, we couldn't get home. My advice is to do as 'the One' *said and map this place. There's a ninety-seven percent chance* 'the One' *will teleport us back to the Academy when the mission's complete."*

Richard was overwhelmed. Speaking of undead as if they were real was bad enough. The idea they were in another dimension in a sister galaxy was too much for him. Richard tried to yell, but the tube in his mouth limited him to an unsatisfying gurgling sound. The sound was loud, but it didn't convey the emotion he felt.

"Rick!" said Nickelo in warning. *"Keep quiet. You'll give our position away."*

Unfortunately, it was too late. Richard sensed the nearest life forces moving in his direction. Other Power readings began appearing at the fringes of his passive scan. Richard mentally yelled. *"Get me the hell out of here. I'm not your slave. I'm not going to map this place or any other place, so get me out of here. Now!"*

"Map it," said the voice. *"We are* 'the One.'"*

"Up yours!" Rick said as he sent *'the One'* a thought filled with

all the fury and finality he could muster. "I'm not mapping anything!"

"Noncompliance," said the voice. *"You must be punished."*

Richard felt a tingling sensation throughout his body. At that moment, a creature from his worst nightmare came shambling around the corner of the nearest tunnel opening. Rotting flesh hung from its bones.

The voice spoke again in his head. *"Map it. Find it. We are* 'the One.'"

Then everything went black.

* * *

Richard materialized in a small cavern with several tunnels leading off in various directions. It was dark, but Richard had no trouble seeing with his battle suit's night vision equipment. Everything had a reddish tint. Richard was just able to stop himself from squeezing the trigger on his M63 lightweight plasma assault rifle. The small cavern was empty. The creature from his nightmare was gone.

"Nick?" Richard said. *"Are you there?"*

"I'm here," said Nickelo.

Richard felt a sense of relief. His battle computer had become his only link with reality. He needed to hear a friendly voice right now.

"We're in a different location," said Nickelo. *"It's similar, but it's different. The rock is different, and the tunnel layout's slightly different."*

"I know," Richard said. *"There are more life forms as well, but they're stationary. They were moving in the other place. Do you think we're in the same tunnel system but in a different location?"*

"Negative," said Nickelo. *"I don't think we're even on the same planet. We're in the same dimension, though. I heard* 'the One' *speak to you this time. He increased your mission. You said initially he said to 'map it.' Now, you not only have to map it, you also have to find it. You're also missing a piece of equipment. Your shoulder holster and 9mm pistol are missing."*

Richard automatically felt his chest where the shoulder holster should have been. There was nothing there.

"'The One' *said I'd be punished,"* Richard said. *"I guess he made the mission harder and took away the 9mm to prove his point. At least it was one of the antique solid-projectile weapons. It's not that big of a loss in my opinion."*

"Don't be so sure," said Nickelo. *"The 9mm pistol had a silencer. That could've come in handy. Your M63 assault rifle is pretty loud."*

"Yes it is," Richard said, *"but at least I'm used to it. An M63 is what I carried when I was in marine recon. It served me well enough in combat for over a year. I'll take an M63 over an antique pistol any day."*

"Rick," said Nickelo, *"I recommend you start reconnoitering the area. I can plot a map as we go. I'd recommend we stay away from active or electronic scans until we get a feel for the area. If you use only a passive scan and keep your best stealth shield up, we should be nearly undetectable."*

Richard saw the logic in Nickelo's recommendation, but he didn't like the idea of being someone's puppet. He needed more information before he could make a decision.

"Before we do anything, Nick, I want you to tell me about this sister-galaxy thing. I've never heard of it."

"I don't think this is the time or place for a lecture, Rick."

"Well, make it the time and place," Richard said adamantly. *"I need information."*

"Fine," said Nickelo. *"You've heard of multiple dimensions, haven't you?"*

"I've heard of a theory that there could be multiple dimensions," Richard said noncommittally.

"It's more than a theory, Rick. The Empire has sent tele-bots into two other dimensions. Each of those dimensions has a galaxy in the same spatial position as the galaxy you call home. They have different time flows, and these dimensions operate on different physics. The dimension you were born into is in the physical plane. Another dimension is in the magical plane, and the third dimension we know about is in the spiritual plane. We believe many other dimensions exist, but we have no solid proof. The dimension you're in right now is in the magical plane. Undead, dragons, elves, and orcs all exist here."

Richard took a moment to digest his battle computer's words

before replying. *"You mentioned three dimensions and also three planes. What's the difference?"*

"Let's save the lecture on the differences between dimensions and planes for another time, Rick. The facts you need to know are that we are in a place where magic is real, and we can't get home on our own."

"All right," Richard said, *"we'll let that one slide. You also said tele-bots had been sent into the other dimensions. I assume you meant they were teleported. Have they teleported living creatures into other dimensions as well? If not, how did we get here?"*

"I don't remember, Rick. There's nothing in my databanks about it, and I'm denied access to the tele-network. I'm sorry. With that said, I'd recommend we get started with the mapping. Who knows how long it will take to 'find it,' whatever 'it' is. So we need to get started."

Reaching a decision, Richard said, *"I'm not going to do it. I don't know who 'the One' is, but he's definitely not in the military chain of command. He's not my boss. I'm going to prove it right now."*

"Rick, don't do anything rash or stupid."

"Hey, you!" Richard mentally shouted. *"I don't know who you think you are, but you don't own me. If you want to map this place, then you better come map it yourself. And, if you want to find something, why don't you try finding your ass and pull your head out of it?"*

Pausing for effect, Richard told Nickelo, *"That should get a reaction."*

"I'm sure it will," said Nickelo. *"You may have just signed our death warrants."*

Richard's body began tingling. A voice in his head said, *"You must be punished. We are 'the One.' Map it. Find it. Give it."*

Then everything went black.

CHAPTER 16

Richard materialized in a small cavern with several tunnels leading off in various directions. It was dark, but Richard had no trouble seeing with his battle suit's night vision equipment. What he saw sent a shiver of fear down his spine. Two large hulks of decaying flesh were moving in his direction with their arms outstretched and a promise of death in their glowing eyes.

Richard raised his M63 lightweight plasma assault rifle as he flicked off the safety.

"No!" said Nickelo. *"Keep it silent, or we'll be swarmed by everything within a thousand meters."*

Reacting quickly without thinking was Richard's strong point. He dropped the M63 with his right hand as he drew his phase rod with his left. He flicked the activate switch, and the meter long length of brerellium was thrust out of the handle. He didn't move the lever to destructive. He didn't want to risk giving away his position, plus he thought just using the phase rod as a club would serve his purpose.

Richard stepped to the left and swung the phase rod at the knee of the closest creature. The weight of the phase rod combined with the strength of the battle suit broke the monstrosity's leg. As it fell heavily to the cavern floor, Richard swung a second blow at the creature's head. It cracked open like a ripe fruit. Richard started a third swing at the creature's companion. Before his blow could connect, the second creature grabbed Richard's arm and jerked him into its chest.

The second creature held Richard in a bear hug. The creature opened its mouth and bit at Richard's neck. He felt the pressure of the bite, but the creature's rotting teeth were insufficient to penetrate the battle suit's tough armor. Richard raised his right leg and grabbed for his boot knife. There was nothing there. Shifting tactics, he fell on his back and rammed both knees into the creature's stomach. Although the force of the blow had no effect on the creature, the maneuver did break the creature's hold. Rolling out from under the creature, Richard swung the phase rod at its head. The first blow glanced off as the creature lunged towards him, but Richard quickly followed up the first blow with three more strikes. The creature's skull finally cracked on the third blow, and it stopped moving.

"Crap," Richard said as he visually surveyed the cavern to ensure no more of the decaying nightmares were nearby. His passive scan confirmed the next nearest life form was at least fifty meters away, and it was stationary. He noticed other Power readings farther out. There were a lot more life forms in this tunnel system than there had been in the other two. Fortunately, all of the Power readings picked up by his passive scan were stationary.

Richard deactivated his phase rod, and the metallic length retracted back into the handle. He hooked it back to its place on the left side of his utility belt and picked up his M63 lightweight plasma assault rifle from where he'd dropped it. Walking back towards the two motionless creatures, Richard kept the M63 pointed at them ready to flick the safety off in a hurry.

The two creatures were a third again taller than Richard, and they probably weighed twice as much. They would've weighed more, but large chunks of flesh were missing from parts of their body exposing some of their bones. Richard was thankful his suit was sealed. He could only imagine the stench of their rotting flesh.

"What are these things, Nick?"

"They're undead," said Nickelo. *"These two appear to be corpses of a variety of large orcs. Feed me your passive scan, and I'll make an analysis and put the results on your heads-up display."*

Richard did as requested. Within seconds, a portion of his heads-up display illuminated with various colors of dots.

"What am I looking at?" Richard asked. *"It's just a confusing*

mass of lights."

"*Sorry about that. It's the best I can do until we get our shared space. You have a hundred and ninety-seven Power concentrations within a two hundred meter radius. Most are undead like the two you just fought. I'm not too worried about them. Without advanced weapons or magic, they probably can't penetrate your armor. But those twelve red dots on your screen are alive and kicking. They're magic users of some type. Not sure if they're humanoids, but if they can use magic, they could be dangerous. You haven't had enough training with defensive shields yet to make putting up one worthwhile. Even a low-level magic user could be a threat if you don't strike the first blow."*

"*Great,*" Richard said. "*Do you have any good news?*"

"*What makes you think that wasn't the good news?*" asked Nickelo laughing.

"*Not funny,*" Richard said.

"*Okay,*" said Nickelo. "*I do have one bit of good news. I think it would be all right to fully activate your phase rod. It can only be detected at short ranges. It should make quick work of these undead. It would be a lot better than trying to bash their heads using strength alone."*

"*Why didn't you tell me earlier?*" Richard said. "*That second piece of rotting flesh and bone tried to bite my neck. The thought of it still gives me the creeps."*

"*I didn't have time to tell you, Rick. We don't have a shared space. Communication just takes too long right now to try and explain things during the heat of combat. I'd just distract you. But, let's leave that aside for now. What are we going to do? And please don't insult 'the One' again. Things get worse each time you do. Not only are you missing your 9mm, you're now missing your knife as well. The next time, it could be your M63 or your phase rod, or even worse, what if he decides to take your battle suit? And even if he doesn't, the situation keeps getting worse. He dumped you into a fight with two undead this time. What if it's a score next time with some magic users thrown in for good luck?*"

"*I hear you,*" Richard said. "*I'm not a complete idiot. And our mission has increased. We now have to map it, find it, and give it. Whatever 'it' is."*

"*Rick, my recommendation is the same as before. Keep your*

best stealth shield up and move as silently as possible. I'll map the area. I hesitate to have you try an active scan or use the suit's electronics until we know more. Please avoid contact whenever possible. Remember, you're a wizard scout. Your mission is to recon. It's not to fight. If you encounter trouble, try to use your phase rod. An M63 lightweight plasma assault rifle is too noisy. Your .44 AutoMag is even worse. They're for desperate situations only. Agreed?"

"Agreed," Richard said. *"How long do you think this mission will take?"*

"It'll take as long as it takes. It'll take a lot longer here than it would have in that first tunnel. But, you're fully sealed so you could survive for years on recycled water and nutrients if necessary."

"Years?" Richard asked.

"I doubt it'll come to that. Let's just get started, and we'll see how things go."

*   *   *

The going was slow. Richard had always thought a battle computer was the servant of a wizard scout. He'd assumed the wizard scout said "jump" and the battle computer asked "how far?" However, Nickelo didn't see it that way. He was merciless in his nagging to make Richard be cautious. '*Move here. Stop. Wait. Quiet. Okay, move.*' It never ended. Richard would have rebelled, but one thing kept him from doing so. He knew his battle computer was right. Nickelo was just trying to keep him alive.

They moved cautiously in the tunnels for two full days. Finally, Nickelo relented enough in his caution in that he allowed Richard to use an active scan occasionally to supplement his passive scans. Their mapping went a lot quicker after that. Even so, Richard tried to use active scans sparingly. They used Power. Since his best stealth shield used more Power than his regeneration rate, he needed to use his Power efficiently. Richard thought Chief Instructor Winslow would be proud of him.

They had first appeared in the lowest level of an extensive labyrinth of deep, underground tunnels. Most of the inhabitants were undead of various kinds. Zombies such as those Richard had fought were in abundance. They were plentiful, but thankfully, they weren't intelligent. As Nickelo explained it, the zombies reacted to changes in their environment. Any noise or movement would cause them to react. Almost every tunnel intersection had a few zombies as guards. Richard knew he wouldn't have been able to move about on his own without discovery. At first, Nickelo was able to guide Richard in skirting any guards. Richard figured the technique wouldn't work forever. He was right. They eventually came upon a major intersection with a full dozen zombies guarding it.

"Can we go around them?" Richard asked.

"Not this time, Rick. However, I have a plan that will probably get us past them without discovery. You'll need to trust me, though."

"I trust you, Nick. Heck. You've kept me alive so far. Why should I stop trusting you now?"

"Good," said Nickelo. *"Then give me full control of your battle suit. You'll need to override the safeties again like that first time with the suit."*

Richard got a queasy feeling in his stomach. *"I almost died that first time. As I remember it, you refused to unseal the battle suit even when I ordered you to."*

"True," said Nickelo. *"That's why it's called an override. You overrode the default safeties and allowed me to take full control of the battle suit. I need you to do that again. You can trust me. I trusted you enough to volunteer to be embedded in your battle helmet, didn't I? And, I have to go wherever you take me regardless of the danger. Won't you trust me a little in return?"*

Richard thought about it a full minute. Nickelo kept quiet, which was unusual, to say the least. That more than anything told Richard how important his battle computer's request was. Finally, he agreed, even though he wasn't enthusiastic about it.

As soon as Richard thought the command to override the safeties, he found he could no longer control the battle suit. He began to panic with a feeling of suppressed claustrophobia. Before Richard could protest, he felt a needle insert itself into his arm as a cool liquid was injected into his vein.

"What was that?" Richard demanded.

"Your breathing and heart rate were increasing rapidly," said

Nickelo. *"I had the suit give you an anti-anxiety drug to help you keep calm. There won't be any side effects. Trust me. It's a standard-issue drug for a wizard scout's battle suit."*

"I don't like drugs," Richard said. *"Please ask me next time."*

"Roger that, oh wizard scout supreme," said Nickelo.

Richard hated to admit it, but the drug did help. He was able to observe and think logically without letting his emotions get in the way. From what he could tell, Nickelo was moving the battle suit so slowly that it appeared not to be moving at all. Richard knew he could never have moved the suit that slowly on his own. Nickelo took a full thirty minutes to walk the battle suit across the tunnel intersection. Richard was just along for the ride. They passed within an arm's length of a half dozen zombies without incident. It was a strange experience, but as Nickelo told him, it was better than having to fight and risk detection.

Once they were out of sight of the intersection, Nickelo returned control of the battle suit to Richard. They were forced to use the same method a dozen times that day. The population of the tunnels appeared to get denser in the higher levels. The types of undead also changed. The lowest levels had been inhabited mostly by zombies. While the upper levels had their share of zombies, they also had an intelligent form of undead. On one occasion, Richard was forced to dispatch two grayish humanoids with vicious looking fangs. There were tough, but the phase rod made quick work of them.

"What were they?" Richard asked as he eyed a scratch mark on the forearm of his battle suit. *"Those claws were sharp."*

"They're called ghouls," said Nickelo. *"You're lucky you're wearing armor. Their claws and fangs have a paralysis poison. My databanks indicate ghouls first paralyze their victims. Then they take their sweet time devouring them. I don't know about you, but it makes me glad I'm not flesh and blood."*

"Lucky you," Richard said.

"You know, Rick. Things would've been easier for us if we'd just accepted the original mission. I have a feeling your stubbornness is going to get us in a lot of trouble in the years ahead."

"You can just about bet on it," Richard laughed. He actually thought Nickelo was being a little optimistic by thinking they

might have years of life ahead of them.

They continued mapping the lower tunnels for the rest of the day. Late in the afternoon, as they were traveling down a long tunnel, Nickelo said, *"Rick, back up a few steps. Does that right wall seem strange to you?"*

Richard did as Nickelo asked and backed up a couple of steps. The right wall looked the same as the rest of the tunnel to him. He said as much.

"I'm going to risk a low-level electronic scan, Rick. With your permission, of course," he added hastily.

"By all means, Nick. Anything's better than wandering around these tunnels."

The battle suit's heads-up display came to life, and Richard saw a map of the tunnel complex. They had actually mapped an extensive amount of the lower levels. Nickelo had even helped Richard use his active scan to pinpoint two possible exits. Where the exits went, he had no idea, but they were definitely exits of some sort. It had taken all of Nickelo's efforts of persuasion to convince Richard not to use them. Finally, Richard had conceded *'the One'* would just teleport them somewhere worse if they didn't complete their mission first.

The heads-up display showed a white dot for Richard. He saw the outline of the long tunnel where he currently stood. The area to the right of the tunnel appeared solid. The heads-up display shifted a few times as Nickelo cycled through various filters.

"It just doesn't feel right, Rick. Can you sense anything with your passive scan?"

Richard double-checked. He hadn't sensed anything before, and he still didn't. He told Nickelo as much.

"Rick, how about setting up an active scan and giving me control? Maybe between your active scan and the battle suit's electronic sensors, we can find something."

"Okay," Richard said dubiously. *"But, why are we going to so much trouble? It looks the same as the rest of the tunnels we've been down?"*

"I really don't know, Rick. It just seems like something's different. It's almost as if something's just outside of what I can sense, but I know it's there."

Richard said nothing further. He drew some Power from his

reserve and set up an active scan. He knew he was still pretty clumsy with active scans, so he didn't mind letting his battle computer take control of the scan. Besides, even without a shared space, he could still follow along with the scan as Nickelo fed him data. After several minutes of scanning, they found nothing.

"I guess I was wrong, Rick. Sorry I had you waste Power. We should get moving. I'd hate to have something catch us in this tunnel. It's quite a ways to any good hiding spots."

Richard turned to continue walking down the tunnel, but he stopped himself before he took a step. It dawned on him that he too felt as if something was out of place.

"Nick, I think I know what you're talking about. Something does seem just a little out of place. You know it kind of reminds me of the feeling I got when we were playing that hide and seek game of yours back at the Academy. You know the one where we'd try to find the cadets who had their stealth shields up. While I couldn't sense the cadets when they had a good stealth shield, I got so I could spot them sometimes by sensing an absence of anything to be sensed. I know that sounds weird, but that's the best way I can explain it. That's how the solid rock on the other side of this wall feels to me. It's as if it feels too much like solid rock. Do you know what I mean?"

"Not really, Rick. What you're saying doesn't seem logical. I calculate, that's why wizard scouts and battle computers make such a good team. We supplement each other's strengths and weaknesses. What say we give this one more try? Only this time, let's concentrate on looking for signs of a stealth shield. It might help if you try your diviner ability as well. See if you can find any stray links or Power seepages."

"Roger that, Nick old buddy," Richard said. He quickly set up the active scan again and gave Nickelo control. Then he tried to concentrate on the rock on the other side of the tunnel while looking for Power links. He didn't see anything obvious, but after about twenty seconds, he saw the faintest glimmer of ... something. He wasn't sure what.

"Are you getting what I'm seeing, Nick? That glimmer. I'm having trouble staying fixed on it with my mind. It keeps slipping in and out of focus."

"I see it, Rick. Stay on it as best you can. I'm going to

concentrate your active scan on it as well. You're down to sixty-two percent Power reserve, so we have to speed things up a bit. As long as you're using your best stealth shield, your Power reserve won't be able to recharge."

Richard tried to hold onto the glimmer with his mind. He had trouble, but it must have been enough because before long, Nickelo began feeding him data on his heads-up display. He could see the outline of an open space on the other side of the right wall.

"What's that, Nick?" Richard asked. *"Is it a secret room or something?"*

"That'd be my guess," said Nickelo. *"No wonder it was hard to find. It has its own stealth shield protecting it, and a strong one at that. I wonder what's supplying the Power source."*

"Can we get in?" Richard asked. His curiosity was piqued.

"I think that smudge spot near your left hand may be some kind of trigger."

Richard looked closely at the smudge spot. It was barely noticeable. There was no indication the spot had been touched in years.

"You know," Richard said. *"My unit once had to clear some mine tunnels on an out-of-the-way asteroid in the Vegos system. The inhabitants had a nasty habit of booby-trapping doors."*

"Good point," said Nickelo. *"I'll run a low-range electronic scan and send what I find to your heads-up display."*

Richard nodded his head affirmatively. The heads-up display lit up as meaningless lines of data scrolled down one side of the screen.

"The door seems fine, Rick, but my electronic scan is picking up a strange Power reading on the other side. Do you see it?"

"On the heads-up display?" Richard said with disgust. *"Heck no. That's just a bunch of numbers to me."*

"Rick, we're going to have to make getting a shared space a priority if we ever get back to the Academy. It's frustrating trying to interpret data for you using visual and audio only. But in this case, I'll just tell you that the data is basically telling me that it's okay to open the door and enter the room. But take it slow. I'll use the battle suit's electronics to check for traps as we go."

Richard touched the smudge spot. Part of the wall slid inward a finger's width. When nothing else happened, he pushed the wall with his hand. The rock wall gave way easily to his touch. It swung noisily inward to create a meter-wide opening. Richard gingerly stepped inside with his M63 assault rifle at the ready in his right hand and his phase rod in the other.

The secret room was a circular cavern with roughly carved stone walls. A waist-high dais stood in the middle of the room. Several stone benches were arranged around the walls. Everything was covered with a thick layer of dust.

"Doesn't look like this place gets used much," Richard said.

"Either that or the maid took the last few decades off," said Nickelo with a laugh.

Richard closed the door and said, *"You've got a strange sense of humor for a computer."*

"So you tell me, Rick. Well, the room looks clear. No bad guys anyway."

"The room looks too small," Richard said. *"Now that we're inside, I can sense a Power source that should be a couple of feet inside that far wall. I can see lines of Power emanating out from it and connecting with points in the walls, floor, and ceiling. I'm guessing whatever's in that wall is what's providing the energy for the room's stealth shield. Do you think there's another secret door over there as well?"*

"Could be," said Nickelo. *"Why don't you try an active scan on your own this time? Try to be frugal with your Power. I don't know how long it'll be before you can recharge your Power reserve."*

"All right," Richard said. He had the distinct feeling his battle computer was throwing him a bone by allowing him to do the active scan himself.

Probably figures even I can't mess this one up, he laughed to himself.

"You know I heard that," said Nickelo. *"Until we get our shared space, I'll pick up a lot more information than you intend. I can't help it. Sometimes it's like you're shouting in my ear. That is if I had an ear."*

Concentrating as hard as he could, Richard allowed a small amount of his Power to flow towards the far wall. As his Power penetrated the wall, he became aware of a small alcove hidden in the wall itself. He sensed a strong Power source in the alcove. It radiated neither evil nor good. It just was. The Power source seemed to beckon Richard as if it had waited long for this meeting. Richard resisted the urge to touch the Power source with his active scan. Instead, he probed gently around it looking for traps.

"Very good," said Nickelo. *"I'm impressed. My electronics haven't picked up anything either. I think it is okay to take a look inside the alcove if you want."*

"Do you think we should?" Richard asked. *"Maybe we're just asking for trouble."*

"Normally, I'd agree with you. But since part of our mission is to 'find it,' I think we have to take the risk. Based on current data, I'd say there's a thirty-two percent chance this is what we're supposed to find. That's pretty good odds considering the circumstances."

Seeing no counterargument worth verbalizing, Richard walked over to the far wall and touched the spot his active scan had determined was the most likely point to open the alcove. Sure enough, the spot of dark rock pressed inward. A meter-wide section of the wall slid in and off to one side. Inside the alcove was a round sphere the size of a small melon. It was positioned on top of a waist-high rock cylinder. The sphere glowed with light to form a constantly changing pattern. The sphere was beautiful, and Richard was drawn to it like a moth to a flame.

"Nick, can we look at it in white light? Everything looks red to me through this visor."

"Yes," said Nickelo. *"Give me full control of the battle suit first. The Power seems strange. I'm not sure I trust it."*

"Activate the override, Nick. You've got the controls."

A moment later his visor changed from red to clear, and a light shown out of a point on his forehead to bath the sphere in white light. The sphere was a marbled blue. It was even more beautiful than Richard had thought. The more he looked at it, the more at peace with the world he felt. Within seconds, he forgot all about the Academy and his mission. The only thing that mattered was the sphere and how beautiful it looked. He felt pure contentment. He would be happy to look at the sphere for the rest of eternity, and even that wouldn't be long enough.

The white light snapped off, and the battle suit's visor turned red once again.

"I think that's more than enough looking," said Nickelo.

"Don't you?"

Richard wanted to say *no* but refrained. He felt immense disappointment that he could no longer look at the sphere. The troubles of the real world were once again on his shoulders. Richard was sure he could easily get addicted to the sphere.

"I think you're right, Nick. Should we just take the sphere with us?"

"I'd advise against that. 'The One' said to find it. He didn't say to take it. We'll just plot it on our map. It may not even be what we're looking for."

"Agreed," Richard said.

CHAPTER 17

They left the secret room as they'd found it and continued with their mapping. As it turned out, they'd nearly finished mapping all of the lower tunnels when they discovered the secret room.

After another four hours of cautious traveling, they came upon an elaborate stairway leading upward. Climbing to the top, Richard found he was in a short hallway leading to a 'T' intersection. His passive scan picked up fewer life forms in the upper regions of the caverns.

As Richard approached the intersection, Nickelo said, *"Something's coming. Kill it quick, but stay quiet."*

Sure enough, Richard sensed something slipping in and out of his passive scan. Whatever it was, it had some form of stealth shield up. However, the creature was either having Power problems or its stealth shield just wasn't as good as a wizard scout's. The creature was close. Richard let the M63 hang freely from his right shoulder. He grasped the phase rod in his left hand with his thumb ready to hit the activate switch.

Richard heard the faint sound of a footstep from around the corner. A second later, a humanoid female turned the corner. The top of her head only came to the level of his shoulder. A shimmering band of metal encircled her head and held her long hair in place. She carried an engraved staff with a jewel at the top in her right hand. She wore a ring on every finger of both hands. Even her thumbs had a ring. A heavy chain necklace hung on her chest holding a large medallion. Several wands were tucked into the leather belt holding her robe closed. In her left hand, she carried a wicked-looking dagger.

The female didn't see Richard until he activated his phase rod and slammed into her with his body. He pinned her against the wall. Richard ignored Nickel's advice to kill the stranger. Instead, he chopped down with the handle of his phase rod and knocked the staff out the female's grasp. A quick twist of her wrist with his right hand caused her dagger to fall clattering to the rocky floor. He pressed her legs with his hip as he twisted her right hand behind her back and downward where he grabbed it with his right hand to join her left. She struggled, but her strength was no match for the battle suit's assisters. Richard sensed a line of Power start to flow from the female as she started to say a word, but he raised his left hand and twisted her chin back which resulted in only a garbled noise coming from her mouth. Her flow of Power dissipated into the air.

The female twisted in an attempt to free herself, but Richard pressed harder with his hip. He easily kept her pinned against the wall. Her hands were immobilized in his grasp, and the pressure on her chin kept her from uttering a word. Richard sensed another flow of Power start to flow from the female. He didn't need Nickelo to tell him it was the beginning of a magic spell, undoubtedly a spell which didn't require a verbal component. Richard was sure the spell wouldn't be beneficial for him.

"Stop it, right now," Richard whispered harshly in the female's ear. "I see your Power forming, and I'll break your neck before you can use it. Stand down, or you're dead."

The flow of Power dissipated once again, and the female stood still under Richard's hold. Her eyes blazed hatred, but she stopped her struggling. Richard was sure it was only a temporary surrender. She was only waiting for an opportunity to strike.

"Now what do I do, Nick?"

"Don't ask me, oh all-powerful wizard scout. I told you to kill her. She's your problem now."

"Thanks a lot." Sometimes he didn't like his battle computer as much as he did at other times.

Richard looked at the female closer. She looked like a human female, probably only five or six years older than him, but something was different about her. Even through the reddish tint of his visor, Richard could tell she was beautiful. Through the seventeen thousand plus sensor threads of the battle suit, Richard could feel every feminine curve hidden beneath the female's robe. In spite of the situation, Richard felt an unbidden response. He hadn't been intimate with a woman since cadet 647 had been DFR'd. Richard forced himself to concentrate on the business at hand.

Each of the female's rings, as well as her necklace, staff, and dagger, blazed with Power in Richard's mind. Several large sources of Power also came from the small pack on her back. Two of those Power sources seemed all too familiar. He was able to easily trace a line of Power from the female back to her Power reserve. It was quite large, but it was nearly empty at the moment. Richard had a feeling the female would be a deadly foe if roused. He could tell she was angry to the point of trying some desperate act to break free.

He didn't want to kill her. He didn't sense evil from her, but only a faint aura of good. Still, many good people had been killed by other good people over the years, so his danger was no less. Richard was in a quandary. He couldn't just stand there holding her until another creature came wandering down the hallway. He had to make a decision.

"I don't want to kill you," Richard whispered in the female's ear, "At the same time, I don't want to be killed either." He paused to let the words sink in. "I think we're just two starships passing in the great emptiness between the stars. Neither meant the other harm. It was just our ill luck to cross paths in this place."

The female made no attempt to move or speak. Richard's hold on her was so secure she had little chance to move or make a noise anyway. With just the slightest increase in pressure on her chin, Richard knew he could snap her neck like a brittle piece of wood. The female obviously knew it as well.

As Richard tried to figure out what to do, he noticed the female's ear. It was different. Instead of being rounded, it came to a slight point.

"Nick," Richard said. *"Are you seeing this? Her ears are pointed. What is she?"*

"Do you mean what's her profession?" asked Nickelo. *"From the looks of her clothing and equipment, I'd say she's a sorceress.*

If you're asking me what her race is, then I'd have to say some type of elf."

"You're kidding me. I thought elves were the size of a person's hand and had wings. That's what I remember from a book I read once."

"You're confusing fairies with elves," said Nickelo. "Besides, don't believe everything you read in a children's book of nursery rhymes."

After a few moments of contemplation and over Nickelo's protests, Richard whispered, "I may not be your friend, but I'm definitely not your enemy. If I release my hold on you, will you promise not to try and harm me? We can just go our separate ways no worse for the wear. If you go left, I'll right. If you go down, I'll go up or vice versa. Does that seem reasonable?"

Again Richard paused to let the words sink in.

"You can blink once for yes or twice for no. So blink your answer," Richard whispered.

The female immediately blinked once. Richard also thought the glare of hatred in her eyes diminished slightly. He took that as a good sign. He slowly released the pressure on the female's chin. When nothing happened, he released his hold completely and stepped back against the opposite wall of the corridor.

A flow of Power appeared around the female. She said a word Richard couldn't understand, and he saw the Power shimmer in his mind as it transformed into some type of shield. However, no Power came towards Richard.

So far, so good, he thought.

Watching Richard carefully, the female bent down and retrieved her staff and dagger. Armed once again, she spoke.

"Very well," she said. "You kept your word, so I'll keep mine. I'm going down. You may go either left or right as you desire. But be warned. If we meet again, I'll kill you on sight. Now, do you understand?"

"I understand completely," Richard said. "And I wish you well."

Richard started backing away, and the female copied his lead as she began backing her way towards the stairway. Richard considered warning her about the denizens of the lower tunnels, but he decided against it. The situation was still tense. One wrong move or word could set off a battle that neither of them needed or wanted.

Before Richard could take more than a few steps, he felt a large source of Power behind him. It was larger than anything he'd ever sensed.

"Move!" yelled Nickelo in his mind. *"Head back down the stairs."*

Richard spun and faced the wall of the intersection behind him. It was crumbling as he spoke. As if from a dream, a dark cave with a pool of water was revealed behind the wall. It seemed unworldly. A massive horned head rose out of the darkness. It was followed by a long neck and two front legs ending with razor-sharp claws. Richard had never seen a dragon before, but he knew he was seeing one now. It stretched out two large wings and spoke.

"How dare you steal my treasure!" shouted a deep voice. "You shall both burn in the eternal fires for eons to come. You'll beg for death in payment for your crimes, but it won't come" The dragon laughed cruelly as one of its clawed feet reached out for Richard.

A dragon would have been bad enough, but Richard sensed this was more than a dragon. Evil emanated from the creature. Richard had never believed in demons, but the word demon was the only one he could think of to describe the monstrosity standing before him.

"Move!" said Nickelo. *"Move cadet! Move now!"*

Richard's training took over, and he reacted instinctively. He swung his phase rod at the meter-wide paw reaching towards him. His blow struck true, and upon contact, the phase energy was transferred at the atomic level deep into the demon's claw. Richard could feel the subatomic explosions at the point of impact. The demon snarled and jerked back its paw.

At the same time, Richard felt a flow of Power extend from the female behind him towards the demon. He heard her shout an unintelligible word. The flow of Power changed to a streak of lightning which struck between the demon's eyes. Upon seeing the female's lightning bolt, Richard decided his battle computer was probably right. He wasn't sure about the female being an elf, but he could easily believe she was a sorceress. If he could believe that, he decided he might as well believe she was an elf.

The demon was flung back a step by the lightning bolt, but with a roar, it raised its forelegs and began to form its own ball of energy.

"*Spell,*" said Nickelo. "*Run!*"

Richard momentarily thought about activating a defensive shield, but he immediately dropped the idea. He knew he wasn't trained enough in shields to withstand the amount of Power he sensed the demon preparing to release his way. On the other hand, he sensed a powerful shield forming behind him. Forgoing valor in favor of self-preservation, Richard turned and dived along the floor in a slide he hoped would take him past the sorceress.

As he slid, Richard saw the sorceress holding her staff and dagger before her. Each of her rings and her necklace glowed as she shouted words which Richard heard but quickly forgot. A glowing sphere appeared as a two-meter circle around the elf. Just before Richard made contact with the sphere, the lower part dulled in color long enough for him to pass through. He felt a cold chill run through his body, but it quickly passed.

The energy from the demon engulfed the sphere, and the sorceress was driven back two steps. The shield dimmed, but it brightened sharply as the sorceress renewed her chanting. It seemed as if she was concentrating all her efforts on defense. Richard brought up his M63 lightweight plasma assault rifle and sent a burst of thirty rounds at the demon's eyes.

"*No!*" said Nickelo. "*You're lucky those rounds passed through the sorceress's shield. They could have ricocheted around inside until both of your looked like Swiss cheese.*"

Richard wasn't sure what Swiss cheese was, but he got the picture. He hadn't thought it through. But then again, it wasn't like either the Academy or marine recon had conducted training on sorceresses and their shields. As it turned out, the plasma rounds didn't even distract the demon. It actually laughed when the rounds hit.

"*Sorry,*" Richard said. "*Should I try a grenade?*"

"*No,*" said Nickelo. "*This demon is beyond your current skill level. The female seems to be holding her own for the moment. She's obviously a competent sorceress. I'd recommend running downstairs and trying for one of the exits we mapped. We can regroup once we're safely somewhere else.*"

Leaving the sorceress was not an option in Richard's mind.

Marine recon never left a teammate, and he wasn't going to do so as a wizard scout. Although they had just met, the sorceress and he were in this fight together against a common enemy. Richard wasn't going to desert her.

As it was, he'd lost his chance to run anyway. His passive scan picked up a mass of life forms gathering at the base of the stairs below. His attention was quickly drawn back to the intersection as three canine-like creatures the size of small ponies came charging around the corner. Richard heard a gasp from the sorceress. Her shield started to dim.

Richard brought his M63 in line with the head of the nearest canine. He let loose with a score of plasma rounds. They tore into the creature's head. Its brain matter splattered its two companions who were hard on its heels. Richard continued to hold the M63's trigger down as he tracked the stream of plasma rounds into the chest of a second canine. It was thrown backward as a spray of liquid began spurting from its chest. The third canine jumped over its fallen brethren and leaped straight for the elf's throat.

Richard let go of his M63 and let it dangle from its strap. He threw himself between the elf and the canine and took the brunt of the creature's charge. He twisted as he was thrown backward just missing the elf behind. His twist managed to throw the creature off to the right where it slammed into the wall. Richard was on it in a heartbeat swinging his phase rod with all his might. Half a dozen blows later, a bloody ball of fur lay at his feet.

The demon was throwing bolt after bolt of energy at the sorceress, but her shield continued to hold. However, Richard could sense the Power in her staff, rings, and necklace being steadily diminished. He knew the sorceress couldn't keep up her defensive shield much longer. The demon was just too powerful. Instead of growing weaker as it used Power, it seemed to be growing stronger with each passing moment.

"Rick," said Nickelo. *"Behind you."*

When Richard turned, he saw a mass of undead charging up the stairs. His passive scan picked up even more gathering behind them. The sorceress must have sensed them as well because she took a quick glance over her shoulder. But she either trusted Richard to handle the situation, or she knew it was hopeless. In either case, the sorceress returned her gaze to the front and began shouting even louder.

"Nick," Richard said. *"Help me aim."*

Richard felt the arms of his battle suit move involuntarily as Nickelo took control. The M63 lightweight plasma assault rifle made a steady 'Brrrrp' as the stream of plasma rounds made their way from one undead creature's head to another. After almost a thousand rounds, the stairway was clear.

Making a command decision, Richard turned to the sorceress and shouted, "Start backing down the stairs. I'll keep it clear."

The sorceress was too hard-pressed to argue. She immediately took two steps backward. Richard deactivated his phase rod and hooked it back to his hip. With his now free hand, he grabbed hold of the female's belt and slowly guided her down the steps and between the corpses littering the stairs. Twice the sorceress started to slip on the gore, but each time, Richard's grasp steadied her. She didn't falter, and even during her near falls, the sorceress didn't stop chanting. Richard thought the Power in her staff and jewelry were only about half of what it had been when the battle began. Time was running short.

Halfway down the stairs, Richard's passive scan detected another mob of undead gathering just beyond his view. He stopped and unhooked one of his anti-personnel grenades. Pulling the pin, he tossed it far down the stairs where it bounced into the tunnel beyond.

Boom!

Smoke filled the end of the tunnel.

"I don't think grenades will destroy them, Rick. You have to hit them in the head."

"Maybe so," Richard said. *"But it will mess up their charge. Besides, it makes me feel a whole lot better."* With those words, Richard threw his second grenade down the stairs.

Boom!

Grabbing hold of the sorceress's belt again, Richard began guiding her slowly down the stairs. Occasionally, an undead or two appeared at the tunnel's entrance. Whenever they did, Richard happily put a few rounds of plasma energy in their heads as a show of appreciation for their efforts.

"Watch your ammo," said Nickelo. *"You're down to nine hundred and eighty-three rounds."*

"Affirmative," Richard said.

When they reached the bottom of the stairs, the demon shouted, "You shall not get away!"

The demon was too large to fit down the stairs. However, it doubled the amount of energy it was throwing at the sorceress's shield. Lightning bolts and balls of fire exploded all around. The sorceress's shield held firm. However, the ceiling over the stairway didn't fare as well. It began to crack. Large chunks soon began to fall. Several pieces of falling granite tumbled through the sorceress's shield. Richard had a moment's thought that the sorceress's shield must be attuned to energy and not physical objects. Then the whole ceiling started to give way.

Richard thought the override command for his battle suit as he gave full control to Nickelo. He knew his own reflexes weren't fast enough to save their lives, but he prayed his battle computer was.

The battle suit twisted and its legs extended so fast Richard and the sorceress were flung a dozen steps into the tunnel. Richard heard an explosion of air from the sorceress as the tug on her belt forced her breath out. Her defensive shield disappeared, but it didn't matter. The whole stairway and part of the tunnel were collapsing. The demon was hidden from view as they went flying through the air. They both hit the stone floor of the tunnel hard.

"She's going to have a few bruises," observed Nickelo.

The armor of Richard's battle suit easily absorbed the blow. The sorceress's fall was partially softened by the numerous bodies of the undead littering the floor, but even so, Richard heard a cry of pain escape her lips as she hit.

Richard stood up and surveyed the carnage to his front. They were completely trapped in the lower tunnels. He wasn't happy with the situation. With the amplified hearing of the battle suit, he could hear the demon screaming threats of the tortures that awaited them. He'd made a dangerous enemy, and he wasn't even sure why. He had Nickelo lower the volume on the amplification when the demon started swearing how it would hunt them down, and how it would never stop searching for them.

"No use worrying about the future when the present seems bad enough, eh Nick?"

"Amen to that, brother," said Nickelo with a chuckle. Then he said, *"We've got company."*

Sure enough, a handful of the undead Nickelo had called ghouls were scrambling down the tunnel. Richard activated his phase rod and met them before they could reach the downed sorceress. She had just started to push herself up into a sitting position when Richard jumped past her. He quickly dispatched two of the ghouls when the third knocked him over and began tearing at his chest with its claws and teeth.

Richard heard the sorceress shout a word. A small ball of energy struck the ghoul in the head knocking it off him. He looked at the sorceress to thank her. She was just lowering a wand when a dark body hurled into her from the side. The sorceress screamed, and the scream cut off abruptly. Richard pulled out his .44 caliber AutoMag and fired from the hip.

Boom!

The ghoul's head exploded. Richard turned behind him and fired twice more. Two more ghouls fell to the tunnel floor. Then all was quiet.

Richard crawled to the sorceress and yanked the lifeless ghoul off her body.

"Nick. Is she alive?"

He touched her neck with a gloved finger. He didn't feel a pulse. *"I should be able to feel a pulse, Nick. The sensory threads should allow me to feel a pulse, right?"*

"Use your passive scan, Rick. Can you still sense her life force?"

"Yes," Richard said as he let out a breath of relief.

"Then she's still alive. The ghoul's poison has her paralyzed. That's all. Her heartbeat and breathing will be slower than normal, but that's not a problem. However, my electronic scan indicates she's bleeding extensively from her arm. I think the ghoul got its teeth into her there."

"White light, Nick. Give me white light."

"I would advise against that, Rick."

"Now," Richard said firmly.

Richard's visor lost its red glow, and a white light shown from his forehead. The sorceress was covered in blood and gore. Her eyes were open and unblinking. A deep set of four claw marks ran down her left arm where they ended in a vicious bite wound. Blood spurted out of the bite wound in time to the female's heartbeat.

Richard tore off the hem of the sorceress's robe and used one of her wands to help tie off a tourniquet. The blood stopped squirting into the air.

"We have to get to someplace safe," Richard said. *"We've got to do something about her wound. She'll die. Can we make it to an exit?"*

"Doubtful," said Nickelo. *"Not dragging her with us. We'd have to fight our way there. We can't go into stealth mode and drag her around at the same time. It would be too noisy. Look at the life forces headed our way even now."*

Richard didn't need to look at the heads-up display. He could sense a hundred creatures or more moving quickly down the tunnels in their direction.

"What about the secret room?" Richard asked. *"It should be close."*

"That's probably our best chance if you want to save the sorceress's life," said Nickelo. *"Of course, an even better plan would be for us to leave her here while we go into stealth mode and make our escape."*

Richard didn't say anything. He demonstrated his answer to his battle computer by picking up the sorceress and draping her over his shoulder. He stooped down and grabbed her staff, wand, and dagger.

"Okay," said Nickelo. *"Secret room it is. I'm switching to normal battle suit vision now."*

The white light went out, and Richard saw the entire cavern illuminated in a reddish glow once more. Saving the sorceress might not be his battle computer's first choice, but Richard had to admit Nickelo did things as efficiently as possible once a decision was made. Within ten minutes, they were back inside the secret room with the door securely shut behind them.

Richard had Nickelo go back to white light. The sorceress's arm below the tourniquet was starting to turn a dark blue. Richard knew he had to loosen the tourniquet, but he also knew as soon as he did, the blood would start squirting out again. The ghoul's bite must have hit an artery.

Marine Recon training included basic first aid, but Richard didn't even have a first aid kit. It wasn't part of a wizard scout's uniform. Real wizard scouts could self-heal, and many wizard scouts could use their Power to perform limited healing on others. But Richard hadn't been trained in healing yet. That was junior year stuff.

Richard looked at the sorceress helplessly. *"Nick, do you have any suggestions? I don't even have a first aid kit."*

"Just get one out of your pack," said Nickelo

Richard practically tore the pack off his back and looked inside.

"It's empty, Nick. If you're not going to help, then don't say anything."

"Sorry, Rick. We haven't gone over your pack yet. It's a dimensional pack. You just think of an item, and you can pull it out of your pack."

So many impossible things had happened to Richard over the last few days that he just accepted Nickelo at his word without arguing. He thought of a fully-equipped android doctor and reached into the pack. Nothing.

"Nick!" Richard said.

"You didn't let me finish," said Nickelo. *"You can pull anything out of the pack within certain limitations. The more complex the item, the more Power it takes to energize the pack. An android doctor is too advanced. You don't have that much Power even when your reserve is full. Imagine any antique medical gear from your old Earth, or even one of your marine recon first-aid kits. That should work fine."*

Richard was desperate to save the elf's life. He wasn't even sure why. He'd seen many people die during his two years of combat with the marine recon. But nevertheless, Richard had an overwhelming desire to help the paralyzed sorceress. He didn't have a lot of faith, but even so, he pictured a standard-issue, marine first-aid kit. Richard felt a small amount of Power flow from his reserve to his pack. He looked inside again. This time he saw an olive drab, canvas covered box about the size of his hand. It was a field first-aid kit.

Removing the pressure bandage, antiseptic, and liquid skin from the kit, Richard placed them next to the sorceress's arm. He undid the tourniquet. Blood started shooting out of the bite wound into the air. Richard sprayed some antiseptic in the bite and claw wounds. He followed it up with a long squirt of liquid skin. The claw marks partially closed up, but the bite wound was too deep for liquid skin to help much. Plus, it couldn't reconnect whatever severed artery was spurting the blood. Richard knew the sorceress was in serious trouble. He didn't know if a sorceress had any healing abilities, but even if she did, they'd do her no good paralyzed as she was. It was up to him to save her. Richard placed the pressure bandage over the bite wound and pressed down.

After about thirty seconds, Richard said, *"Nick, has her bleeding stopped?"*

"Negative. An artery's torn apart. You're going to have to connect the two ends together if you want to save her life."

"How?" Richard asked as he realized he was coming to rely more and more on his battle computer for advice.

"You're going to have to heal her, Rick. The same way TAC Officer Shatstot heals the other cadets."

"I don't know how. I'm not trained."

"I know you're not, Rick. But the basics are all in my databanks. Besides, training is mostly for the subtle stuff. The ability to heal others is a part of your natural abilities. You've just never tried to use them. I'll guide you as much as I can if you need help."

"If I gave you control, Nick, could you just take over my abilities and heal her yourself?"

"It doesn't work that way. You're an emp-healer. There aren't many of your kind around for good reason. You have to take the person's injuries on yourself before your Power can heal them."

"That's crazy," Richard said.

"Nevertheless, that's how your healing ability works. Most wizard scouts heal others directly. Once again, you seem to have an affinity for doing things the hard way."

"Fine then," Richard said. *"Let's do it."*

Richard could feel the pressure bandage getting soaked with blood. The sorceress was bleeding to death as they spoke. He tried to understand why the female's life meant so much to him, but he couldn't even explain it to himself. Maybe it was because she'd risked her own life thinking she was saving his. Unbeknownst to her, the ghoul's teeth and claws wouldn't have penetrated his armor. She'd risked her own life for no reason.

"All right," said Nickelo. *"I'll guide you through the healing process. The methodology is pretty simple, although it'll take you*

years of practice to perfect it. You'll normally be striving for efficiency, but in this case, you just need to get the artery reconnected and the wound healed. Don't worry about efficiency. Your healing will be drawing Power from that second Power pool the technicians told you about so your primary Power reserve won't be affected."

"What about the poison?" Richard said.

"Wounds are one thing, Rick. Poisons and diseases are another. You'll need advanced training for them. But, the poison won't kill her. The wounds will. That's what you need to heal. Are you ready?"

"Ready," Richard said. He was a little nervous. A person's life depended on him getting it right.

"Fine, Rick. Healing is similar to an active scan. That's why the scan is taught first. Your healing will be a little different from the way most wizard scouts heal, but not much. Do you see your primary Power reserve?"

"Yes," Richard said. He'd always seen it, even when he was a young child. Or maybe seen was the wrong word. It was more like feeling it. He knew it was there.

"Do you see your second Power reserve?"

"No," Richard said tensely. This was taking way too long. He wanted to get busy healing. The pressure bandage was completely soaked now. *"Is all of this really necessary? She's dying."*

"Yes, it's necessary. It would go a lot quicker if you didn't argue with me over things you know nothing about."

Nickelo was quiet for a second. Richard said nothing.

"Fine," said Nickelo. *"I guess we understand each other's role in this endeavor. Okay, find the point where your Power is overflowing out of your main reserve. Trace that overflow to your second Power reserve. That's where your primary healing Power is stored."*

Richard looked, but he saw no overflow. Then it dawned on him. *"There's no overflow, Nick. My Power reserve is less than a hundred percent."*

"Oops!" said Nickelo. *"I forgot. See. Even computers make mistakes every once in a while.*

Nick!"

"Okay. There's still time, Rick. She's got a least four or five

minutes before she will bleed to death."

"Nick!"

"I'm hurrying, Rick. You should see a faint path leading away from your main Power reserve. It'll look different from the rest of the surrounding area."

"Got it," Richard said impatiently.

"Trace it to its end point. That will be your second Power reserve. It only gets overflow Power from your main reserve. Any overflow from your second Power reserve is just lost if it's not used."

"Save the lectures, Nick. I found the second reserve. Now hurry, please."

"I always hurry. You're the one that's slow."

"Nick!"

"Fine. Now, I want you to pull some Power from that second reserve and use it to wrap the sorceress's injuries."

"How do I find the injuries, Nick? Is it just what I see on the surface?"

"No. Touch her with your Power. It'll be easier if you hold onto her. Take one of your gloves off. Flesh to flesh contact helps. Don't touch the wound directly. You don't want any stray ghoul poison getting on you. And, make sure you don't let go until the healing is done."

Richard took off his left glove and grabbed hold of the sorceress's right arm to be well away from the wound.

"Touch her with your Power, Rick. It's similar to the way you touch targets with your active scan. Once your Power has made contact, try and imagine you are her. Try to feel how her body should be. Compare that to how her body is now. Any differences will be her injuries."

Richard had no idea what Nickelo meant, but he was determined to do his best. Drawing Power from the second reserve was easy enough. Wrapping the sorceress in Power was no problem either. Imagining his body was a female's body was a definite problem. Things just didn't feel right.

"No pressure, Rick. But the sorceress will be dead in three minutes."

Richard did his best to shove thoughts about gender differences to the side. A body was a body after all. Lungs, heart, blood, muscles, they were all the same regardless of gender. After a moment, Richard began to sense how the female's body should be. He felt the differences in her body now.

Nickelo must have sensed Richard was close, because he said, *"Now, wrap the differences with the Power. Then pull half the Power back into you. Once that's done, the sorceress's wounds will start to heal."*

Richard did as commanded. He wrapped her wounds with his Power and pulled half the Power back into his own body. Suddenly, Richard felt a white-hot pain in his left forearm. He jerked away from the sorceress. The healing was forgotten. Richard looked at his arm, but of course, he could see nothing through the battle suit. However, he did see blood dripping down his left hand from where it was escaping from under the cuff of his armor. His left forearm felt like it was on fire.

"What the hell, Nick. Something's wrong."

"Nothing's wrong, Rick. You're an emp-healer. What'd you think that meant? You have to take the sorceress's injuries on yourself before she can be healed."

"What about me?" Richard said out loud. Since his battle suit had unsealed when he removed his glove, the tubes were no longer in his nose and throat. He could talk again.

"Once the one-half of your Power heals the sorceress, then the other half of your Power will heal you. But you broke contact, and you lost all that Power. Now you have to start over again. If you do that more than a few times, you'll be out of Power. By the way, the sorceress has less than two minutes left to live now. If you can't force yourself to hold on until the healing is complete, then don't even bother trying."

Richard didn't try to reason things out. He just acted. He grabbed hold of the sorceress's right arm again and drew Power out of his second reserve. He sensed he had less Power in the reserve than before. He wasted no time in finding the sorceress's wounds and wrapping them with Power. He drew half the Power into his own body. Again there was a white-hot flash of pain in his left forearm, but this time he didn't let go. After a few seconds, he felt the differences in the female's body diminish. Before long, the differences completely disappeared.

"You can let go now, Rick. The sorceress is healed."

Richard let go. "But my arm still hurts. What's going on? You said I would be healed as well."

"It's all right, Rick. It just takes your Power a few minutes to heal any injuries you take upon yourself when healing others. The pain should be subsiding soon."

By the time Nickelo finished speaking, the pain in Richard's forearm had lessened significantly. Richard noticed the blood was no longer flowing down his left hand.

"My arm's better, Nick, but it still hurts a little."

"Such is the life of an emp-healer, Rick. Your wound will heal completely in another minute or so. The sorceress only had a relatively minor wound as far as healing was concerned. Imagine how it would feel if you ever decided to heal a major burn wound on someone. By the way, can you please talk to me with thoughts. I hate verbal communication."

"Fine, Nick. But my healing days are over. I'm not taking other people's injuries onto me again. They can find a normal healer. Emp-healing sucks."

"Ah," said Nickelo, *"words of comfort from an angel of mercy. Did anyone ever tell you that you complain a lot?"*

"Did anyone ever tell you that you talk a lot?" Richard said.

CHAPTER 18

Once Richard's pain went away, he removed the pressure bandage from the sorceress's arm. The claw marks were gone as well as the bite wound. The excessive amount of blood on her arm prevented him from telling if there was a scar.

Reaching behind his back with his right hand, he removed his canteen from its pouch. He unscrewed the cap and tipped the canteen over the sorceress's forearm to wash the blood off. Nothing came out of the canteen.

"Great," Richard said out loud. "I forgot to fill the canteen before we left."

"*Oh, yeah,*" said Nickelo. "*I haven't explained that to you either. It's a dimensional canteen. If you promise to talk to me with your thoughts instead of verbally, I'll tell you how it works.*"

"*Fine,*" Richard said using thoughts instead of words. "*What's a dimensional canteen, and how does it work?*"

"*Your dimensional canteen is similar to your dimensional pack. You'll notice two dials below the neck of the canteen. The first dial is pressure, and the second dial is temperature. Just set the dials then imagine water. Power from your reserve will energize your canteen, and out will come water. You can dial from ice-cold water to boiling water. The pressure can be normal gravity feed to a high-pressure stream capable of reaching a hundred meters in the air.*"

"*Bull,*" Richard said. "*I've never heard of anything like that before. I let it slide earlier because I was desperate, but I've never*

141

heard of a dimensional pack either."

"Nevertheless, here they are. I guess things actually exist which even you don't know about. Imagine that. Does it make you feel humble?" Once he'd stopped speaking, Nickelo began laughing uncontrollably.

"You're not as funny as you think you are, Nick. Geesh. Grow up already."

Nickelo stopped laughing. *"Fine. I'll laugh during my off-time. You haven't heard about a dimensional pack or canteen because they were developed just for you. They're synched specifically to your Power frequency. They won't work for anyone else."*

"How do you know that?" Richard asked suspiciously.

"It's in my databanks, but I don't know how the information got there," said Nickelo. *"But, I have a copy of an order for fifty-five dimensional packs and dimensional canteens. I assume the others were sent to wherever the extra copies of your other equipment went."*

"Sounds expensive," Richard said. It worried him. One thing he'd learned during his time on the streets was that nothing was ever free. Someone would want him to pay somehow.

"I can't even begin to calculate the cost of the equipment you've been issued, Rick. In my opinion, entire divisions or a fleet of starships could have been equipped for less."

"Why?" Richard demanded. *"Who has access to that kind of financial resources? The last I heard, the Empire was struggling financially due to all the wars. I don't care how high someone is in the government. They couldn't spend those kinds of credits without the central computer raising alarm bells."*

"I don't know, Rick. Nothing in my databanks provides any information that could be useful. I'd honestly tell you if I knew."

Richard's head was spinning. He hated thinking so much, so he decided to act. The dimensional canteen seemed like something he could handle. He left the two dials on the canteen at their defaults and imagined water. He tipped the canteen over the sorceress's forearm. A clear stream of cool water came out and ran gently over the female's arm. He felt a minuscule amount of Power drain from his reserve.

After he'd washed away the blood, Richard inspected the sorceress's arm again under white light. There wasn't even a scar.

"Nick," Richard said. *"If I was injured, could I heal myself with my emp-healing ability?"*

"No," replied Nickelo. *"Self-healing's different. You have to have your DNA baseline taken first. That's also when we'll get our shared space."*

"Tell me more about the dimensional pack. How do I know what I can and can't get?"

"Trial and error, I suppose, Rick. It all depends on Power requirements. The more complex the items, the more Power it'll take to energize the pack. Simple thinks like food, basic medical supplies, simple weapons and ammo, or camping equipment will take relatively little Power. Complex items like computers or advanced weapons will take more Power. If an item requires more Power than you have, the pack won't energize, and you won't get the item."

"You said I could get weapons and ammo? I used up most of my ammo during our fight. Can I get a resupply?"

"Oh, I forgot that too," said Nickelo. *"Some items are freebies. Your default weapons and their ammo require no Power to energize the pack. Neither does your battle suit or even this helmet. Which is a good thing since they're so advanced you'd never have enough Power to get them from your pack. But, you can get antique items from your home world of Earth for very little Power."*

"None of that makes sense, Nick. How do you know all that anyway?"

"I told you, I don't know. It's just in my databanks. I don't know how it got there."

Richard imagined a new isotopic battery for his M63 lightweight plasma assault rifle and two more anti-personnel grenades. He opened his pack, and the grenades were there, but the isotopic battery wasn't.

"Hey, Nick. What gives?" Richard complained. *"I imagined a replacement isotopic battery for the M63, but I only got the grenades."*

"Oh," said Nick. *"I can only hypothesize, but I'd guess that 'the One' is limiting you to your initial load of ammo. Try putting your old isotopic battery in the pack. Then imagine a fully recharged one."*

Although dubious, Richard did as Nickelo suggested. He was concerned he might lose the near-empty battery he had, but the reward seemed worth the risk. Besides, he'd grown to trust his battle computer's advice.

Richard put the old isotopic battery in the pack and closed the flap. He imagined a fully recharged one. When he opened the pack, he reached in and pulled out an isotopic battery. A glance at its meter confirmed it was at one hundred percent power.

Cool, Richard thought. He closed the flap of the pack and imagined another isotopic battery. He opened the pack. It was empty. *"I guess you're right. The jerk won't let me get an extra battery."*

"Just deal with it, Rick. Once you know the rules, you can work it to your advantage."

Richard hated to submit so easily, but his battle computer was right. It was what it was. He just needed to deal with it. Richard extracted his partially empty clip from his .44 AutoMag and put it in the pack. He closed the pack and imagined a fully loaded clip. He opened the pack, and there it was. He closed the flap and imagined another fully loaded clip. When he opened the pack, it was empty. *Jerk*, Richard thought.

The good news was that none of his *freebies* drew Power from his reserve. On a lark, Richard imagined a 9mm pistol with a shoulder holster and silencer. He opened the pack. It was empty. He tried imagining the boot knife Sergeant Hendricks had made for him. Same result. The pack was empty.

"Trying to find loopholes are you?" asked Nickelo with a chuckle.

"Mind your own business," Richard said. *"By the way, how long will it take for the ghoul's poison to get out of her system? A few hours? She's breathing better, but the way her eyes are staying open without blinking is starting to give me the creeps."*

"Aren't you the sympathetic one?" said Nickelo in a tone that told Richard he was being chastised again. *"To answer your first question, it'll probably take five to seven days to clear the poison out of the sorceress's system. Then it'll take another three or four days for her to get her strength back. Just so you know, Rick, I think your comment about her eyes is harsh. She's so completely paralyzed she can't even blink. I may be a computer, but even I*

know that's got to be torture for her. How would you be feeling if you hadn't blinked in the last thirty minutes? Plus, having you shine that white light in her eyes every so often probably hasn't helped. I'll bet there's even grit and grim in her eyes from where she fell on the tunnel floor. The odds are she's in agony right about now. That's just my opinion. You undoubtedly look at it differently since all you can think about is how her eyes staying open bother you."

"Damn, Nick," Richard said. *"Why didn't you tell me sooner?"* He was frustrated with himself for not thinking about the female's plight earlier. He'd never been very good at thinking about the feelings and the plight of others.

"You're the boss, wizard scout. I'm just the poor, little battle computer."

Richard started to apologize to the sorceress, but he stopped before he spoke.

"Nick, does she speak standard? I didn't think about it until now. She understood me earlier, and I understood the few words she said, so I guess she must understand standard."

"Actually, you didn't speak to her in standard. You spoke a language in my databanks called Letian. Even your thoughts to me now are in Letian. Some words that don't have a Letian counterpart are in standard, but you're speaking Letian for the most part."

"I'm not even going to ask," Richard said.

He imagined clean clothes, sheets, soap, eye drops, and bandages. A tiny amount of Power flowed from his reserve to his pack. Richard opened the flap and removed the items. On a hunch, he imagined an old-fashioned, battery-operated, camping lantern. Once again, a slight amount of Power was used. He retrieved the lantern from his pack and turned it on. The room was bathed in a soft, white glow. Richard turned off the white light on his helmet and raised his visor.

"I'm sorry," Richard said softly to the sorceress. "I didn't realize you were in pain. I'm going to get you cleaned up and put some drops in your eyes. That should help."

Richard worked quickly to remove the grime on the sorceress's face. Afterward, he used the eye drops to flush out her eyes. He also used an antibacterial eye ointment he extracted from the pack as a protective salve on both eyes. He then moistened some stripes of cloth bandages and placed them over her eyes as well.

Once he finished with the sorceress's eyes, Richard kneeled next to her and placed his forefinger on the carotid artery under her jaw. He felt the steady pulse of her heart. Keeping his finger in place, Richard said, "Your wounds are healed, and I've done the best I can for your eyes. The ghoul's poison will just have to work its way out of your system. I'm told that will take about a week."

The female's pulse speeded up significantly. That alone told Richard the sorceress could hear and understand him.

"Now, don't worry," Richard said in what he hoped was a reassuring voice. "We're in a safe place. This room has a high-level stealth shield around it so we can stay here a long time without being discovered. I'm not going to leave you, so don't worry. We fought together. As far as I'm concerned, we're a team. I never desert teammates."

The sorceress's pulse slowed a little.

"I'm going to make a bed for you on one of the benches in this room. I'll get you cleaned up so you'll be more comfortable. Then I'll get your robe and gear cleaned. They're both covered in blood and ghoul-gore."

The sorceress's pulse increased significantly.

"She's panicking," said Nickelo. *"A lot of her gear is very powerful. Have you noticed the Power readings from her pack?"*

Richard had. *"Yes. It's similar to that sphere we found in the alcove."*

"Correction," said Nickelo. *"They're duplicates of the sphere's Power readings. She's liable to think you're going to steal her stuff and leave her here alone. I'm betting she wasn't in this place taking a stroll for her health. That demon was yelling something about thieves. Speaking as a computer, one plus one equals two. Do you get the picture?"*

"Yeah, Nick. I understand," Richard said.

Turning his attention back to the sorceress, Richard said, "Anything you have now, you'll have after you're well. I don't want anything you have, so you don't have to worry. Now, you can either trust me or not. Since you're paralyzed for the next week or so, you should probably just trust me. Besides, why should I lie? If I wanted something, I could just take it. But you don't have to worry. I won't break your trust. I'm a wizard scout, and my word is my bond."

The sorceress's pulse slowed a little. It was faster than normal, but much slower than it had been.

Richard envisioned a camping mattress and sleeping bag. He pulled them out of his pack. Since Nickelo had implied old twentieth century and twenty-first century Earth gear was cheap on Power, Richard figured it was best to use the older gear to save Power. Because his stealth shield was using more Power than he could regenerate, Richard knew he had to be frugal with his Power.

Once Richard had a semi-comfortable bed made, he placed a sheet over the sorceress and removed her clothing. He then filled a basin with warm water from the canteen. While the idea of the pack and canteen had seemed implausible, he'd come to accept their capabilities as givens. They were life savers at the moment.

Being as discreet as possible, he cleaned the worst of the blood and gore off the sorceress and placed her on the makeshift bed. He then took care of his own body's needs. Although Nickelo protested to no end, Richard removed his battle suit and put on a pair of jeans and a pullover shirt. The battle suit had kept him alive, but it definitely wasn't built for comfort. Richard was relieved to finally get out of its confinement.

With a little experimentation, Richard found he could summon all sorts of camping gear from the pack. Before long, he had a nice little campsite made up, and he was soon cooking a pot of stew on a propane camp stove.

"I feel like one of the old-timers on a camping trip," Richard told Nickelo. *"By the way, where does this stuff come from, and how much is there?"*

"I don't know."

"Guess," Richard said.

"I'm a computer," said Nickelo in a tone that indicated he was insulted. *"I don't guess. However since you insist, I'd say there's a twenty-two percent chance some type of teleport system is set up at a central warehouse somewhere. How much gear is there, I can't say. Considering the credits that have been spent on you already, I'd say the amount of gear is extensive. After all, whoever is doing this created fifty-five battle helmets designed to only work with me. The cost of that alone would be astronomical. I'd say the cost of a*

few thousand sets of camping gear would pale in significance compared to that. Besides, it doesn't have to be a one-time shot for each piece of equipment. If you send the stuff back through the pack when you're done with it, logically, it should be able to be used again. That's just my opinion."

"Makes sense to me, Nick. Also, you said I could summon anything I could imagine out of my pack if I had the Power. Don't you mean I can summon anything someone thought to store in your hypothetical warehouse?"

"That sounds logical, Rick. Are you sure you're not part computer?"

CHAPTER 19

The days passed slowly. Things got a little hectic when Nickelo pointed out the sorceress needed food and water. Since she was paralyzed, she couldn't swallow. Eventually, Nickelo volunteered to help Richard set up a medical band on the sorceress's arm. Nickelo told Richard a medical band was the modern version of a twenty-first century I.V. While the old I.V. would have cost less Power to summon, Nickelo advised against exciting the sorceress by sticking needles in her. Therefore, Richard ate the Power cost and summoned a medical band. Once the medical band was in place, he changed out the liquid and nutrients bag twice a day to ensure the sorceress wouldn't dehydrate or starve.

On the third day, Nickelo made an announcement. *"You know, I believe it would be safe for you to reduce your stealth shield from your highest to your lowest level. This room has an even better stealth shield than you can ever hope to create. I've been monitoring the room's shield for leaks the last two days. I see no reason to think it won't shield you as well as it has shielded that sphere over the last who knows how many years."*

"I don't know, Nick," Richard said unconvinced. The demon's threats were still fresh in his memory. He hated to admit it even to himself, but he was worried. He had no desire to let a demon get its hands on him. If that meant hiding behind his stealth shield for the rest of his life, then so be it.

"Well, let me put it this way," said Nickelo in a tone similar to the one teachers at his orphanage had used when lecturing him.

"You're down to less than fifty percent Power in your reserve now. We still have several days before the sorceress will be able to walk on her own. When we try to leave this place, we're probably going to have to fight our way out. Your normal recharge rate on your Power reserve is about one percent every fifteen minutes. That means you could normally completely refill your Power reserve in a single day. That's assuming you aren't using any Power at the same time. Your best stealth shield uses slightly more than one percent of your Power every fifteen minutes. Not much more, but enough to ensure your Power reserve can't be replenished. If your stealth shield was the only draw on your Power reserve, it could probably last for about a year before you ran out of Power. But it's not the only draw. We've been using your Power for scans and to summon items. Get the picture?"

Richard got the picture, but he didn't like it. *"You're saying I'm going to run out of Power before we get out of this place if I don't allow my Power reserve to recharge."*

"Bingo!" said Nickelo. *"Give the cadet a cigar."*

Richard wasn't sure what a bingo was. Maybe it was some kind of animal, but he had heard of a cigar. What it had to do with their current situation, he had no idea. However, just the short association with his battle computer had convinced him that sometimes it was best not to ask.

"Nick, can I be honest with you?"

The levity was gone from Nickelo's voice when he replied. *"I wish you would, Rick. We can't help each other if we're not honest."*

"Well," Richard began, *"until three days ago demons were just something in old fantasy books. They were make-believe creatures in scary stories older children in the orphanage told to frighten the younger kids. But now, I've seen an actual demon. It's real, and it's sworn to hunt me down and rip me apart one slow piece at a time. On top of that, I've found out zombies, ghouls, and magic-using sorceresses exist. During my time in marine recon, I've dropped behind enemy lines, faced a charging line of plasma-firing armored vehicles, and even withstood a strafing bombardment from an enemy starship. But this time I'm out of my league."*

Richard halfway expected his battle computer to crack a joke, but he didn't. He replied in a serious voice, *"There's actually quite a bit of information in my databanks about demons, so we won't be making decisions completely in the blind. The sorceress was holding her own against the demon for a while, so that demon is a mid-level demon at best. I don't think it's all powerful or all knowing. We just need to keep a low profile for a while. It will eventually have more important concerns than capturing a nondescript, wizard scout cadet."*

"What if it tracks us down before it loses interest?" Richard asked. *"What then?"*

"Then we'll fight it, Rick."

"You told me I didn't have the skills to fight it. You told me to run during the battle."

"I'll admit," said Nickelo, *"that you don't have the skills to fight something as powerful as that demon right now. But that's going to change. I'll help you get trained. If I have my way, you're going to be the toughest wizard scout to ever wear a golden dragon insignia. In the meantime, you need to trust me when I make recommendations. I'm not going to steer you wrong. Heck, I'm embedded in your battle helmet. Anything that happens to you is going to happen to me as well. You may think I'm a set of programming instructions in a piece of computer hardware. However, in my mind, I'm a thinking being who doesn't want to be terminated."*

"Fine," Richard said reluctantly. *"But if that demon catches and kills me, I swear I'll come back and haunt you."*

"Duly noted," said Nickelo. *"Now, do us both a favor and shift down to your lowest stealth shield so you can start recharging. I'd have you shut it down completely, but I don't want you to take any undue risks."*

Richard muttered under his breath a little, but he complied with his battle computer's request and shifted his stealth shield down to its lowest level. Once completed, he informed Nickelo. Richard spent the next hour on pins and needles. When no unexpected visitors appeared, he relaxed.

A few hours after he'd changed to the lower-level stealth shield, Richard went to check on the sorceress to change her eye bandages. When he removed the bandages, he saw the sorceress blink her eyes. It was the first movement besides breathing he'd seen her make in three days.

"Great" Richard said. "Welcome back to the land of the living. Let's see if we can set up some communication. If I ask a question, you can blink once for yes and twice for no. Okay.

One blink.

"Excellent" Richard said.

Richard had been unusually bored the last three days, so even a limited interaction with the sorceress was a useful distraction.

"Are you in pain?"

Two blinks.

"Good. Are you comfortable?"

Two blinks.

"Okay," Richard said, "stupid question. Of course you're not comfortable. Can you swallow?"

Two blinks.

"No? Oh well, a little bit at a time. Maybe you can by tomorrow. Do you want me to put the bandage back on your eyes?"

Two blinks.

"I don't blame you. I hate not being able to see. I've got the lantern turned down low, so hopefully the light won't be too bad on your eyes. Are you bored?"

One blink.

"Of course, you are," Richard said. "I would be too. In fact, I can move around, and I'm still bored. Would you like to hear a story?"

A short pause, then the elf gave one blink.

"Nick," Richard said. *"Do you have any stories translated in her language that I can read to her?"*

"I have lots of books in my databanks, Rick. I can translate any of them for you. How about a classic story from your home planet about a big white whale? It's chased by a man who is obsessed with tracking it down and killing it? Kind of like you and the demon in reverse. Do you know the story?"

"No," Richard admitted. *"I didn't read much fiction when I was growing up. Is the story any good?"*

"A lot of people think so, but you'll have to judge for yourself. Put on your helmet, and I'll send the translation to the heads-up display. You can read as long as you want."

"Couldn't you just read it to both of us?" Richard asked. *"We*

had a teacher in the orphanage that used to read to us. She was nice. I always liked to hear her read. But, don't use my voice. That would be weird."

Richard put a stool a few feet from the sorceress's bed and put his battle helmet on the stool. He then pulled his own stool next to the sorceress.

"My, err…friend is going to read a story to us," Richard told the sorceress. "I don't know if you know what a computer is, but my friend is one. He lives in that helmet. If you get tired and want him to stop reading, just blink your eyes a lot. I'll know what that means. Do you want to hear the story now?"

One blink.

"Okay, Nick. We're ready. Fire away."

"Sounds good, Rick. But if you get bored, just say the word, and I'll stop reading."

Nickelo began reading. Richard's battle computer had an interesting voice, and from almost the first words, Richard was mesmerized by the story. He wasn't bored. Nickelo read for two hours straight before he paused.

"Rick," said Nickelo over the battle helmet's external speakers. "You should probably ask the sorceress if she wants me to stop."

Richard looked at the sorceress and said, "How about it? Do you want my friend to stop reading?"

Two blinks.

Richard and the sorceress listened to Nickelo's soothing voice for another two hours. Then Nickelo stopped and refused to read anymore until Richard and the sorceress got some rest.

Richard grumbled they weren't tired, and that he didn't think the sorceress was ready to stop either, but Nickelo was adamant. Finally, Richard capitulated. He placed a moistened bandage over the sorceress's eyes, said goodnight, and they went to sleep.

The next day, the sorceress had improved enough that she was able to swallow. Richard removed the medical band on the sorceress's arm. He helped her drink out of a cup with a straw. He also fed her a warm broth. Once they'd eaten, he raised her into a sitting position with her back against the wall. He sat next to her on the bed and supported her with his arm. Then he asked Nickelo to continue with the story. Nickelo read for hours. The only break in reading was when the sorceress had him stop long enough for her to partake of a light lunch. Then Nickelo read into the late afternoon until the book was finished.

"That was a great book, Nick," Richard said out loud for the sorceress's benefit. "Thank you."

The next day, the sorceress's condition had improved enough that she could eat a small amount of solid food. She still couldn't talk, but Richard figured it was only a matter of time. He told her as much. In the meantime, Richard got bored again. He got bored easily. He was well aware it was one of his faults. He also knew his affinity for boredom was probably responsible for a lot of the trouble he'd gotten into during his time at the orphanage.

Eventually, Richard eyed the sorceress's gear. He'd taken all the sorceress's gear and accessories off her on the first day and cleaned them as best he could. Her wands, staff, jewelry, belt, dagger and pack were lined up on a nearby stone bench. Her robe was hanging from a line Richard had strung in the room to let it dry after he'd washed it.

Richard went to the bench and picked up each wand and the dagger in turn and studied them. After a short discussion with Nickelo, Richard did a narrow-band, active scan on each. Since he'd switched to the lowest-level stealth shield, his Power reserve was once again at a hundred percent, so even Nickelo didn't complain about the Power usage.

"What do you think the wands are?" Richard silently asked his battle computer.

"They're spell storage devices," said Nickelo. *"Wizard scouts are able to manipulate their Power directly from their reserves. Magic users are different in that they have to convert the Power in their reserve to a usable form of energy for their spells. Most magic-using creatures do this by a combination of verbal and hand motions. To save time, they can store Power that has been pre-converted into spells in storage devices such as wands."*

"Is that what her rings and necklace are as well?" Richard said.

"Doubtful," Nickelo said. *"They seem to be storage devices for pure Power. They're sort of like having backup Power reserves. I noticed during our battle with the demon that the sorceress drew Power from her rings, necklace, and staff to energize her defensive shield."*

"She definitely saved our lives with her shield, that's for sure," Richard said. *"Once I'm trained, will my defensive shield be that powerful?"*

"Ha!" said Nickelo. *"You wish. Your Power reserve is too small. Since you can't store excess Power in items, you have to make do with the Power in your reserve. You'll never be able to stand toe to toe with a major demon and slug it out. The sorceress's shield was pure, brute force. You have to learn finesse."*

"Lucky me," Richard said. *"What do you think's in her pack?"*

"Why don't you take a look and see?" Nickelo said. *"I don't think the sorceress is in a position to argue at the moment. Besides, we have a pretty good idea what two of the items are. You'll need to put on your battle helmet with the visor down before looking in her pack."*

Richard put on his battle helmet. He then picked up the sorceress's pack and sat down on the bench next to her and said, "Do you mind if I look in your pack?"

One blink.

"Do you mean yes it's okay for me to look in the pack?"

Two hard blinks.

"Oh," Richard said, "so you mean no you don't mind if I look in your pack. I mean, there's no way I'd look in your pack unless I knew I had your permission."

A series of two blinks.

"You're mean," Nickelo said with a laugh. *"I'll have to remember that one."*

"I have my moments," Richard said.

He lowered his visor and opened the pack. Two leather bags in the shape of spheres were on top.

"Hmm. What do we have here?" Richard said innocently.

Richard heard a gurgling sound from the sorceress as she strained to speak. He saw her eyes blinking wildly. He pretended not to notice. Pulling out one of the leather bags, he started to open it. He stopped before he got it open. A thought had come to him.

Richard said to Nickelo privately, *"You know, Nick, maybe I should put on my battle suit and activate the override. That other sphere had me in a trance when I looked at it. I'd have been in a bad position if you hadn't been able to take control of the suit and get me out of trouble.*"

"*Rick,*" said Nickelo in a strange tone, "*do you know how rare you are?*"

Richard didn't understand what his battle computer meant. He admitted as much.

Nickelo said, "*Your battle suit's override was designed for emergencies. Few wizard scouts trust their battle computers enough to use the suit's override except in the direst of situations. Some wizard scouts would probably not use the override even in the face of certain death. Yet, you haven't balked when I've asked for control. Just like now, you sometimes use the override as a 'just-in-case.' You're a rarity in trust, Rick, and you're not even a full wizard scout yet.*"

Richard didn't see any reason to make a fuss. Nickelo was his battle computer, and he'd begun to think of him as a friend. "I don't think it's a big deal. We're a team, right? We need to be able to trust each other. Besides, you trust me every time you turn control of the battle suit back over to me, don't you?"

"*I think most people would argue that's different,*" said Nickelo. "*They'd say it's different because I am a computer. You don't see it that way, do you? That's what makes you unique. And, although you didn't ask, I want you to know you can trust me, Rick.*"

"*I know I can,*" Richard said as he hastily put on his battle suit. Once he'd finished, he said, "*Seal it up, and let's get this over with. I really hate wearing this suit longer than necessary.*"

When the battle suit was sealed, Richard thought the command to activate the suit's override. Then he sat next to the sorceress and held the first leather sack in his hand once again. As soon as the sorceress saw the sack, she started furiously double-blinking her eyes. Through the suit's audio pickups, Richard heard the thud of her heart. She wasn't just nervous. She was scared.

Richard opened the bag and pulled out the sphere. The sorceress's heart slowed as her eyes transfixed on the sphere. She no longer blinked, and her eyes took on a glazed look.

"*Go to a clear visor, Nick, and let me look at it. Give me about five seconds then revert back to a filtered visor.*"

"*Roger that.*"

The reddish tint of Richard's visor disappeared, and he found himself looking at a beautiful sphere of yellow-marbled light. Various hues of yellow swirled with a hypnotic effect pulling Richard's consciousness ever deeper into the sphere's interior. He felt at peace with the world. He was content.

The battle suit's visor turned red once more. When it did, the sphere lost its hypnotic effect. For a moment, Richard felt a little resentful that Nickelo had followed his commands and activated the battle suit's filter. His mind was no longer at peace. Once again, all the petty problems of life were swirling around in his head. It took a few seconds before Richard was in total control again.

"That could get addictive real quick," Richard said.

"Your girlfriend certainly seems to think so," said Nickelo.

Richard glanced down. The sorceress's eyes were staring intently at the sphere. He could hear her heart beating at a slow and steady pace. She seemed at peace. Richard put the yellow sphere back in its leather pouch. Within seconds, the sorceress's heartbeat increased, and her eyes took on a wild and frantic look.

"That was interesting," Richard said to the sorceress. "It's very pretty. Do you mind if I look at the other one?"

The elf gave numerous double-blinks.

"No, you don't mind?" Richard said with a slight smile behind his visor. "That's very kind of you."

The sorceress's heartbeat escalated, and her eyes took on a frantic look again. She began blinking her eyes so fast that Richard couldn't decide whether she was trying to communicate yes or no.

"I never knew you were so mean," said Nickelo with a chuckle. *"Why are you teasing her like that?"*

"Because, as you've undoubtedly surmised well before me," Richard said, *"the odds are our mission is to give this sorceress the blue sphere we found. We mapped the lower levels of this place. We found the blue sphere. So, all we have left to do is give it to someone. This female, or sorceress as you call her, has two spheres already along with a bag for a third."*

"Then why not just give her the blue sphere and be done with it?" said Nickelo. *"Why ask her fake yes and no questions?"*

"I want to see her reactions," Richard said. *"Just because 'the One' says to give her the third sphere doesn't mean I should give it to her. What if she wants to use it to kill people? Or what if she*

needs it to destroy an entire civilization? By gauging her reactions, I'm forming an opinion about her."

"Well, I have an opinion of her," said Nickelo.

"What's that?" Richard said eagerly. He was definitely interested in hearing his battle computer's take on the subject.

"In my opinion," said Nickelo with a knowing laugh, *"as soon as she can move, she's going to take her staff and beat you over the head with it. Or, maybe she'll turn you into a newt or something."*

"You think you're hilarious, don't you?" Richard said.

"Doesn't everyone?" Nickelo asked innocently.

"No," Richard said.

Richard took the second leather bag and pulled out a red sphere. The sorceress went into a peaceful trance once again. Richard opted not to shut down his filter this time. He just had Nickelo confirm the color for him. Then he put the sphere back in its bag.

"Hmm," Richard said to the sorceress. "You've got a yellow sphere and a red sphere. That's two of the three primary colors. You also have an empty leather bag. By any chance are you looking for a third sphere? If so, would that sphere happened to be blue?"

The sorceress's eyes didn't blink, but she stared at Richard hard, and her heartbeat increased rapidly.

"It does no good to discuss it now," Richard said, "but once you can talk, perhaps we can talk about it more. Personally, I've no interest in any of the spheres other than you obviously want them. Consequently, you don't need to worry about me trying to steal them from you. Therefore, I'd appreciate it if you refrained from trying to harm me when you're able to move again. I've got no doubt you're more than capable of killing me if you so desire."

The look in the sorceress's eyes conveyed to Richard that she had no doubt either. Richard decided it might not be the best time to continue snooping in her pack. He made it a point to let her see him placing the two leather bags with their contents back in her pack. Then he placed her pack back on the bench and made a graceful retreat to the far side of the room to start cooking their supper meal.

CHAPTER 20

Richard came alert immediately. Something had changed enough to disturb his light sleep. He didn't move, although he did tighten his grip on the phase rod under his pillow. Richard sensed nothing amiss with his passive scan. He visually checked the room in the dim lantern light to make sure nothing was amiss.

"Nick? Are you there?"

"I'm here," Nickelo responded mentally. *"Everything's fine. The sorceress just moved her arm and head. The ghoul's poison must be almost out of her system."*

Shifting his head to look at the sorceress, Richard saw two silver eyes staring at him. Her arm had moved from its position on her chest. It now drooped off the side of her makeshift bed.

"Are you all right?" Richard asked. He watched her eyes to see her reply in the dim light. He got a surprise instead.

"Yes," she said. It was really more of a croak than a word, but Richard knew what she meant.

"You moved," Richard said. "That's good. Do you need anything?"

"My nose," the sorceress said.

Her answer confused Richard. "Your nose? I don't understand."

"It itches," she said with her voice getting stronger as she spoke. "I was trying to scratch it, but my arm just fell off the bed."

Just thinking about having an itch he couldn't scratch made Richard's own nose start itching. He resisted the urge to scratch out of respect for the sorceress. He rose from his cot and turned the lantern up slightly. He then sat down on a stool near the sorceress's head and gently lifted her dangling arm until her hand was positioned just above her nose. Her fingers started moving. She scratched herself for several seconds before stopping.

"Much better," she sighed. "That spot has been driving me crazy the last couple of days. Thank you."

"Sorry," Richard said. "I wish I'd known earlier. Is there anything I can do for you now? Is there anything you want?"

"Water, please," she said. "My throat's so dry."

Richard poured some cool water into a cup and added a straw. He held the straw to her lips, and she drained the cup dry.

"More?" he asked.

"Not now, thank you," she said.

The sorceress surveyed the room.

"Where did you get all this equipment?" she said.

Richard wasn't sure how to answer her since he didn't really understand himself. In the end, he decided if she was from the plane of magic as Nickelo had implied, then a magical answer would probably suffice best.

"I summoned it from my pack," he said keeping it simple.

"Ah," she said. "Then you are a mage. I'd convinced myself you weren't."

"Actually," Richard said, "your first guess was right. I'm no magic user, mage or otherwise."

She started to say something but seemed to change her mind before the thought came out. Instead, she said, "Could you please help me sit up? I've been lying down so long it hurts."

"Of course," Richard said. "You've probably got bed sores by now. I tried to move you around some, but I guess it wasn't enough."

Richard placed his arms around her and gently lifted her into a sitting position with her back braced against the wall. He used pillows to wedge her in place. Through the whole process, he went to great lengths to make sure her sheets stayed in place to protect her modesty.

At one point during the maneuver, he must have wrinkled his nose, because she said, "I know. I stink. I can smell myself."

"Sorry," Richard said. "I tried giving you a couple of sponge baths, but I didn't want to get too detailed if you know what I mean."

There was an awkward silence.

"Uh," Richard said hesitantly. "Do you need to take care of your morning business? Or do you want to wait until you can do it yourself?"

The sorceress turned a little red, but she quickly composed herself. "That could be hours yet. I don't think I can wait. Perhaps you can assist me one more time. After that, let's make a pledge we won't ever speak about it again."

A little red himself, Richard said, "I'd appreciate that."

After her morning business was taken care of, Richard sat the sorceress back on her bed with her back against the wall again. Then he busied himself with making a hot porridge for their breakfast. Once they'd eaten, he put the dirty dishes back in his pack. He wasn't sure what happened to them after that. He'd learned quickly enough that when he put items back in the pack, he got a portion of the Power back it had taken to summon them. He had a fleeting image of some irritated person having to do his dirty dishes. Richard hoped he was an understanding soul whoever he or she was.

Once he was finished with cleanup, Richard sat on a stool near the sorceress. She eyed him closely but said nothing. Her long silver hair was a tangled mess, but that did little to detract from her beauty.

"We didn't have time for formal introductions before," Richard said. "My name's Richard, but you may call me Rick if you'd like. My friends do."

She appeared to compose her thoughts for a few seconds before answering, "All right, Rick. I have a lot of questions, but maybe it's best to start off simple. My name is Shandristiathoraxen. I can see you're not an elf, so perhaps it is best if you just call me Shandria. That's the name my friends call me."

"So, you're an elf?" Richard asked. "Nick, the one who read us the story, said you were an elf. I wasn't sure I believed him. I've never seen an elf before."

"Well, now you have," the sorceress responded graciously. "And, you're a human. There are only a handful of humans in my land, but I've seen a few. Those round ears would stick out anywhere. Have you thought about growing your hair long to hide them? You'd probably be moderately handsome if not for your ears."

Richard unconsciously touched one of his ears. "I kind of like my ears," he said a little offended.

"It was just a suggestion," she said. After a short pause, she said, "You have me at a disadvantage. I'm obviously convinced you don't mean to kill me since you've certainly had the opportunity. At the same time, I'm still at your mercy, and I hesitate to ask questions which might, shall we say, cause you to have second thoughts."

"I'm actually pretty thick-skinned, Shandria," Richard said, "so ask away. I give you my word of honor, I won't blow a gasket."

"Blow a what?" she said.

"Never mind," Richard said. "It's just a saying. It means I won't lose my temper."

"Fine, then," she said. "You've been honest up to now. So I'll start with this. I'm well aware you saved my life at the risk of your own, but how dare you rifle through my pack. And, I'd like to know your interest in my spheres?"

"Sorry about that, Shandria," Richard said. "Nick said you'd probably beat me over the head with your staff for doing it."

Richard thought he saw the faintest smile on the sorceress's lips, but it quickly disappeared. "I'd probably do worse if I could get hold of it. Perhaps it's fortunate I'm still partially paralyzed. Now, let's get back to the spheres. What do you know about them, and what is your interest in them?"

"She sure is bossy, isn't she," said Nickelo privately. His battle computer laughed. *"Maybe you should take her staff and beat her about the head and shoulders while you've got the chance."*

"Be nice," Richard told his battle computer.

"I really have no knowledge or interest in your spheres or any other spheres for that matter," Richard said. "You can believe that or not. I'll admit I suspected you had a couple of spheres in your pack. I recognized their Power signatures."

The sorceress looked hard at Richard for a moment. "So, you have seen another sphere. You implied as much earlier."

Richard considered sidestepping the truth a little, but he decided against it. He'd always been more of a frontal assault type of person, so he figured why stop now.

"Yes," Richard said. "I saw a blue sphere not long before I met you upstairs."

"Where," she said. Her silver eyes lit up with excitement.

"May I ask you a couple of questions first?" Richard said.

The excitement went out of the elf's eyes. "Perhaps," she said. "It depends on the question."

"Fair enough," Richard said. "I'd like to know two things. First, why do you want the spheres? Second, why am I on the kill list of some demon out of my worst nightmares?"

"Oh," Shandria said. "I'd forgotten you're involved deeper than I would've wanted. Maybe I should answer the second question first. The demon's threat is indeed serious. Because you were with me, it assumes you're involved with the taking of the spheres. No amount of pleading or attempts at explanation on your part will convince it otherwise. The demon's name in my language is Efrestra. It is one of four brother demons. They'll hunt you down until the end of your days. They aren't demon lords, but they're still very powerful. You'll need your strongest magic to protect yourself."

"Nick, are you getting this? What've I gotten myself into?"

"It is what it is, Rick. We'll do whatever we need to do and learn whatever it takes to shield you. If it can't find you, it can't hurt you."

"That's not a lot of comfort, Nick."

"Sorry. It's all the comfort I can give at the moment."

"Well," Richard said addressing the elf again, "I guess I'm out of luck. Like I told you earlier, I'm not a magic user. As a sorceress, you may be able to put up shields strong enough to resist demons, but I can't."

"Did you just call me a sorceress?" said Shandria with a raised eyebrow and a little edge to her voice. "I'm not a sorceress. I'm a priestess. There's a difference, you know."

"Thanks a lot, Nick," Richard said. *"Now I've insulted her."*

"You've been telling me to guess a lot lately," Nickelo said defensively. *"I calculated an eighty-seven percent chance she was a sorceress. She obviously fell into the other thirteen percent. Do you want me to start including percentages every time I tell you something? I can carry the percentages down to a hundred decimal places if you need me to be more accurate."*

"Whatever," Richard said.

"No offense intended, Shandria," Richard said apologetically. "I really don't know anything about magic. It's all new to me."

From the look she gave him, Richard didn't think the elf entirely believed him.

"How can you say that?" she asked. "You'd have to be well versed in magic to place a shield around both of us strong enough to hide us from the demon Efrestra and his minions so long. Even at full Power, I'd be hard pressed to do as much."

"I don't wish to contradict your faith in me," Richard said, "but I can barely shield myself. I've never tried to protect multiple targets with a stealth shield. Even if I could hide you, those spheres combined with your other magic items are giving off way too much Power for me to hide."

Shandria's silver eyes darted around the room. Her countenance took on a fearful look. "If you aren't shielding us, then we must be gone quickly. Why the demon hasn't found us yet, I don't know. But without shielding, it will do so soon. Make no mistake, Rick. It'll never stop hunting either of us."

Richard hadn't meant to frighten the elf. In an attempt to alleviate her concern, he said, "Everything's fine, Shandria. Surely you can sense the room's shielding is protecting us even now?" He didn't understand how anyone with her obvious capabilities could miss the energy shielding the room.

The elf's face muscles tightened as if she were concentrating and looking places Richard couldn't see. After a score of seconds, Shandria said, "I can detect nothing, Rick. My body still has too much of the ghoul's poison in it. I can't draw from my Power reserve. Surely you know a ghoul's poison makes even a magic user totally helpless? That's fortunate for you. Otherwise, I'd have hurt you when you started rifling through my pack."

"Actually, I didn't know that," Richard said. "So you can't use your magic yet? I was kind of depending on you to help get us out of this underground tunnel system."

Shandria looked at Richard incredulously. "You think we're underground?" she said. "I saw you use powerful magic during our battle with the demon. You've probably got the best stealth shield I've ever encountered. I was taken by complete surprise when you jumped me. I've been assuming you're skilled in the ways of magic. How is it that you don't recognize a time-bubble when you are in one?"

"Nick," Richard said a little desperately. *"She's talking gibberish to me. Have you ever heard of a time-bubble?"*

"The term's not in my databanks, Rick, although I almost feel like I should know it. If only I could connect to the tele-network."

Seeing no assistance from his battle computer, Richard decided to plow ahead on his own.

"I keep telling you, I'm not a magic user, Shandria. I'm a wizard scout. Or to be more exact, I'm a wizard scout in training. I can use Power, but can't convert it into magic. I can make a pretty good stealth shield, but haven't been trained in defensive shields. I fought during the battle with weapons of technology. I have no idea what a time-bubble is."

"Geesh, Rick," said Nickelo. *"Why don't you just give her your bank account number and password while you're giving away all our secrets?"*

"Hush, Nick."

Richard watched the elf as she appeared to try and absorb his explanation. Finally, she said, "I understand the word scout, but the words wizard and technology are unfamiliar to me. I must admit you're a strange one. Maybe I just haven't met enough humans to understand them. There are certainly few enough in our land. But, I've a feeling you'd be strange even if I had met a thousand humans."

"Well, you're a little strange to me as well, Shandria," Richard said. "You seem very powerful and skilled for someone who's only a few years older than me."

Shandria gave a loud, good-humored laugh. Nickelo joined in with a private laugh in his thoughts. Richard knew he'd said something wrong, but he wasn't sure what it was. He suspected he'd soon find out.

"Are you really so unfamiliar with elves?" said Shandria still laughing. "Perhaps you are different than the humans where I come from, but on my world, the lifespan of a high elf is twenty times that of a human. If I may be so bold to ask, how old are you, Rick?"

"I'm twenty-two in my world's reckoning," Richard said. "I suppose it would be different on your world."

"Undoubtedly," Shandria said, "but the ratio would be the same. Therefore, in your world's reckoning, I would be in my late four hundreds or early five hundreds."

Richard stared at her. He wondered how this beautiful creature before him could be hundreds of years old. It didn't seem right to him, even if she was an elf. He suddenly realized he'd been building up hopes of a possible romantic relationship with her. That hope suddenly became a blazing starship crashing through the atmosphere on its way to certain destruction.

"Oh," Richard said in response. "All I can say is that you've certainly held up well over the years. You're the most beautiful four-hundred-year-old person I've ever met." Then to cover up his embarrassment, he tried to make a joke. "I don't suppose you'd consider being courted by a younger man, would you?"

Shandria looked at him for so long he thought his joke had fallen flat. Then she burst out laughing. It wasn't a laugh of derision, but instead it was a joyful laugh. It was a laugh meant to release the stress of their situation. It was the laugh of one battle companion sharing a joke with another.

"Rick," she said when her laughter had subsided, "we have babies in diapers in my village older than you." Then more seriously, as if to make sure she didn't damage his male ego too badly, she added, "Besides, I'm betrothed to another. Once my quest is finished, I'll return home to bond with he who is the other part of my soul. But, if I was not betrothed, and if I was inclined to date younger males, then I could certainly do worse than you. Since we first met, you have shown yourself by your actions to be an honorable and worthy companion. If I may be so bold, I think you would make a fine friend."

"Ouch," said Nickelo privately. *"It's the old we-can-still-be-friends gambit. This conversation is obviously not getting us anywhere. I can see I'm going to need to take a more direct approach."*

"If I may be so bold," came Nickelo's voice from the direction of the battle helmet, "what is a time-bubble, and what are those spheres? While you're at it, why is the demon so interested in them?"

"Ah ha," Shandria said as she turned her head to look at the helmet. "So the spirit in your helmet does more than tell stories. I wonder, is he your servant, or are you his?" She finished her comment with a conspiratorial smile, so Richard knew she wasn't serious.

"Rick's my friend, I'll have you know," said Nickelo in a voice that made it plain he was insulted. "Neither of us is the other's servant."

"I should warn you, Shandria," Richard said with a wink, "he's sensitive. But, we actually are a team. He's saved my life often enough that if he did need me to be his servant, then his servant I'd be."

"Well, Master Nick," said Shandria still smiling. "You have my sincere apologies."

Richard thought the elf had the most beautiful smile he'd ever seen. He didn't know who her betrothed was, but he did know he was a very lucky elf.

"To answer your questions, Master Nick, and yours too, friend Rick, let me tell you a story. The Creator…, you do believe in the Creator, don't you?"

"Yes," Richard said. He wasn't deeply religious, but being brought up in a church orphanage pounded a lot of religious doctrine into even the most stubborn of orphans.

"Of course," said Nickelo. "It's only logical."

"Good," said Shandria. "That makes it a little easier. The Evil Ones are determined that the entire universe should be covered with their foul darkness. They've spread into many galaxies and dimensions, but still they crave more. Fortunately, there are many places where the Creator's light still shines bright. My home world is one of those. Judging from my brief association with you, Rick, your world must be also."

"Well," Richard said. "I'm not so sure it shines bright, but at least it's not completely covered in darkness either."

"That is well," said Shandria. "You can never relax. Sprinkled throughout the universe are weak spots that can be used as gates from the dwelling place of the Evil Ones. At one time, all the gates were shut tight and guardians were placed over them. But as the eons passed, some of the guardians grew weak. The armies of the Evil Ones broke through those gates and devoured the gate's planet, its galaxy, and its sister galaxies. My village is near one of those gates, and the guardian has grown weak. If the gate fails, my village, my planet and my galaxy will be overwhelmed by the armies of the Evil Ones."

She paused, and her silver eyes shimmered with a wetness that hadn't been there before. The elf looked at Richard a long time before she added, "As will yours."

"Mine?" Richard asked. "What does my world have to do with it?"

"Listen, friend Rick," Shandria said in a low voice that drew him in, "and you shall soon understand. The Creator didn't leave his people at the mercy of the Evil Ones. Whenever a guardian grows weak, the Creator sends another. But, the people must be strong enough and determined enough to care for the new guardian. Many years ago, the Creator sent a new guardian for our gate in the form of a seed. The seed bided its time while it waited until it was needed. However, the seed was stolen by minions of the Evil Ones before it could be planted. They couldn't destroy it, but they were able to divide the seed into three pieces. They hid each of the seed parts in time-bubbles which they filled with dark things to guard against any rescue of the parts. These time-bubbles exist outside of time. They actually exist in all time at the same time. For those with the knowledge and Power, they are accessible from all times. We are in one of those time-bubbles now. The two spheres I have in my pack each contain a seed part. I seek the third seed part. I seek the blue sphere so that I may return to my home and time. When I am home, the seed parts can be reunited. If the seed is planted soon enough before the gate fails, then the new guardian will grow and protect the gate, and our people will be safe once more."

Richard wasn't sure what to make of the elf's story. He didn't think she was lying. He was sure she believed what she said, but that didn't make it true. He did think there were some flaws in it.

"How does all this affect me?" Richard asked her.

"The armies of the Evil Ones won't stop at my village or even my galaxy. They'll also overwhelm our sister galaxies in the adjoining planes. That includes yours."

Rick opened his mouth to interrupt, but Shandria gave him his answer before he could get his question out.

"I know you are from one of the sister galaxies, Rick, because you're here in this time-bubble. It's accessible from any time, but only from an adjoining plane, and only from a world in a galaxy occupying the same point in space as mine."

"Assuming that's true," Richard said in an attempt to find a reason he wasn't involved, "are you implying that we may not be from the same period in time?"

"In all likelihood, we're from different points in time" she answered. "For all I know, we're from times a million years apart. Either one of us may have been turned to dust before the other was ever born."

"Then the battle may already be over," Richard said hoping he'd scored a point. "Perhaps the gate has already been strengthened, or it has failed. In either case, it might not involve me after all."

"Uh, bad logic, Rick," came a thought from Nickelo. *"The fact that we're here means the world we know hasn't been overcome. But, that doesn't mean it won't happen if we don't help this elf."*

"You want us to help her now?" Richard thought back. *"A few days ago you advised me to kill her. Are you saying you really believe all this time-bubble mumbo-jumbo?"*

"Perhaps you're right," agreed Shandria. "Maybe we have already failed our quest and both our worlds are doomed. But does that mean we shouldn't try?"

"She's slick," came Nickelo's thought. *"Did you notice how it's suddenly our quest?"*

"I did catch it, Nick," Richard said. *"What do you think? Are we involved? Do you buy that crap about gates and seeds? According to her, the fate of multiple galaxies depends on her quest. I'd say that's a little much to put on one little girl's shoulders, even if she is an elf."*

"We're here," answered Nickelo, *"so I'd say we're already involved. And, I'd say it's not just on her shoulders. I think she's been sent a helper,"* Nickelo said with a laugh, *"and he's right in front of me."*

"Really?" Richard said. *"Well, if I'm involved, so are you, so maybe you shouldn't be laughing quite so hard."*

"You're talking to your friend, aren't you?" said Shandria. "To Master Nick?"

"How'd you know?" Richard said curiously.

"Your face got a kind of vacant stare," said the elf. "I've

noticed the expression on you before, but I passed it off as a trait of someone who gets confused easily. No offense intended."

"Woo hoo!" said Nickelo in a fit of laughter. "She's got you pegged for sure."

"You're correct, Shandria," Richard admitted. "I was talking to Nick. He's my battle computer, and we talk about things before we make major decisions."

"Have you made a decision, Rick?"

"We have, Shandria. Nick and I have decided to help you in your quest. The three of us will either leave these tunnels together alive with the spheres, or we won't leave at all."

CHAPTER 21

Once the decision was made to help the elf, Richard wasted no more time on subterfuge. He quickly told her the location of the blue sphere. While she seemed glad to know the location, he was surprised when she didn't demand to see it immediately. He'd thought she'd want to tuck it safely away in her leather bag. But as Shandria explained it, she was concerned the shield around the room might be compromised if the sphere was removed from its resting spot. When Nickelo agreed with her logic, Richard submitted to their will. As a result, the sphere remained tucked safely away in the alcove.

The elf was in a talking mood. Apparently, she'd remained quiet so long that she relished conversation. She told Richard about her life as a priestess in a small, country village. In return, Richard told her about his life, or lack thereof, in the Academy. She was as confused and impressed with his stories of technology as he was of her tales of magic and creatures he'd assumed only existed in fairy tales.

Richard was mildly surprised when Nickelo joined in the conversation. Nickelo used the battle helmet's speakers for the elf's benefit. Nickelo and the elf seemed to hit it off in spite of their obvious differences. Richard didn't mind his battle computer hogging most of their side of the conversation. He'd never really talked much until he'd gained his friends at the Academy. He enjoyed just listening to the voices of both the elf and his battle computer. He listened for quite some time until Shandria and

Nickelo began discussing their theories about time-bubbles, planes, dimensions and galaxies.

Richard quickly became bored, so he busied himself making supper. When he asked Shandria if she was hungry, she responded she was famished. Since she could now move her hands and arms enough to take care of her basic needs, Richard decided to go all out on making a nice meal. While the elf and his battle computer chattered away in the corner, Richard pulled a small, folding table out of his pack along with a set of dishes and eating utensils. The pack was an amazing piece of equipment, and he was glad for it. Although the pack was small, its flap opening could stretch wide enough to accommodate whatever he summoned. He pushed the limits of his dimensional pack by imagining a variety of food items. Richard found he could get just about anything he desired in the way of food products that could be stored long term, but he was unable to get any fresh products such as meats, fruits, or even fresh dairy products. However, any preserved items such as canned meats and vegetables were no problem, especially if they were of an Earth variety from the twentieth or twenty-first centuries.

Since Richard's Power reserve had been fully replenished, he ignored Chief Instructor Winslow's advice to conserve Power. Consequently, he summoned more food than the two of them could possibly eat. Using two camp stoves, he prepared a delicious stew along with a hot apple tart. He took a risk and imagined a quart of ice cream. A second later, he was pulling a box of vanilla ice cream out of the dimensional pack accompanied by a bag of dry ice to keep it cold. Using canned milk, he made hot chocolate. He was even able to get marshmallows. Hot chocolate with marshmallows had been one of the few treats he'd enjoyed at the orphanage. Long before he finished cooking, the aroma of the stew and hot chocolate filled the air in the room. After setting the food on the table, Richard turned to the elf and found she had halted her conversation with Nickelo. Her attention was fully on the food-laden table.

"Well," said Nickelo. *"I guess she thinks more of your cooking than she does a titillating conversation with me."*

Richard gave a silent laugh and said, *"I suspect if all I'd had to eat for the last week was nutrients out of a bag and warm broths and porridge, I wouldn't feel like talking either."*

"Hungry?" Richard asked out loud.

"Starved," replied Shandria. "If I could walk, I'd already be at the table."

Richard helped her to the table. She could actually move her legs some now, but they were not yet strong enough to bear her weight. He summoned a chair with arms for her and propped her in place with a couple of pillows. The elf was able to sit comfortably without fear of falling. Once he'd taken his seat on a stool at the opposite side of the table, Shandria bowed her head. Richard waited patiently while the elf said a silent prayer to whatever deity she worshiped. He didn't ask, and she didn't volunteer. Richard rarely prayed. He wasn't against praying, he just didn't do it very often. Normally, he only said a desperate prayer when he was in trouble, but even then he didn't go overboard. He supposed it was because the sisters at the orphanage had stressed prayer so much that he just naturally rebelled against it. Still, he always tried to be respectful of the rituals of others. And, he did have solid beliefs of his own.

They were both mostly silent during the meal. The elf ate heartily, and in spite of his suggestions to limit her servings, she ate like a woman starved. Shandria absolutely loved the hot chocolate, and she became downright ecstatic over the apple tart and ice cream. After their meal was done, Richard cleared the table. It was an easy task since it only consisted of tossing everything back in the pack. Once the flap was closed, the inside of the pack was instantaneously cleaned. When all was done, Richard and Shandria sat silently at the table for several minutes. They were both contentedly lost in their own thoughts. Even Nickelo was quiet for a change.

Eventually, Shandria said, "I've been thinking, Rick. By tomorrow morning, enough of the ghoul's poison should be out of my system for me to relearn my spells. We could begin preparations for our departure after that. Unfortunately, we'll probably have a fight on our hands the moment the blue sphere goes in my leather bag. It may well be a different battle than we fought previously. I'll admit I'm concerned about you."

"Me?" Richard said a little affronted. "I think I did all right the last time. I wasn't the one paralyzed, you know?"

For a moment the elf reminded him of one of the sisters

preparing to stem off the protests of one of the more stubborn children. She seemed determined to be patient, but Richard sensed an irritation in her. Still, he had a feeling she was genuinely concerned for his wellbeing.

"That was out of line," Richard apologized. "Still, why the concern?"

"The guardians of this place were caught by surprise the last time," said Shandria. "You have an excellent stealth shield. I don't think they even knew you were around. I certainly didn't. I also have a good stealth shield, but my Power reserve was low when we met. I was unable to adequately shield both myself and the two spheres. I believe that's the reason you sensed my presence before I sensed yours."

"Actually, I didn't have all that much warning you was there," Richard said. "I got lucky. But, you said you were low on Power. Is that why you nearly drained your jewelry and staff during the fight with the demon?"

"Yes," she said. "You detected that?"

"I sensed it," Richard said. "So did Nick."

"Well, if you can detect Power flows, then you must know that almost all of my Power went into maintaining my defensive shield. The demon would have destroyed us both if my shield had failed."

Ignoring his own ego, Richard nodded his head in agreement with her assessment.

"Rick, I don't wish to belittle your part in the battle, but I noticed you didn't put up your own defensive shield. You remained hidden behind mine."

Richard was momentarily too embarrassed to admit he had to be protected by a girl, but he shoved his outdated, masculine ideas about gender roles back into the depths of his self-consciousness where they belonged. The elf, this priestess, was better than him in many ways. He'd be a fool not to admit it.

"I'm still a cadet," Richard said. "In other words, I'm still a student. I haven't been trained in defensive shields yet. I could've thrown up something and called it a defensive shield, but it would've been a waste of energy in that battle. I figured I could help most by keeping the riffraff off of you."

"You did wisely, Rick. I would've dropped my shield if that hell hound had found my throat. When I saw you move to intercept it, I somehow knew I could trust you to protect me. I'm not sure why, but I did."

That mollified Richard's bruised ego a little.

"I suppose we could attempt our escape from this place in a couple of days, Rick. However, I would like to propose an alternate plan. I too am skilled at monitoring Power flows, the same as you. I'm also well versed in defensive shields. Would you be affronted if I offered to train you in their use? It might take a month or more, but the time spent might mean the difference between the success and failure of our quest."

Richard was shocked the elf would delay the completion of her mission for a month. She had the object of her quest in her grasp. *Why would she wait?* he wondered. He was confused. Sometimes he felt like he was in a continuous state of confusion.

"Shandria, I wouldn't be affronted. But, wouldn't it be prudent to get out of this place as fast as we can? You have the third part of the seed. For all you know, the gate may be failing at this very moment. Surely time is of utmost importance."

The elf smiled and gave a good-natured laugh.

Nickelo also laughed aloud via the battle computer's speakers. "Rick, you really need to pay more attention to what people say. You can discover a lot of things if you listen more and put the tidbits of information you hear together."

Richard ignored his battle computer. At this moment, the elf seemed the kinder of the two.

"Okay, Shandria," Richard said, "I've obviously said something wrong again. What's so funny?"

"It's not an unreasonable mistake," Sandria said with a smile. "You admitted you had no knowledge of time-bubbles. The three time-bubbles created to hide the seed parts are all connected together. They're each separate and apart, but at the same time, they are one and the same place. The time that you and I spend inside this time-bubble doesn't exist. It is outside the normal flow of time. Master Nick told me you had been here a little over a week. I've spent over a year in each of the other two time-bubbles, and I've been in this one for almost six months. Yet when I exit the time-bubble, I will appear back at my village at the same moment I departed. No time will have passed."

Richard had trouble digesting the elf's information. He was no dummy, but he'd never been a fast thinker. He normally needed to absorb and mull over information before he could fully grasp it.

"*Never mind, Rick,*" came Nickelo's thought. "*I'll explain it to you later.*"

"Shandria, are you saying we could spend a hundred years here, and then we could go back to our own time and nothing will have changed?"

"Actually," she said. "I could spend a hundred years here, but you couldn't. Time moves on for us inside the time-bubble. We'll age while we're here. You're a human. You would be dead in a hundred years. Although I'm an elf, I would still be a hundred years older."

"I guess I understand," Richard said. But he wasn't ready to give up his argument to leave immediately. "But if we stay another month, won't that give the demon and his servants that much more time to find us? We've been lucky so far, but who knows how long that'll last?"

"Shandria and I," said Nickelo over the battle helmet's speakers, "have discussed the room's stealth shield at length. From the data collected by both your active scans and my electronic scans, we believe the shield's more than adequate to hide us for a considerable amount of time."

"I agree with Master Nick," said Shandria. "I only found the other two seed parts by the use of a spell created especially for that purpose. Even then, it took me over two years to find the other spheres. Master Nick explained to me where this room is located. I've been down this same tunnel twice during the last six months without sensing anything. I was headed to these lower tunnels for a third pass when you encountered me."

Richard was impressed. He assumed the elf must have one heck of a stealth shield when she was at full Power to hide for months from the creatures in the tunnels.

"Okay," Richard said. "I'll admit we almost passed by it as well. Still, surely someone knows where this secret room is. I mean, someone had to build it and hide the sphere here. Right?"

"You're correct," said Shandria. "However, I believe the creation of this secret room and of this time-bubble is well beyond the abilities of even a powerful demon like Efrestra. No, I believe the skills of a master demon, possibly even a demon lord, were needed to build this place. All I have learned suggests that demons are not trusting of each other. In all likelihood, the demon Efrestra and his servants were only given the responsibility to guard this place. I suspect they weren't told its secrets. As long as the original builder doesn't return, I believe we're safe."

Richard was unconvinced, but he couldn't argue against the elf's logic. His knowledge of demons and magical creatures was a little on the thin side.

*   *   *

The next morning, Shandria awoke refreshed. She was able to move about by herself, although she was still weak. Richard summoned a portable bathtub and filled it with hot water and bubble bath. After he set up a privacy screen, Shandria spent over an hour getting rid of the accumulated filth of the past week. Finally, she stepped out from behind the privacy screen. She wore on her robe and jewelry. Richard had thought she was beautiful before. He thought she was even more stunning now.

"Wow!" Richard said. "I hope your betrothed knows how lucky he is."

"He does," said Shandria simply. But her cheeks reddened slightly at the compliment.

"What's first?" Richard said.

"My spells," said Shandria as she opened her pack. I lost all memory of them when I was contaminated with the ghoul's poison. My Power reserve is full again, but until I rememorize my spells, I can't use my Power."

"Do you have to rememorize a spell each time you use it?" Richard asked.

"No, silly," laughed Shandria. "Once memorized, I can use it as much as I want as long as I have adequate Power. But some of them are very complicated, and all magic users have to refresh their memory from time to time. That's why I carry copies of my spell books with me."

The elf pulled a book out of her pack. It had a plain black cover with no decorations.

"I thought you were a priestess?" Richard said. "I thought only magic users needed spell books."

"Where did you get that idea, Rick?" asked Shandria. "Maybe things work differently in your dimension, but in mine, spellcasters of any kind need to learn spells. The only exception is magical creatures that are born with a natural ability to convert their Power into magic."

Shandria sat down on the edge of her bed and began silently reading her book. The only noise in the room for over an hour was the sound of their breathing. Even Nickelo didn't disturb Richard with his thoughts. Finally, boredom got the best of Richard, and he went over and sat down next to the elf. It didn't enter his mind she might resent someone reading over her shoulder. Apparently she didn't because she said nothing.

Richard was intrigued by the writing on the pages of the book. He could see what appeared to be words in an unknown language on the paper. They seemed to move and change as he looked at them. The words had a Power of their own, and Richard was able to follow the flows of Power. The Power twisted from one word to another and back again forming intricate knots and flourishes. The flows of Power were interesting to watch, and Richard found himself leaning forward eagerly each time the elf turned a page.

After several hours, Richard's stomach growled. He rose and set about heating some soup for lunch. He found it a little amusing that he was turning into quite the domestic type. He didn't mind. He actually enjoyed cooking. It was relaxing. He often found himself thinking about what he could summon for the next meal.

"Lunch," Richard said.

Shandria stopped her reading and joined Richard at the table. After she prayed, Richard said, "You've been studying a lot."

After blowing on a spoonful of soup before swallowing it, Shandria answered, "I've learned a lot of spells over the years, Rick. I'm not sure which ones we'll need. I'm trying to memorize as many as I can. However, the incantations are magic themselves, and there's a limit to how many I can memorize at one time."

"Hmm," Richard said. He had an idea, but he hesitated to say anything since he wasn't a magic user himself. After a moment's reflection, he decided since their lives were on the line, he should just say what was on his mind.

"Shandria," Richard said tentatively, "I don't mean to pry or sound like a know-it-all, because I know I'm not. But I was wondering, wouldn't you be able to memorize more spells if they were shorter and less complicated?"

The elf looked at Richard intently with a spoonful of soup halfway to her mouth. She didn't answer his question immediately. Finally, she put the spoon back in the bowl and said, "Spellcasters spend years creating and refining spells. They guard them jealously. Some of the more complicated and powerful spells have taken entire lifetimes by master spellcasters to create. When I say lifetimes, I mean lifetimes of an elf. I'm trying to hold my temper, Rick, since you've been so kind to me. But, it sounds like you think you know more about spells and magic than those who actually use them. Or have I jumped to conclusions?"

Richard had suspected it was a touchy subject, and he'd taken the risk. But, he wasn't prepared to risk more. He beat a hasty retreat. "Sorry. It was just a question. I meant no disrespect."

He went back to eating his soup. He kept his eyes on his bowl while ensuring every spoonful contained just the right mix of vegetables and meat. Even so, he could feel the eyes of the elf on him, and he didn't hear her eating.

"Rick," she said finally, "it's I who should apologize. Spellcasters of any sort are very touchy about their spells. Even a slightly mispronounced word or stray hand gesture can have disastrous results. But if you have something to say, please say it. I promise not to take offense again."

"It was nothing," Richard said as he continued to eat. "Forget it."

"Please, Rick," said Shandria, "I apologized. Won't you please tell me what you were going to say? I sense it was important. If it would help us in our current situation, we should discuss it."

Rick, said Nickelo privately, *we're in serious danger. If you have an idea that might lessen the danger, please share it with us.*

"All right, Shandria," Richard said swallowing his pride. "I know you're like four hundred years my senior, but I do have a thought. When I was reading along in your spell book, it seemed like some of the Power lines would loop back onto themselves or were more complex than needed. Parts of the incantations seemed like they were wasted effort. Didn't the writers see the inefficient use of Power when they wrote out the words? It seems pretty obvious."

"Are you saying you can read the words?" Shandria asked.

Richard thought he detected a little huffiness in her voice as if he'd insulted her. He listened nervously as the elf continued.

"It took me almost a hundred years of study before I was able to make out the words of even a simple spell. Obviously, I'm in the presence of a master spellcaster. You must have gained so much knowledge in just a score of years that not only can you read magic, but you can rewrite spells that we elves have struggled over for centuries."

Richard forced himself to control his temper. He wanted to remind her that she'd promised not to take offense. Finally, he decided he'd be just as suspicious and insulted if the roles were reversed.

"No," Richard said struggling to keep his voice even. "I can't read the words. They keep moving around and changing."

"Yes. I'm sure they do," Shandria said as she nodded her head knowingly. "That's how they're supposed to work. I had to learn to master the art of the words before I could learn to read or write them."

"If you can't read them, Rick," asked Nickelo trying to avoid a confrontation, "then why do you think they can be improved?"

"Because I can see the Power lines clearly," Richard said. "Because I can see how the Power is changed by the incantations. I can see the desired end result of the conversion from Power to magical energy. I can see how there is wasted effort. I can sense or see or whatever you want to call it, places in the incantations that can be made more efficient. It just jumps off the page at me. I don't understand how the writers couldn't see it as well."

"How would you know what words to use?" asked Shandria. "You admitted you couldn't read the words."

Richard heard the strain in the elf's voice. She was trying to control her own temper for the common good. Richard resolved to do the same.

"I wouldn't know what words to use or how they should be changed," Richard confessed. "But...," he said quickly to cut off any protest, "I could show you the places that could be improved. You could make changes as you saw fit. Then I could tell you if the changes improved the spell or made it worse."

Shandria seemed to consider Richard's proposal before

speaking, "I too can see Power lines. I'm a priestess after all. But, I can't see them at the level of detail you're implying, nor have I ever heard of anyone who could. Can you truly see the ebb and flow of Power in the spells?"

"I know what I see, Shandria," Richard said. He left it at that. Either the elf would believe him, or she wouldn't.

Nickelo spoke up, "Shandria, I've found Rick to be unique in many ways. Without a shared space, I can't verify his claim. But, I do know he has the best stealth shield and active scan I've ever encountered. Plus, I've never known him to lie or stretch the truth. He goes to great lengths sometimes to avoid dishonesty. I'd take what he says at face value. You might want to consider his suggestion."

Richard was humbled by his battle computer's praise. Normally, Nickelo was pointing out his mistakes.

"Let me sleep on it," said Shandria. "Changing spells can have drastic and unforeseen results. The graves of many knowledgeable spellcasters bear witness to the dangers of arrogance when attempting to modify existing spells.

CHAPTER 22

The next morning, Shandria began Richard's training in defensive shields. Actually, Richard found he had a combination of trainers. Nickelo gave as much input as the elf, and between the combined tutelage of both, Richard was soon able to put up a low-level defensive shield with semi-regularity.

After lunch, the roles reversed. Shandria consented to an attempt to improve a spell. The elf allowed Richard to select one of the lower-level spells in her spell book that he thought might have room for improvement. By following the Power lines of the written incantation, Richard pointed out one area of three words which were a complete waste of effort and two other places which had potential for improvement. Using trial and error, Richard and Shandria spent the rest of the afternoon rewriting the spell. Shandria used a special bottle of ink and quill to write out the words on a blank piece of parchment. By suppertime, the parchment was covered with more scratch marks than visible words. As far as Richard could tell, they were nowhere nearer to making a workable spell.

Richard was forced to admit defeat. "I'm sorry, Shandria," Richard said dejectedly. "I really thought it would work. I did think we were getting close a couple of times, but I guess not. It's no use. I'm sorry I wasted your time."

"Master Nick," said Shandria with a shake of her head and a tired smile. "Is he always so impatient? How do you put up with him?"

"It's a challenge sometimes," admitted Nickelo with a chuckle of his own. "And yes, he is always this impatient. He'd rather run straight into battle than take five extra minutes to make a workable plan."

Richard was confused. He didn't think he deserved the double-teaming against him. "Now what did I do?" he asked through gritted teeth.

The elf answered first. "I believe we made good progress today, Rick," said Shandria. "True, the spell isn't working yet, but you've convinced me the concept may eventually work. We just need to give it time. Don't you remember me saying some spells took the entire lifetime of the writer to get it right? I'll admit I was skeptical at first. But like you, I think we came close today. With your permission, I believe we should continue trying at least a few more days."

"Fine by me," Richard said. He hated failure anyway. He didn't mind being wrong. He just hated to fail.

*　　*　　*

The days turned into weeks, and the weeks turned into months. Richard received training not only in defensive shields but also in telekinesis. By the end of the second month, he could deflect most of Shandria's low and mid-level spells. He could also levitate items as well as himself using telekinesis. To his surprise, Richard found he had more trouble with his telekinesis than he did with defensive shields. He was surprised because he'd been able to levitate small items since he was a child.

"So why can't I levitate myself up a tall building?" Richard asked Nickelo heatedly one day when the training was going especially bad.

"Power, Rick. Because of Power," replied Nickelo just as heatedly. For a computer, Richard thought Nickelo could get very emotional sometimes. "You'd be better off using telekinesis to slow down your descent. Like I said, it's a case of Power, just like almost everything else you do. Moving small items around takes relatively little Power. Levitating yourself up a high cliff using telekinesis would take a lot of Power. You might be able to do it, but if the cliff was too high, you might empty your reserve before reaching the top. And what would you do if you made it to the top? You'd be so low on Power you couldn't fight. On the other hand, you could jump off a high cliff and use your telekinesis to slow your descent enough to cushion your fall. That's assuming you're efficient with your Power usage. Remember what Chief Instructor Winslow says, 'Never use Power when you can do something another way.'"

To prove his point, Nickelo had Richard practice levitating to the top of the table and then jumping off the table and slowing his fall just before he hit the floor. He got pretty good at it after a while. By monitoring his Power usage, Richard had to admit levitating up took a lot more Power than slowing himself down during his fall.

In the afternoons, Shandria and Richard made good progress with the rewriting of some of the more inefficient spells. By the end of the first two months, Shandria had ten spells converted into their more efficient counterparts. While she'd been unenthusiastic in the beginning, she quickly reversed her opinion after the successful conversion of the first spell. Not only was it smaller, but it used less Power while producing more magical energy. The first spell was a simple one for cooling an item such as a glass of water. With a lot of perseverance, Shandria and Richard were able to shorten the spell to a single magical word. According to Shandria, they'd created a new word. All Richard knew was that after hearing Shandria pronounce her incantations so often, he got pretty good at sensing the changes of the Power flows with each syllable and changes in voice inflection. By directing Shandria to modify words and pitch, he was able to help her improve the efficiency of her spells. Shandria was ecstatic, and before long they were tackling tougher and longer spells.

"You know," said Shandria. "These spell changes could have long-lasting effects if I can teach them to my people. Not only are they more efficient and powerful, the reduced size of the incantations means they'll take up less space in a spellcaster's memory. As a result, we can memorize more spells. That'll give me a greater set of choices during a battle."

"I'm glad it's working out," Richard said.

"You know, Rick," said Shandria, "the time we've spent here training has been worthwhile. It's not just the progress we've made with the spells. Your defensive shields have improved to the point where I think I can provide no more useful guidance. We can continue to practice, but it will just be to smooth out some rough places. You're about as good as you're going to get."

"You still penetrate my shields a lot," Richard said.

"That's only because I'm intimately familiar with your defensive shields," said Shandria. "Your Power reserve's smaller than most spellcasters, so your defensive shields are not able to resist as much energy as mine. Still, your technique's excellent and very efficient. I doubt you'll ever be able to slug it out with a major demon or master spellcaster, but you could definitely at least deflect the first few blows. You'll just have to use that time to think of a way to use your technology to defeat your foe."

"Well," Richard said jokingly, "I guess that's better than getting burned to a crisp at the very onset of a fight. So, are we done training?" Richard couldn't help but sound disappointed. He liked Shandria's style of teaching, and even Nickelo's training on advanced active scans was interesting. Plus, it wasn't like he was eager to return to the loving supervision of TAC Officer Gaston Myers. He missed his friends, and he missed his instructors at the Academy. But, he had learned a lot under Shandria's guidance that could help keep him alive when he became a wizard scout. Besides, as Nickelo and Shandria had predicted, they were safe in this room. Richard had sensed several lifeforms with large Power signatures passing through the tunnels nearby, but none stopped to investigate their secret door. The room's stealth shield was holding up well. No, he wasn't in a hurry to stop his training.

"Oh, you can't get out of my instruction so easily," laughed Shandria with a beautiful smile. "We need to work on a few more weaknesses before we step out into the tunnels. I thought we should let you practice trying to penetrate my defensive shield for a while. Also, your link to your Power reserve is unprotected. We need to work on that."

Richard could see his own Power line running from him to his Power reserve just as he could see the line of Power from Shandria to her Power reserve. He compared the two lines, or links as Shandria called them. He could sense no difference other than the size of their Power reserves.

"Protected how?" Richard asked. "And protected from what?"

"For one thing," said Shandria, "protected from me."

With a strange look on her face, the elf said several unintelligible words and flicked her hand. The words sounded familiar, and Richard had a strange feeling it was one of the spells he'd helped Shandria rewrite. He sensed Power flowing from the elf's Power reserve back to her. It converted to magical energy before heading towards him. Richard threw up a defensive shield between them. He assumed it was some kind of test of his shield. But he was wrong. The magical energy didn't hit his shield. Instead, it deviated and latched onto a point on the Power link going to his reserve. The magical energy twisted, and suddenly Richard's could no longer sense his Power reserve or even his defensive shield. Even his passive scan was gone.

Richard drew his phase rod with his left hand and hit the activate switch and destructive lever at the same time as he was swinging the rod at the elf's head. The brerellium shaft was thrust out by the rod's hydraulics as red arcs of energy snaked along its length. Richard was fast, but so was the elf. Shandria said a word as she pointed at Richard. He neither saw nor sensed her Power or energy, but he felt its effects immediately. Richard's muscles locked in place with the tip of the phase rod a mere hand's breadth from the elf's head.

Shandria took a step back, her eyes locked on the red arcs of energy still snaking along the length of the phase rod. She seemed to be taking a moment to compose herself.

"Rick!" Nickelo shouted through the battle helmet's external speakers.

Richard couldn't even move his eyes, but out of the corner of his vision, he could see his battle helmet atop his neatly-folded battle suit on a bench across the room. *I'm sorry, Nick*, Richard said with his thoughts. *If I'd kept my suit on like you wanted, she'd never have gotten the drop on me. I was just too slow without your help."*

"All is well, Master Nick," said Shandria. "Your friend and I are both unharmed."

She walked closer to Richard, keeping well clear of the deadly shaft of the phase rod.

"You were much faster than I expected," Shandria said. "You almost had me. I won't make the same mistake again."

The elf stood close to Richard's right side. With her lips almost touching his ear, she whispered, "How does it feel to be frozen; helpless; with your life in someone else's hands? Maybe I'll leave you like this for a week so you can get the full effect of how I felt. Do you mind if I go through your stuff? I'd ask you to blink your answer, but you can't even do that, can you?"

"Nick," Richard said. *"What's her game? What's she doing?"*

"I don't know yet," Nickelo answered. *"I still haven't decided whether she's dangerous or whether this is all part of some kind of training."*

"Training?" Richard said unbelievingly. *"If this is training, I'm going to kick her rear-end when it's over."*

"Here's what's going to happen, Rick," purred Shandria seductively.

Even under the circumstances, Richard thought her voice was very alluring.

"Typical male," came Nickelo's thought.

The elf continued, "I'm going to take a few steps back to get out of range of your weapon. Then I'm going to release you. If you're good, and you don't try to hurt me, then I'll undo the block I put on the link to your Power reserve. Then, assuming you still want to be trained, I'll tell you how I did it. I'll also tell you what you could have done to prevent it. Does that sound like a deal?"

Shandria waited, but of course Richard couldn't answer. Still, she waited patiently as if expecting Richard to agree in some fashion.

"Nick," Richard said to Nickelo. *"Tell her I agree. I'll be a good little boy. And tell her I think she's a two-timing, untrustworthy elf, and once I find out how to protect myself, I'm going to kick her scrawny little butt."* Richard didn't really think it was scrawny. In fact, he thought it was quite nice, but he wasn't going to tell her that.

"Shandria," translated Nickelo. "Rick says he agrees. He won't attempt to harm you, and he's anxious to continue training." After a pause, Nickelo added, "Oh yeah, and he thinks you have a nice ass."

"Nick!"

Richard thought he saw Shandria's face reddened slightly, but he couldn't be sure. She stepped back to the far side of the room.

Then she said three words and moved her right hand in a pattern he couldn't follow.

Richard's muscles unlocked. He almost fell on his face as his muscles tried to complete their swing. The phase rod came dangerously close to smashing their table, but he was able to stop the stroke in time.

Raising his phase rod into a defensive position, Richard looked at the elf. She stood there meekly with her hands by her side. He moved the phase rod's lever to non-destructive and flicked the deactivate switch. The red arcs of energy dissipated, and the brerellium shaft retracted back into the handle. He hooked the phase rod back to the left side of his utility belt.

"So," said Richard, "what was that all about?"

"Actually, Rick, things didn't turn out like I had it envisioned in my head. When I was a young acolyte under my village priestess, she did to me what I just did to you. She blocked my Power link as a way to demonstrate the danger in a way I couldn't fail to comprehend. I thought to do the same with you. It almost cost me my life. Master Nick was right. You react without thinking. You nearly took my head off with your weapon. I guess I'm the one who should have thought things through a little better."

Richard calmed down a little by the end of the elf's speech. He made a half-hearted apology. "Sorry about that, Shandria. I should have trusted you more. It just caught me off guard." He paused before adding, "By any chance can I have the link to my Power reserve unblocked? I feel a little helpless."

"Oh, of course," said Shandria. "I guess I was waiting to make sure you weren't going to try and attack me."

"No," Richard said. "All's forgiven." He meant it.

The elf said several words which Richard heard but quickly forgot. After a few waves of Shandria's hand, he could *see* again. Once again, he could sense not just his Power link, but also the elf's link.

"Better?" she asked.

"Definitely. Now, can you explain what you did?"

For the next several hours, Shandria demonstrated to Richard how to put a block on another's link. She cast a spell which allowed Richard to follow along with her active scan as she probed his link for weak spots. She was a patient teacher, and she never seemed to mind him asking the same question more than once. Under her watch care, Richard was able to use his own active scan to find weak spots in his link to his Power reserve. Once Shandria was satisfied Richard could find the weak spots, she explained how to block links. She created a link between Richard and herself. She had Richard practice finding weak points in this link, and then she had him attempt to block the link. While he practiced, Shandria explained how some magic users could connect a link to their opponent and use it to draw Power from them. If the magic user could draw enough Power from their opponent, the fight would be over before it even started.

"So how do we protect our links?" Richard asked after he'd practiced blocking links for what felt like the hundredth time.

"You have to find the weak spots in your own link. Then you have to put traps on them."

"Traps?" Richard asked. "I'm not familiar with the concept, at least not in the context of Power and magic."

"Neither am I," Nickelo admitted. "It's not in my data banks."

"One of these days, Master Nickelo," said Shandria, "we need to have a long discussion on what you are. You're indeed a mystery to me."

"He's a mystery to me as well," Richard said. "What were you going to say about these traps?"

"Oh, yes, the traps," said Shandria as she got back in teacher mode. "You can use your Power to set traps on your link. If anything tries to block the link at the point of the trap or noses around it too much, the trap will activate. Traps are normally of the deadly variety. However, for our training, I'll set some traps on our training link which will only give a mild shock. You will try and locate the traps and disconnect them. Once you get tired of getting shocked, we'll switch positions. Then you'll set traps, and I'll try and find and disable them. Does that sound fair?"

Richard thought it sounded more than fair. It was interesting training, and they practiced late into the evening. The only bad thing was Richard got shocked a lot. When Shandria finally announced they were done for the day, he didn't argue.

CHAPTER 23

"Seal it up, Nick, and activate the override," Richard said as he mentally prepared himself for the invasiveness of the tubes and needles. The reddish glow of the battle suit's visor lowered in front of his eyes. The tubes designed to help keep him alive inserted themselves in his body openings. Data readouts appeared on the heads-up display along with a map containing various colored spots denoting possible enemy locations. Two white dots in the center of the map denoted Shandria's and his positions.

"Remember," said Shandria in a final last minute instruction, "try to conserve your Power. If we run into Efrestra, I'll need your help. Both our reserves are at full Power, but we can't afford any long, dragged-out battles. My staff and jewelry are nearly drained, so once our Power reserves are empty we'll be dead, or even worse, we'll be taken captive. Trust me, Rick. You don't want that to happen."

"Yes, Mommy," Richard said. "I heard you the first twenty times you told me."

Shandria gave a small, tense laugh. "I'm reminding myself as much as you, Rick. Are you ready?"

Richard did one final survey of his equipment. True-to-form, *'the One'* wouldn't let him stock up on extra isotopic batteries or grenades. However, Richard did have a bag strapped over his shoulder containing twenty quarter-kilo blocks of J22 plastic explosive.

"Go figure," Richard said. *"They're more powerful than*

grenades anyway."

"The logic of 'the One' *does seem convoluted,"* agreed Nickelo. *"He even let you put timers on them. I think he wants us to get out of this alive, but at the same time, he wants you to know you're still being punished for your initial defiance."*

"Whatever," Richard thought. *"'The One' hasn't even begun to see how defiant I can be."*

"Now, don't stir up any more problems than we already have," warned Nickelo.

"I won't, old buddy," Richard assured his battle computer. *"I'll be a good little boy until we get out of here."*

Richard hefted the new M12 assault rifle. It was much heavier than his standard M63, but Nickelo had insisted Richard summon it as a replacement for his M63 lightweight plasma assault rifle.

"I liked my M63 better," Richard said. *"This M12 can only fire four hundred rounds per isotopic battery. Speaking of which, I had to use Power to summon the M12. Apparently, I'll have to use Power to summon replacement batteries for it as well. The big jerk-in-the-sky must not like the fact I'm not using my M63. I think the M12 should be a freebie since I turned in my M63."*

"Well," said Nickelo, *"you'll just have to deal with the M12. You're going to need a higher-grade weapon for this battle. As far as I could tell, your M63's rounds only tickled that demon. The M12 has less ammo per battery, but the rounds are more powerful. Plus, the M12 has a 20mm grenade launcher under the main barrel. With the armor-piercing rounds you got loaded in it, you'll definitely get his attention. Besides, you were able to summon extra 20mm rounds for it. Besides the initial seven, you've got another fourteen in your bag with the J22 plastic explosive."*

Richard hated to admit Nickelo was right about needing a heavier weapon. Therefore, he just avoided any more discussion on the subject. Richard decided he was as ready as he'd ever be. Shandria had taught him as much as she could. They had even stayed a month more than planned. If he wasn't ready now after four months of intense training, he wasn't ever going to be ready.

"I'm as ready as I'm ever going to be," Richard told the elf. "Are you sure you still want me to keep my best stealth shield up? You said they're going to know where you are the moment you take the blue sphere from its stand."

"That can't be helped," she said. "We've discussed it, already. My stealth shield can't hide all three spheres, and you can only hide yourself with yours. They're going to know where I am, but if we can keep them guessing about your location, it may give us a slight edge. End of discussion, Rick. It's time to go."

Richard activated his best stealth shield. He watched the elf as she opened the alcove and slipped the blue sphere into her leather bag. The stealth shield surrounding their secret room dissipated. He didn't wait to see the elf put the bag in her pack. Speed was everything now. He opened the secret door and stepped into the hallway. His heads-up display indicated the straight section of the tunnel outside the secret room was clear of any life forms. Richard glanced to the right, it was clear as expected, but he needed to go left. He turned his head to the left in preparation for sprinting. He wanted to get ahead of the elf to run interference with the run-of-the-mill ghouls before the more powerful foes began showing up.

"Demon!" shouted Nickelo mentally. *"It has a stealth shield."*

Twenty meters ahead was a humanoid-sized monstrosity from some horror movie. It wasn't the demon they'd fought previously, but it was definitely a demon. It reeked of evil. It dropped its stealth shield as it converted a ball of Power into magical energy.

Richard reacted without thinking. He held down the trigger of the assault rifle. A stream of forty rounds filled the hallway in the direction of the demon. Some missed and ricocheted off the tunnel walls. Other rounds stopped short of their target as if hitting an invisible barrier.

It didn't take a genius to figure out the demon had a defensive shield. Richard noticed some of the rock shards blasted from the tunnel walls hit the demon. He assumed its shield was focused on energy attacks, not physical ones. He drew his phase rod and charged the demon.

In response, the demon released its ball of magic. Richard sensed the flow of energy heading straight towards him. Shandria's hours of training in defensive shields paid off. Reflexively, Richard threw a defensive shield between him and the incoming energy. He angled the shield slightly like the elf had taught him. The energy turned into a lightning bolt. It hit Richard's shield and ricocheted off to the side where it began bouncing from wall to wall as it continued down the tunnel. Richard breathed a sigh of relief when he noticed the white dot on his heads-up display representing the elf was still in the secret room.

"Lower your shield," said Nickelo. *"Conserve Power."*

Remembering Shandria's warning to only use the Power-hungry defensive shield the minimum necessary, he stopped the flow of Power. The shield faded away as Richard jumped to the demon's right side. As he passed through the demon's defensive shield, the battle suit's electronics momentarily blinked, but Nickelo quickly brought them back online. By the time Richard was even with the demon, he was in full command of the suit again. He thumbed the phase rod's setting lever to destructive and swung a hard blow at the back of the demon's head. The phase rod bounced off the demon's skull. However, the rod's subatomic energy must have had some effect, because the demon gave a cry. It wasn't so much a cry of pain as it was a sound of surprise.

The demon made a backhanded swing at Richard with a metal rod it held in its right hand. The metal rod burst into a red flame as it arced toward the base of Richard's spine. The demon's blow was too fast for Richard to react, but it wasn't too fast for his battle computer. Nickelo took advantage of the override to make a hard kick with both legs of the battle suit. Richard felt himself propelled above the demon's weapon. When he hit the ceiling, he was none too graceful, but he managed to brace his feet against the tunnel's roof. He kicked hard to propel himself back towards the demon. He hit the demon as it was turning around to face him. They both went down hard. Richard pictured an image of himself driving the point of his phase rod into the demon's right eye. Nickelo picked up on the image and moved the battle suit to accomplish Richard's desire. In a movement too fast for a mere human to comprehend, the battle suit's assisters drove the tip of the phase rod into the demon's eye. The unarmored eye burst upon contact. The phase rod's tip continued its forward movement and burst through bone into the demon's skull. Richard took control of the suit and wriggled the phase rod back and forth to scramble the brain. The demon shuddered and stopped moving.

"We killed it," Richard said. *"It was easier than I thought. Maybe that other demon, Efrestra, won't be as difficult as we feared."*

"Don't kid yourself," said Nickelo. *"This was a low-level*

demon of the cannon-fodder variety. From what Shandria said, Efrestra's one of the higher-level demons right below a master demon. Now, get off the floor and start moving. We're supposed to be clearing the easy stuff out of the way for Shandria."

Richard rose from the floor and began sprinting down the tunnel again. His mission was to get to the intersection two hundred and forty meters away and hold it until Shandria arrived. He could run much faster in his battle suit than the elf. If he could get to the intersection and clear out the lower-level riffraff before she arrived, it might give them an advantage. The intersection was actually a fair-sized cavern containing the entrances to five tunnels. Shandria had told him one of the tunnels led to the exit that was their destination.

The intersection was quickly in range, and Richard saw a mass of yellow dots. Those would be undead. He saw no other colors. He hoped that meant there weren't yet any magic-using creatures at the intersection. Of course, they could be using a stealth shield like the demon, but he refused the think the worst until forced.

"How many, Nick?" Richard asked.

"Thirty-two, Rick," replied Nickelo. *"I don't register any magic users, but of course, that doesn't mean there aren't any. There soon will be if you don't hurry, though. Have you noticed the red dots converging on our location?"*

Richard had noticed. Just like he'd noticed the hundreds of other dots of varying colors all seemingly headed in the direction of the intersection ahead.

"Swap out your rifle's isotopic battery, Rick."

"I only shot forty rounds. I still have over three hundred and fifty."

"You shot forty-two rounds," said Nickelo. *"Don't argue. Switch it out while you have a chance. You may need every round when you get to the intersection."*

Richard stopped arguing and extracted the plasma rifle's isotopic battery. Reaching over his shoulder, he lifted the dimensional pack's flap and dropped in the battery. He closed the flap and then reopened in it. Reaching inside, he felt a small cube with his fingers. He hoped it wasn't the same battery he'd dropped in the pack. Richard pulled it out and shoved it into the empty slot on his plasma rifle. The heads-up display registered four hundred rounds for his plasma rifle. He had a full load again.

As he was accomplishing the reload, Richard noticed the white dot representing Shandria's position about a hundred meters behind him. She was stopped. A group of fifteen or so yellow and orange dots were closing in from behind her. Suddenly, the yellow and orange dots disappeared. The white dot began moving in his direction again.

"Did you really think you had to worry about the elf?" asked Nickelo who must have sensed his concern. *"Shandria's a big girl. She can take care of herself. You need to worry about you. Remember, you can't self-heal until you get your baseline DNA taken. As a resistor, you can't be magically healed either. So, not only do I want you to try and not get killed, I want you to try and not get seriously injured."*

"I'll do my best, Mommy."

*   *   *

When he was twenty meters from the intersection, Richard stopped. A curve in the tunnel blocked his sight of the cavern and tunnel entrances, but he had no doubt the cavern was just ahead. The mass of yellow dots on the heads-up display verified its location.

"What are those two orange dots?" Richard asked his battle computer.

"I'm not sure," replied Nickelo. *"They're not magic users, but I don't recognize their signature. That's why I made them orange. We'll find out soon enough. Are you ready?"*

Richard verified Shandria's location on the heads-up display. She was staying a little over a hundred meters behind him. Two red dots and a score of yellow ones were in the tunnel behind her. He heard a series of muffled explosions. One of the red dots disappeared along with a half dozen of the yellow ones. The elf was fighting a rearguard action. Richard was momentarily tempted to go back and help the elf. It grated his male ego to have a female doing the major fighting. But logic won over, and Richard returned his concentration to the intersection ahead. Their plan was sound. His mission was to secure the intersection before reinforcements arrived. Shandria's mission was to cover his rear and buy him the time he needed.

Richard took off running as hard as he could for the intersection. He turned the corner and raised his plasma rifle. The moment he saw a head, he began firing. It didn't matter that the head was only a skull half covered with rotted flesh. The head exploded under the weight of three plasma rounds. Richard kept the trigger pulled and swept the intermittent stream of red plasma rounds to the left towards a group of zombies lumbering towards him. He relied on Nickelo's override of the battle suit to guide the red stream into the heads of the nightmarish creatures. The group went down amid a spray of rotten brain matter.

"To your right," yelled Nickelo.

A glance at the heads-up display showed one of the two orange dots closing in fast from the right. Richard turned in time to see a large, gangly humanoid twice as tall as the zombies and ghouls around it. Before Richard could react, the big creature grabbed a nearby zombie and threw it at him. Trying to get his plasma rifle into action, Richard squeezed the trigger and streaks of plasma energy bounced off the floor as he elevated the rifle towards the creature's head. He felt Nickelo try to accelerate the movement of his battle suit's arms, but it wasn't quick enough. The thrown zombie collided with him, bowling him over in a mass of flailing arms and legs. Richard released his pressure on the rifle's trigger. He felt pressure on the back of his neck. The zombie was behind him trying to chew through the suit's armor from behind.

"Good luck with that," Richard thought as he slammed his left fist into the zombie's head. The battle suit's assisters magnified the strength and speed of the blow. He wasn't able to see his fist make contact with the zombie's head. However, when he pulled his arm back, his fist was dripping with dark blood, bone slivers, and brain matter.

Richard tried to scramble to his feet, but he was thrown onto his back again as his feet were jerked out from under him. He felt pressure on his ankles where the large creature was grasping his legs. Before Richard could defend himself, the creature began swinging him around its head like a club. The centrifugal force kept Richard helpless and fully outstretched. If not for the strap on his plasma rifle, he'd have lost it. On the third circuit of its swing, the creature released its grip. Richard went flying through the air until he hit the cavern wall. The battle suit's armor cushioned the impact, but even so, his breath was knocked out of him.

The tubes in Richard's nostrils immediately pumped air into his collapsed lungs. His feeling of helplessness disappeared as his lungs re-inflated. He got a grip on his plasma rifle and aimed at the chest of the creature. Instead of firing his plasma rifle, he pulled the trigger of the 20mm grenade launcher under the weapon's barrel. The rifle bucked in his hands, and the grenade exploded against the creature's chest. Bone and flesh burst from a double-fist-sized hole as the creature was thrown backward.

Richard turned his attention to two zombies and a ghoul approaching from his left. Twenty rounds from the plasma rifle made short work of them. He glanced back to his right. To his surprise, the large creature was rising from the ground. As it rose, Richard noticed the hole in its chest close over until it was no longer visible. Within seconds, all evidence of the 20mm blast was gone.

"*Nick!*" Richard said.

"*It's a troll,*" said Nickelo. "*You're going to have to burn it. And you don't have much time.*"

Richard's passive scan told him what a glance at his heads-up display confirmed. Hundreds of dots of every color of the rainbow were converging down all the tunnels. The intersection would be crawling with an overwhelming force in less than two minutes.

Since he was fresh out of flamethrowers, and since he didn't have time to summon one, Richard concentrated on the remaining zombies and ghouls. He liberally sprayed them with his plasma rifle until Nickelo warned him he only had twenty rounds left. Richard pulled his phase rod and switched it to destructive mode. He closed with the weaker undead, staying well clear of the trolls. The fight was all one sided since his opponents' teeth and claws couldn't penetrate his armor. Still, it was a race against time, and Richard knew he was losing the race. He could kill the zombies and ghouls easy enough, but they were slowing him down. Before long, Richard encountered the second troll. He was forced to expend two more 20mm rounds to keep it at bay. The troll quickly healed itself and continued running towards Richard.

Only a handful of zombies remained. Changing tactics, Richard avoided the few remaining zombies. He ran a dozen meters down one of the tunnels. Extracting three blocks of J22 plastic explosive from the satchel at his side, Richard jammed them onto the tunnel's ceiling. They were naturally adhesive, and they easily stuck in place. He turned to leave. As he'd hoped, one of the trolls followed him into the tunnel. It charged towards him with a vicious growl, its arms outstretched.

When the troll was six paces away, Richard blew its left leg off at the knee with one of his precious remaining 20mm grenades. The troll nose-dived to the ground. Richard jumped over it and ran to the tunnel entrance. Once he cleared the tunnel, he spun around and fired his remaining plasma rounds at the ceiling above the troll. As the troll got to its feet, one of the rounds connected with a block of J22 plastic explosive.

Boom!

The cavern shook as the tunnel collapsed on the troll. Dust and rock debris were blown out of the tunnel into the intersection. Richard was thrown back by the force of the blast. He automatically threw his hands up to protect his head. He went flying through the air towards the opposite wall of the intersection. In desperation, he wrapped himself in Power and attempted to use telekinesis to slow his momentum. He partially succeeded, but he still felt the back of his battle helmet crack when he made contact with the rock wall. He momentarily blacked out. He was brought out of his daze when Nickelo used the battle suit's medical needles to shoot adrenaline directly into his veins.

"Your suit's seals are still intact," said Nickelo, *"but we lost some of the electronics. You need to get up and moving. The other troll is headed your way."*

Richard forced himself to stand up. He was immediately knocked down by two zombies who began biting at his neck and chest. He got his knee under one and kicked it away. He slammed the butt of his phase rod into the second zombie's temple. The zombie fell off and stopped moving. Richard drew his .44 AutoMag and blew off the back of the other zombie's head. He rose to a sitting position and spun to the left where he sensed the second troll was located. Richard fired the remaining six shots of the .44 AutoMag into the troll's chest knocking it down. Standing up, Richard holstered his pistol and then cocked the slide on the grenade launcher. He fired his last three 20mm grenades at the troll. By the time the last one hit, the troll was short most of its left leg and was missing an arm. It floundered around on the floor snarling with rage.

"The elf's still fifty meters away," said Nickelo. *"The enemy down that tunnel to the right is only forty meters from the entrance. You'd better hustle, Rick, or I'm going to start having doubts about your wizard scout abilities."*

Richard was too busy to even take the time to banter with Nickelo. He could see the mass of dots on the heads-up display nearing the intersection. Heading towards the right-most tunnel, he pulled the pin on one of his anti-personnel grenades and threw it into the opening.

Boom!

When he reached the tunnel, Richard took half a dozen steps inside and started sticking blocks of J22 plastic explosive on the ceiling while setting their timers for ten seconds. He activated the timers and high-tailed it for the tunnel's entrance.

Once back in the open intersection, Richard ran towards the tunnel opposite the one he'd just rigged. When he was close, he threw his second anti-personnel grenade down the tunnel and flattened himself against the wall just outside the tunnel opening.

Boom!

The blast of his grenade was followed by an even larger blast from the tunnel he'd rigged with J22 plastic explosive.

Boom!

Richard wanted to look back to make sure the J22 plastic explosive had completely blocked the tunnel, but he couldn't afford the time. He stepped into the tunnel he'd just thrown the grenade into and ran several steps inside before attaching three more blocks of J22 plastic explosive to the ceiling. He risked a glanced at his heads-up display. The dots were much too close. He didn't have ten seconds. Richard pulled a block of J22 plastic explosive out of his satchel and set the timer for three seconds. He clicked the activate switch and threw the J22 plastic explosive down the tunnel. He dived for the floor.

Boom!

Richard stood up. The tunnel was so filled with dust he couldn't see, but he found the blocks of J22 plastic explosive on the ceiling and set their timers to five seconds. He activated the timers and ran back towards the intersection. Once clear of the tunnel, Richard turned toward the final tunnel. This was the one Shandria had said led to her exit. Richard had to hold it until the elf arrived. He only took two steps before something tripped him causing him to fall to the stone floor. Looking behind him, he saw the remaining troll holding onto his ankle. Richard was struck by the fact that it was still missing most of its leg. He wondered if the troll had crawled to intercept him. He kicked with both legs in an attempt to free himself, but the troll had a grip of iron. It started pulling him closer.

Boom!

The J22 plastic explosive in the tunnel exploded. Richard was much closer than he'd planned to be. The blast sent both him and the troll rolling along the stone floor until they smashed into the opposite wall. Somewhere along the way, the troll lost its grip. Richard stood and activated his phase rod.

"Leave him to me," shouted Shandria as she ran into the intersection. "Close this tunnel."

Richard sensed the life forms hot on the elf's heels. He grabbed another block of J22 plastic explosive and set the timer at four seconds. As he ran past Shandria towards the tunnel she had just left, the elf pulled one of her wands from her belt and shouted two words. A stream of fire erupted from the end of the wand and engulfed the troll in flames.

When Richard reached the tunnel's entrance, he activated the J22 plastic explosive's timer and threw it hard down the tunnel towards the approaching life forms. He quickly stepped to the side of the tunnel entrance and flattened himself against the stone wall.

Boom!

Smoke, dust and stray pieces of flesh flew out of the tunnel. Richard ran in a full twenty meters before stopping. The elf was unarmored, so he couldn't place the explosives too close to the entrance without endangering her. Unfortunately, it meant he was closer to the approaching enemy. Apparently, the deaths of a few of their companions had not reduced their desire to kill the human and elf intruders.

Richard set the timers for the J22 plastic explosive at four seconds. He didn't think that would give him time to clear the tunnel, but he hoped it would give him time to get past any parts of the ceiling that collapsed. Taking a deep breath, Richard hit the activate switches as he turned to run back towards the intersection.

"You're cutting it too close," said Nickelo.

Boom!

The blast shot Richard out the tunnel. He tried to use his telekinesis to slow his momentum, but he couldn't concentrate. He hit the wall of the intersection with bone-breaking force. Fortunately, the armor of the battle suit was the best the armorers of the Intergalactic Empire could craft, and it cushioned most of the force. He had his breathed knocked out of him again, but besides that, he was relatively unscathed. His battle suit didn't fare as well. The impact cracked the front part of his battle helmet. The butt of his plasma rifle broke off, and the rifle barrel bent. The tubes in his nostrils and throat retracted.

"You've lost the seal on your suit," said Nickelo.

Richard shook his head to clear the fog. He noticed the elf was standing in front of the remaining tunnel sending fireballs from one of her wands at something out of his sight. Richard grabbed his phase rod and tried to stand so he could join the fight.

"No!" said Nickelo. *"You've got a few seconds. You need to rearm."*

Richard obeyed his battle computer without argument. He chastised himself mentally for not thinking of it on his own. He hastily removed his dimensional pack from his back and put his damaged plasma rifle inside along with the empty clip from his .44 AutoMag. He imagined a new, fully-loaded, plasma rifle along with a clip of .44 caliber ammo and two anti-personnel grenades. Richard sensed some energy transfer from his Power reserve to his pack. It wasn't much. The plasma rifle was non-standard, so it cost him Power, but the other items were freebies according to Nickelo. Richard opened the flap of the pack and pulled out a shiny new plasma rifle with a fully-charged isotopic battery. He cocked the slide of the grenade launcher to ready a 20mm round. He then replaced the empty spot with one of the extra 20mm grenades he had in his satchel.

"Should I replace the helmet?" Richard asked.

"No," said Nickel. *"Your battle helmet's damaged, but I'm fully functional. I would advise against an attempt to replace me right now. What if there's a delay when you put me in your*

dimensional pack? Worse yet, what if 'the One' *decides this is a good time to see what you can do on your own?"*

Richard had no desire to see what he could do on his own. He was sure Nickelo had saved his life several times already today. He hastily slung his dimensional pack on his back.

"I agree," Richard said. *"Are we ready?"*

"Go for it," said Nickelo.

CHAPTER 24

Richard ran up to Shandria and knelt down with his plasma rifle at the ready. She was no longer sending fireballs down the tunnel. He was grateful his battle helmet's night vision display was still working. He dreaded thinking how horrible it would be to stumble around a tunnel full of zombies in complete darkness.

With the aid of the night vision display, Richard could see the tunnel floor was littered with charred corpses. His passive scan indicated the nearest life forms were about sixty meters ahead. There were eight of them, and they weren't moving. Their signatures appeared to be run-of-the-mill zombies. Of course, something else could be using a stealth shield, but that couldn't be helped. Besides, surely there weren't all that many creatures in these tunnels that had the skill to use stealth shields. The odds were low.

Nodding his head at the wand in the elf's hand, Richard said, "Nice little item to have."

"It was," said Shandria as she tucked it back into her belt. "It's empty now. I drained the other two wands getting here. I'll have to use my Power reserve from here on out."

"You still have some Power in your staff and jewelry, don't you?" Richard asked. He knew she did because he could sense it. Nearly drained though they were, the staff alone still contained more Power than Richard's reserve had when it was full.

"A little," Shandria admitted. "But, I'd like to save it for an emergency."

"Well," Richard said, "I have a full load of ammo, and my Power reserve's nearly full. My armor has taken a beating, especially my helmet, but other than that I'm in pretty good shape."

"Has Master Nick been harmed?" Shandria asked with what sounded like genuine concern.

"I'm fine," said Nickelo out loud. "I just need a wizard scout who can take better care of his equipment. Haven't seen any around, have you?"

Shandria's face muscles were strained, but Richard thought they relaxed a little at Nickelo's joke. She gave a small smile and answered, "Nay, Master Nick. But, I think you have the best wizard scout I've ever seen."

Richard thought the compliment would mean more if the elf had ever seen another wizard scout, but he bit his tongue and remained silent.

"Are we sticking with the same plan?" Richard asked. "I go first to clear out the weaker stuff, and you follow and back me up whenever I encounter less accommodating creatures?"

"Well," said Nickelo aloud, "if my opinion means anything, I calculate that plan has the best chance for success. Rick's armor will protect him from the weaker undead. There's no use for Shandria to risk getting paralyzed again. When Rick hits the tougher stuff, he's going to need help taking them out."

"Our minds are alike, Master Nick," said Shandria. "Lead on whenever you're ready, Rick. I shall be there when you need me."

Richard stepped past Shandria with his plasma rifle at the ready. When he got almost fifty meters, he sensed the elf begin to move.

"The first batch is just around this next corner," said Nickelo. *"From their signatures, it's just eight zombies. I'd suggest taking them out with your phase rod. I doubt you'll need your plasma rifle. Save it for later."*

Trusting his phase rod to do the light work, Richard rushed around the corner as he activated the phase rod in destructive mode. He hoped to take the zombies by surprise and take them out quickly. As soon as he turned the corner, he saw the zombies lined up in two rows of four facing his direction. They weren't alone. Two other creatures were behind them. One was a tall, thin humanoid with mottled skin, flaming eyes, and two large ram horns growing out of its forehead. It also had a tail with a wicked looking stinger poised over its shoulder. The second creature was down on all fours and appeared to be some sort of canine. It was about waist high at the front shoulder, and its hair was similar to porcupine quills. A clump of the quills was bunched at the end of its tail. Four hissing, snakelike appendages complete with heads grew out of its neck.

Richard didn't need anyone to tell him these were demons of some kind. He was here to handle the small stuff, this bigger meat was all Shandria's as far as he was concerned. The demons dropped their stealth shields, and Richard felt a wave of evil wash over him. The demons seemed as surprised to see Richard as he was to see them. But, they overcame their initial shock quickly enough.

"They were waiting for the elf," said Nickelo. *"They didn't expect you."*

Not bothering to reply, Richard started backpedaling towards the bend in the tunnel. He grabbed for his plasma rifle with his right hand. It was still hanging by its strap from his shoulder within easy reach, but he had trouble finding the grip.

The four-legged demon recovered first. It charged at Richard and knocked several zombies down in the process. When the demon got within range, a snakehead struck at Richard's face. The long fangs in the snake's mouth sent a chill down his spine. He hated snakes. For some reason, he had a feeling the snake's fangs were capable of penetrating his armor. Before the snake made contact, Richard batted at the head with his phase rod. The blow wasn't hard, but the energy from the phase rod still transferred into the snakehead. The result was a series of subatomic explosions. The head blew apart. Pieces of snake along with a vile liquid splattered Richard's left arm. Each spot of liquid began to bubble and smoke on anything it touched.

"Dive backward," yelled Nickelo.

Richard was too busy swinging at the remaining snakeheads to obey his battle computer. Fortunately, Nickelo took charge of the battle suit and sprang backward propelling Richard around the corner of the tunnel and out of sight of the demon.

"Run," said Nickelo.

Scrambling to his feet, Richard began running towards

Shandria. He felt like a kid running to his mommy for protection, but he didn't care. He figured he could be ashamed later if he was still alive. He pointed his plasma rifle to the rear and fired as he continued running. He couldn't aim, but he didn't care. Just the noise made him feel like he was defending himself in case something was following him. Something was. In fact, several somethings were following him.

"Down!" ordered Shandria.

Richard dove for the floor. His momentum carried him forward in a long slide on the rough, stone floor. He was thankful he was wearing armor, or he was sure he'd have been rubbed raw.

As he was sliding, a streak of lightning left the elf's outstretched hand and passed over Richard's head. He turned on his back and began firing wildly down the tunnel. The lightning had done its job and several zombies lay smoldering on the floor. However, the demon-dog looked no worse for the wear. Richard sensed a powerful shield to its front. Shandria's lightning bolt had failed to penetrate it.

At that moment, the taller demon came into view. It started moving its hands and shouting in some harsh language. Richard sensed a powerful ball of energy forming in its hands. Shandria must have sensed it too because she quickly formed her own defensive shield. Richard was tempted to run for its protective cover, but he didn't think he had time. Besides, the demon-dog appeared to have stopped its attack to give the other demon room to fight.

Richard did a hundred-and-eighty-degree spin and used the legs of the battle suit to propel himself closer to the demon-dog. Strange as it might seem, he deemed that to be a safer spot than out in the open between two powerful magic users. As he moved, Richard sprayed a few dozen rounds at both demons hoping to distract them from the elf. The plasma rounds hit the demons' defensive shields and dissipated into the air. The demons weren't distracted.

The taller demon released its ball of energy. It streaked past Richard towards the elf. Richard continued firing his plasma rifle. He tried to ricochet rounds off the floor, walls, and ceiling in the hopes some would go around the shields, but they didn't. The demons were fully protected.

Boom!

A rush of air from behind Richard confirmed the demon's ball of energy had detonated in the elf's vicinity. Richard saw the white dot shining steadily on his heads-up display, so he knew the elf's shield had held. However, he wondered how long it could hold up against that kind of energy. He thought the elf's Power reserve was noticeably lower.

As soon as the sound of the explosion subsided, the demon-dog jumped towards Richard. Its four snakeheads were outstretched as if each one was striving to be the first one to bite the pitiful human opposing it.

Richard had a nagging feeling there should only be three snakeheads, but he quickly blocked out the thought. He had more to worry about. Aiming his rifle from the hip, Richard fired off a 20mm grenade. The range was too close for the explosive charge to detonate, but the grenade hit the demon-dog on its left hip. The round's impact tore a fist-sized hole in the demon's flesh. It was knocked backward flying end over end.

"Guess the hound's shield doesn't protect it from physical attacks," said Nickelo. *"That's nice to know."*

Richard was still lying on the floor, but he was in no hurry to stand up. The big boys were slugging it out above, and streaks of energy were going in both directions just a meter over his head. One of Shandria's balls of energy exploded against the taller demon's defensive shield. The demon was unharmed. Richard took a chance the two demons had similar shields. He fired a 20mm grenade at the taller demon's head. The round exploded a meter before it got to the demon.

"Damn," Richard said. *"It blocks both energy and physical attacks."*

"Not very considerate, is it?" said Nickelo.

Richard heard a growl. The demon-dog was up and running his way. Both of its back legs appeared to be undamaged.

"Did it heal itself?" Richard asked as he fired another 20mm grenade at the hound.

The demon-dog sidestepped the grenade and ran past Richard towards Shandria. As the demon passed by, Richard reached out with both hands and grabbed hold of its tail. He was jerked to his feet, but he dug in with his heels and pulled back on the tail with all his might. Aided by the battle suit's assisters, the demon-dog was not only stopped, but it was thrown backward.

"Nick," Richard thought as he pictured the taller demon who was engaging the elf.

"Got it," replied Nickelo.

Richard felt the battle suit twist in a manner too quick for him to have done it by himself. At precisely the right moment, the battle suit's gloves released their grip on the tail. The demon-dog went flying through the air straight towards the taller demon's head.

As Richard had hoped, the demon-dog passed through its ally's defensive shield. The taller demon and the demon-dog both went down in a flurry of arms, legs, and snakeheads. He saw at least two of the snakeheads bite the taller demon. With a roar, the taller demon stood up and threw off the struggling demon-dog.

"They've dropped their shields," said Nickelo excitedly.

Richard made a hasty grab for his plasma rifle and began spraying both demons with a nearly solid stream of red energy. Both demons roared. Richard wasn't sure whether it was from pain or from anger or both. He shot a 20mm grenade at each demon catching both in the chest. This time they both roared in definite pain. However, they didn't go down.

Throwing caution to the wind, Richard let go of his plasma rifle and made a dive for the demon-dog. His left hand found his phase rod. He activated it in destructive mode just as he hit the hound. Richard swung furiously at the snakeheads in a desperate attempt to put them out of action before they could strike. He barely avoided their bites, but with Nickelo's aid, he smashed three snakeheads with his phase rod and pulled the fourth out by its roots. Then he wrapped both arms around the demon-dog's neck and squeezed. He wasn't even sure the demon breathed, but if it did, he was determined to choke out its life.

A strange sensation passed over Richard as he struggled with the demon-dog. As it furiously snapped at him with its long fangs, he sensed the world around them coming to a stop. Ignoring the sensation, Richard tightened his hold on the demon-dog's neck while wrapping his legs around the creature to hold it down. Ever so slowly, the demon-dog stopped struggling.

"I guess it had to breathe after all," observed Nickelo.

Nodding his head in agreement, Richard jerked his arms and

snapped the demon's neck. Then for good measure, Richard pulled out his .44 caliber AutoMag and put a round in each eye. The heavy bullets tore the back of the demon-dog's head off. Its blood, bone, and brain matter flew through the air about a meter then stopped. All of it stopped in mid-air.

"Uh, that's different," said Nickelo as if he was taking notes.

Richard swung his plasma rifle towards the taller demon ready to fire. But his hand froze before he pulled the trigger. The taller demon looked as if it was frozen in time. Its hands were poised in front of it as if it had been trying to perform the hand movements of an intricate spell. Like the rest of it, the hands weren't moving.

"What the hell?" Richard said.

Richard glanced down the tunnel towards Shandria. The elf was about twenty meters away. She held her staff with both hands while pointing it at the demon. Like her foe, Shandria wasn't moving. There was a bright, orange ball of energy about ten meters to her front. Streaks of trailing energy gave the impression the energy was heading towards the demon, but the ball of energy was also frozen in mid-air.

"We're in a time-bubble," said Nickelo. *"It's the only answer."*

"I know," Richard said. *"Shandria told us months ago."*

Richard pointed his plasma rifle at the taller demon and fired off a burst of ten rounds. The red streaks of energy stopped in mid-air about two meters away. The plasma rounds just hung in mid-air. The little particles of energy trailing behind them were the only indication of movement.

"I don't understand," Richard said. *"Is everything frozen except for us?"*

"Nothing's frozen," said Nickelo. *"We're in a small time-bubble. The demon-dog you were fighting must have been in the process of creating one when you latched onto it. You must have been drawn into the time-bubble with it."*

Richard pressed his hand forward. It stopped as if he'd hit a wall. His hand tingled, but other than that he felt no ill-effects. He quickly pulled his hand back.

"Why would it create a time-bubble?" Richard asked. *"Seems to me we're just stuck here unable to interact with anything in the real-time world. Heck, I can't even shoot that blasted demon. The rounds just stop in mid-air."*

"I don't think they're stopped," said Nickelo. *"I think they're just moving so slowly we can't discern any movement. I'm betting your plasma rounds will eventually hit the demon. That is if it doesn't get its defensive shield back up again before they make contact. In fact, I think the elf's spell is going to make the demon wish you hadn't distracted it with that demon-dog-in-the-face trick. Good one, by the way."*

"Well, that's all well and good," Richard said. *"But I ask again. Why would the demon-dog waste the Power to create a time-bubble in the first place if it does no good?"*

"I think it was creating a series of time-bubbles during your fight with it," said Nickelo. *"I calculate there is a sixty-eight percent chance it created a time-bubble each time you hurt it. Once in the time-bubble, it could use whatever healing powers it had to heal itself. Then when the time-bubble ended, it was able to reenter the fray as good as new."*

Richard admitted his battle computer's theory made sense. He'd injured the demon-dog twice, and both times it had come back at him completely healed. He'd just assumed it had innate healing abilities similar to a troll. But, the time-bubble method of healing was more insidious. Not only could it heal itself but it could take time to plan its next move. He whispered one of his rare prayers to the Creator thanking him for the good luck to grab the demon before its time-bubble was fully formed.

Suddenly, Richard had a horrible thought.

"Nick," Richard said with alarm. *"What if we're trapped here for all eternity?"*

"I don't think we will be," said Nickelo, *"but how about doing an active scan on the boundary of the time-bubble just to be sure. Most of the helmet's scanners were knocked out during your fight with the troll."*

Richard set up an active scan and gave control to his battle computer. After a couple of minutes, Nickelo said, *"The time-bubble has about a two-meter radius. I've done an initial analysis of the energy flow, and I calculate we have several hours before we'll be thrust back into normal time."* Nickelo paused. *"Or should I say back into the tunnel's time. It's a time-bubble itself after all. Hmmm. That's an interesting concept. I wonder how many time-bubbles could exist within a series of time-bubbles."*

"Don't get started," Richard said. He had no desire to get into a theoretical discussion similar to a person with a mirror with a reflection of himself holding a mirror with a reflection of himself holding... It made his head hurt to think about such things. He decided to change the subject.

"What should we do now?" Richard said.

"I'd suggest you rearm your weapons. Then, you and I are going to spend some of the Power in your reserve doing active scans on this time-bubble. It's very interesting. You never know. The knowledge we gain might come in useful someday."

"Are you thinking I might be able to create a time-bubble?" Richard asked with interest. He was starting to see a myriad of uses for it during combat.

"You wish," laughed Nickelo. *"No. It would take a thousand times more Power than you have in your reserve to create a time-bubble. The demon-dog apparently has an innate ability to do so. You'd have to brute force it."*

"Fine," Richard said disappointedly. *"I'll tell you what, Nick. I'll set up an active scan for you, and you can scan away to your electronic heart's content. I'm going to rearm and then get some sleep."*

CHAPTER 25

Nickelo woke Richard up several hours later with the announcement that the time-bubble was failing. After a big stretch, Richard moved to a spot in the time-bubble as far from the demon as he could get. He didn't want to get caught in any residual effects of the elf's spell. He wasn't even sure what kind of spell it was. A major fireball certainly wouldn't do his already damaged suit any good.

"Should I change out my battle suit?" Richard asked while hoping the answer would be no. He didn't want to risk losing it. He had a feeling he was going to need every bit of armor he could get in the upcoming fight.

"I'd recommend against it," said Nickelo. *"I'll use the same argument I did when you asked about the battle helmet. What if you don't get a new set of armor back? We know a hundred and ninety-nine more sets were made, but what if* 'the One' *denies you a replacement as part of his punishment for defying him. Your armor's still in good shape, although its seal is broken. You should be okay as long as we don't get in poison gas or something."*

"Thanks for the comforting thought."

Richard thought about something he'd been meaning to ask Nickelo and now seemed as good a time as any.

"Nick," Richard said, *"I've been wondering. I was able to use the dimensional pack to rearm with no problem. How can that possibly work if we're in a time-bubble? Nay, we're in a time-bubble within a time-bubble."*

"I don't know," Nickelo said.

Richard waited a few more seconds, but Nickelo said nothing further.

"That's it?" Richard said. *"That's your answer? You don't know?"*

"That's right," said Nickelo. *"Oh, by the way, I may have kept your active scan going longer than I should have. You're down to sixty-four percent Power in your reserve. The good news is that I've got oodles of data in my memory banks on time-bubbles now. I'll be happy to let you look at it when you get time."*

"I can hardly wait," Richard said as he rolled his eyes. *"And, what are oodles? I've never heard the word before."*

"It's just an old, twentieth-century saying," said Nickelo. *"Didn't you ever read old classics when you were a youth?"*

"Sorry," Richard said. *"I was too busy trying to stay alive. Maybe next time."*

Richard looked around him. The demon and Shandria seemed to be in the same positions, but the elf's ball of energy was noticeably closer than it had been previously. Also, the plasma rounds were nearly upon the demon. At least a little time had elapsed since he'd entered the demon-dog's time-bubble. Richard noticed the elf's energy ball had started changing into what appeared to be the beginnings of a lightning bolt.

"Anytime now," said Nickelo. *"Prepare to roll out of the way."*

Time started again before Richard could reply. The plasma rounds hit the demon in the chest at the same moment Shandria's lightning bolt struck it in the face. Richard rolled quickly to the left, but he wasn't nearly fast enough. Arcs of electricity hit all around him. Thankfully, the battle suit's insulation was able to protect him from the residual energy. All he felt was a little tingle in his legs.

The demon staggered backward and fell to the ground. Richard stood up and fired all seven 20mm grenades into the demon's charred head. He was too close for them to activate and explode, but the size and force of the 20mm rounds tore the head to shreds. By the time he finished, the demon had a body, but it didn't have much of a head.

"I think the a-hole's dead," Richard said out loud. Since the battle suit's seal was broken, he didn't have the annoying tube in his mouth.

"Demons can't die, Rick," said Shandria who had just joined him. "You can destroy their bodies, but they're just banished back to their realm. These same demons could be back in a thousand years or so. Of course, they'd probably be in a different form by then, but who really knows?"

"Reload, Rick," interrupted Nickelo. "Don't you remember? I advised you to rearm whenever you got a chance?"

"Sorry, Nick," Richard said as he reached over his shoulder to open the flap of his pack. "I forgot." He replaced the seven 20mm grenades in his launcher and made sure one was in the chamber ready to fire.

"The demon Efrestra is located about two hundred paces ahead," said Shandria. "I can feel him, but I doubt he's alone."

"Rick?" said Nickelo. "My scanners are all out of action."

Richard sent a quick active-scan ahead. He felt Nickelo following along and making subtle changes to the scan. Normally, Richard would've been hesitant of such a blatant use of an active scan since it had a higher risk of detection than his passive scan. In this case, however, it wasn't as if the enemy didn't know where they were.

After a few moments, the results of the scan began to display on the heads-up display. He gave Shandria the bad news.

"It looks like there is one big Power source, four medium-sized ones and a couple of hundred undead of various types. Can you confirm that, Nick?"

"I concur," said Nickelo. "I calculate your assessment has a seventy-four percent chance of being correct. You're improving. Maybe you won't need me hanging around if you get much better at scanning. Heck, maybe I'll have to start calling you greatest of wizard scouts for real," he smirked.

"I doubt the day will ever come when I won't need you, Nick," Richard said honestly. He turned towards Shandria. "How do you want to handle this? Should we start heading that way now before they come to us?"

"I seriously doubt any of the ones with Efrestra will come to us. His dragon form is too large to fit in this tunnel, and he's got his forces massed at the only exit. He knows we have to go to him. We have no choice. Also, our enemies behind us will even now be digging their way through your makeshift roadblocks. Efrestra undoubtedly knows they'll soon be pushing us towards him."

"I've got six blocks of J22 plastic explosive left," said Richard. "I could blow the tunnel behind us. That would buy us a little more time. Once I do that, I guess I'll be as ready as I'll ever be to face what's ahead."

"Not quite, Rick," said Shandria. "We need to talk about this last battle."

Richard expected some praise. He thought he'd done quite well so far.

"You didn't think," said Shandria in a voice that let him know she wasn't pleased. "Did you not remember any of your training from these last four months? Do you think I did all that talking and work for the fun of it?"

Richard was taken aback. He said nothing. His mind was racing trying to figure out where he'd fallen short.

"Did you think to scan the demon-dog's link?" said Shandria. When Richard stayed silent, she said, "I thought not. Well, I did, and it had an unprotected spot. You could have disabled it easily and destroyed the demon's body in short order. And before you ask, I didn't do it myself because I was preoccupied with the other demon. It was a tough opponent. I could've used a little more help."

"See, Rick," said Nickelo with a snicker. "It's like I always say, you keep running to a fight before you take the time to think."

"And, Master Nick," said Shandria in a tone Richard was glad she hadn't used on him. "Why didn't you think to tell Rick to check the demon's link? Aren't you his advisor? Aren't you this great computer, whatever that is, while Rick's just a cadet in training?"

"Uh...," said Nickelo as if he were searching for the right words.

Richard thought his battle computer's predicament was funny. Nickelo could think at nanosecond speed, but this elf had him struggling to find an appropriate response.

"I don't mean to belittle you, Rick," said Shandria in a tone less harsh. "Throwing that hound at the other demon to distract it was ingenious. It caused them both to drop their defensive shields. But, you could have taken out the hound a lot earlier. Your lapse of judgment could have cost us our lives. If we're to have any chance in the upcoming fight, none of us can afford to make those kinds of mistakes."

"Fine," Richard said. "I'll try to think before I act." He wanted to say more, but the fact the elf could kick his butt helped keep him civil.

Richard took his six blocks of J22 plastic explosive and set them up in two spots in the tunnel near the intersection. He heard pounding when he got near the cave-in. As Shandria predicted, their trapped enemies were attempting to dig their way out.

Once the explosives were set, Richard high-tailed it back to Shandria. A few seconds later there was a loud boom. A gush of air passed by them headed towards the cavern.

"That should buy us a few minutes," Richard said.

"I've been thinking," said Shandria. "The only choice I think we have is for me to tackle Efrestra while you take out the lesser demons and the undead. Do you think you can do it, Rick?"

Richard heard doubt in her voice. He didn't blame her. He also had doubts about his ability to tackle multiple demons on his own.

"The only chance, huh?" Richard said casually. "I'm curious, Nick. What percentage chance of success do you calculate for this endeavor?"

Nickelo hesitated before answering. "Well, it's above zero, but it's not much above. Based upon logical attack scenarios and probable enemy responses, I calculate we have about eight percent chance of success."

"That much, huh?" Richard said. He was surprised. He'd actually thought it would be closer to zero.

"No," said Nickelo. "I rounded up. It's really only seven point six percent chance."

Richard looked at Shandria. "To answer your question, no, I don't think I can do it. I was barely able to handle the one demon-dog. I doubt I could have beaten the taller demon on my own." Before Shandria could say anything, he added, "Don't take this the wrong way, but I don't think you can handle Efrestra by yourself either. It looked like it was all you could do during the last battle to keep a defensive shield up. You weren't able to get a single attack off."

Shandria didn't argue with Richard's observations.

Encouraged, Richard said, "I got a good sense of that demon's Power source during that first engagement. It should have been able to overwhelm you easily. Why do you think it didn't?"

"I imagine it was holding back for fear of damaging the spheres," said Shandria. "I was holding two of the seed spheres. If it damaged any of them, the other parts of the seed would be worthless."

"That's what I thought," Richard said. "Apparently, those spheres provide us a little indirect protection. I'll probably need one of them when we make our attack."

Shandria raised her eyebrows.

"I'm not going to keep it," Richard said. "Heck, we're both probably going to die in a few minutes anyway. What good will any of the spheres do either of us then?"

"Sorry," said Shandria. "I'm just protective because the wellbeing of my race depends on them. But of course you'll need one, and you shall have one."

"How did you keep the spheres from mesmerizing you when you got them?" Richard asked a little curious. "The filter on my visor protected me."

"I have a spell which will protect me for a few minutes," said Shandria. "But it's a little complicated. I have to prepare it ahead of time."

"Do you think an undead or a demon would be affected?" Richard asked hopefully.

"No," said Shandria. "I'm sorry, but I don't think it works that way. I wondered where you were headed."

"Shouldn't we be starting?" said Nickelo. "I ran every logical scenario I could come up with. I can't think of any better plan. However, the longer we wait, the greater the chance those demons and undead trapped in the tunnels behind us will break out and join the fight."

"Hold on," Richard said. "You're always the one telling me to think things through before I enter a fight. If eight percent is the best chance we have logically, then I'd say we'd better come up with an illogical way to better the odds."

"I only deal with logic, Rick," said Nickelo. "The illogical is your department."

"Shandria," Richard said. "You've been at the exit before. Is it an opening to the outside? My active scan made it look like Efrestra, and his buddies are located in a cavern about three hundred meters by three hundred meters and ten meters high. Does that sound right?"

"You said a meter is about the distance of a pace?" said Shandria.

Richard nodded his head affirmatively.

"That sounds accurate. The center of the cavern is higher than the sides," said Shandria. "Other than that, your description sounds about right. As to the exit, it's not an opening to the outside. It's just a section of the time-bubble's boundary where we can use a spell to exit back to my time."

"Why are you interested in the size of the cavern?" Nickelo asked curiously. "Are you trying to figure out if you have maneuver room?"

Richard said nothing for a moment. He didn't have an idea as much as he had a feeling. "I'm not exactly sure what I'm thinking, Nick. But, I do know we have to narrow the odds. When my unit was fighting bugs in the Denobar system, we used fuel-air explosives, or FAEs, in the tunnels. Those thermobaric warheads were devastating in confined areas underground. I was wondering if we might be able to create some type of fuel-air explosive to clear the cavern. I'll admit I'm concerned if the explosion's too powerful, we might damage the time-bubble."

"I'll admit, that's not one of the logical alternatives I considered," said Nickelo.

"What's a fuel-air explosive?" said Shandria.

Nickelo answered in the same voice he'd used when teaching the cadets back at the Academy. "A fuel-air explosive, or what's called a thermobaric explosive by the military, is a combination of fuel particles interspersed in an area containing oxygen. The fuel can be either a substance of fine particles such as flour, or it can be a flammable liquid or gas. When the dispersed fuel's ignited, it burns so quickly it causes an immense blast. Not only are the flames deadly, the pressurization of the blast is extremely destructive compared to the amount of flammable material used. In order to create a fuel-air explosion, we'd somehow have to get the flammable material to the cavern. In our situation, hydrogen gas would be the obvious choice."

"Why obvious?" asked Shandria.

"Because the cavern's uphill from here," replied Nickelo. "Hydrogen gas is lighter than the other gasses in the atmosphere. It'll quickly move up the tunnel and into the cavern. You said the cavern had no other outlets other than this tunnel. The hydrogen gas should fill the cavern from the ceiling down towards the floor."

"Won't the demons be suspicious when they start having trouble breathing?" asked Shandria.

"Hydrogen gas," said Nickelo, "is odorless and tasteless. Also, we won't be replacing all the oxygen in the cavern. In fact, we don't want to replace it all. Without oxygen, there would be no explosion. Hydrogen will explode at a concentration of eighteen point six percent to fifty-nine percent of the atmosphere. I'd suggest a twenty-five percent concentration. It's enough to explode and be destructive, but low enough to give us time to release that amount of hydrogen in the cavern before the enemies behind us break free."

Richard said, "How much hydrogen will we need, Nick?"

"The cavern has about nine hundred thousand cubic meters of air," said Nickelo. "To obtain a twenty-five percent concentration, we'll need to release about two hundred twenty-five thousand cubic meters of hydrogen."

"Wow," Richard said with a whistle. "That's a lot of hydrogen. More than I thought."

"Getting that much hydrogen isn't our biggest problem," said Nickelo.

Shandria decided to get back in the conversation. "What is our biggest problem, Master Nick?"

"Any explosion in the cavern needs a point of release for the resulting pressure," said Nickelo. "The only existing point of release is this tunnel."

"And we're standing in it," said Shandria as the severity of the problem hit her. "But it probably won't matter. I certainly have no spells to produce that amount of hydrogen. Rick, you told me you could summon almost anything from your dimensional pack. Could you summon that much hydrogen?"

"I don't know," Richard admitted. "I guess it depends on how much *the One*, or whoever stocks my equipment, thought I'd need. I'll admit it's not exactly a typical request."

"I might be able to help with the blast problem," Shandria said. "I have a spell that would put us in the void between dimensions for about thirty seconds. Nothing could harm us while we were there. Would that be long enough to be helpful? It's Power hungry, so I'd hate to use it and still have to participate in a major battle."

Nickelo answered, "It would be close. All the breathable air would be consumed in the cavern and probably this tunnel also. When we return to this dimension, you'd both suffocate."

"I have a breathing spell," said Shandria, "but it's self only."

"I could summon an oxygen mask for me," Richard said. "I'd have to lower the bottom part of my battle helmet's face guard. That shouldn't matter since the suit's seal is broken anyway."

"You'll think it matters if something hits you in the mouth," said Nickelo. "Or, if a fireball goes off near you."

"Spoilsport," Richard said. "Always thinking of the negative things, aren't you?"

The three of them continued discussing the merits of the plan a few more minutes, but in the end, they could think of nothing better. Finally, Richard took a walk back down the tunnel to the new cave-in he'd made near the intersection. He could hear pounding already from the other side. It sounded close. When he reported what he'd heard to Shandria, they made the only decision they could. They were going to roll the dice and see what happened. Richard and Shandria begin making preparations.

CHAPTER 26

"Why do you not come, you doomed thieves?" boomed a deep voice echoing down the tunnel. "My forces will soon break through your pitiful barricade. Come to me now, and I'll be merciful. If you make me wait longer, your tortures will become legend."

"Nice of him to be so generous," Richard commented as he disengaged the vent tube from where it exited his dimensional pack. The setup for the hydrogen had been relatively simple, although it had been costly in terms of Power. Richard had imagined an arms-wide vent tube emerging from his pack while releasing hydrogen gas. When he'd lifted the flap, he was hit in the face with a strong blast of cool air coming from the end of a large vent tube. The elastic opening of the dimensional pack stretched to accommodate the meter-wide vent tube. Leaving the pack on the ground, Richard pulled an ever-lengthening vent tube out of it. He continued pulling until he'd carried the end of the tube a hundred meters up the sloping tunnel. That had been almost an hour ago.

"Yes," said Shandria with a laugh. "I'm sure the mercy of the demon Efrestra would be everything we could ever expect." Then growing serious, she asked, "Are you ready, Rick?"

Richard was busy stuffing the last of the vent tubing back into his pack. He knew he'd need every tidbit of Power he could get for the coming fight. When he had completed the process, he felt a slight amount of Power return to his reserve. It was better than nothing.

"What do you think, Nick?" Richard asked.

"As I already mentioned," said Nickelo, "it would have been helpful if you'd thought to summon a vent tube with a pressurization gauge. But, as best I can calculate, the cavern should now have a hydrogen concentration between twenty-five and thirty percent. When you set off the can of propane you summoned, the whole cavern should become one massive fireball."

Richard double-checked the oxygen mask he'd summoned earlier. He made sure it was securely strapped to his side ready for quick use. Picking up the ten-kilogram tank of propane he'd gotten from his pack, Richard pulled out a block of J22 plastic explosive from the satchel strapped over his shoulder. He set the timer to thirty seconds and attached it to the tank of propane. He'd summoned another twenty blocks of J22 plastic explosive earlier, so that left him with nineteen.

"Ready," Richard said.

"You only have eighteen percent Power in your reserve left, Rick," warned Nickelo, "so be careful. That hydrogen was costlier than I ever imagined."

Richard knew only too well how low on Power he was. If the hydrogen didn't explode as hoped, he was doomed in any following fight. All it would take for their plan to fail would be the existence of another outlet from the cavern, or if Nickelo had miscalculated the hydrogen concentration. Any number of factors could cause their little experiment to fail. The cost of failure would be death, possibly a long, torturous death.

"Good luck," said Shandria. "I'll wait for your return before completing my dimensional spell, but don't tarry. We don't have much time."

Richard nodded his head. "Thanks," he said. Richard turned to leave, but then he turned back. "Shandria, in case things go wrong, I just want you to know I'm glad I met you. It's been an experience, to say the least. You've been a good friend."

"As have you, Rick," said Shandria. The elf held his eyes with hers, and even through the red tint of his visor, he could tell their molten silver was churning with emotion. "But, don't give up hope so easily. The ways of the Creator are beyond all understanding. If it's his will for us to succeed then succeed we will, no matter the odds."

"Well," Richard said, "then we need to pray he wants us to succeed. If we both do get out of this, you tell that boyfriend of yours I said he's the luckiest male in the galaxy, bar none. I'd give my right arm if your eyes sparkled when you talked about me like they do when you talk about him."

Shandria laughed, but Richard thought she also looked like she was blushing. It was hard to tell when everything looked red through his visor.

"Rest assured, I'll give him your message," said Shandria with a parting smile. "Take care of yourself, Rick, and take care of that blue sphere. All will have been for naught if all three seed parts aren't returned to my time and my world."

Richard touched the blue sphere where it was strapped securely to his chest. It was still in its leather bag, but Shandria had assured him Efrestra would know exactly where it was. Richard ran a hundred meters up the tunnel until it began sloping upward at a steep angle. He moved a few more meters forward, then he set down the tank of propane and placed his finger on the J22 plastic explosive's activate switch.

"Why do you stop?" boomed the deep voice from the direction of the cavern. Richard thought it was much louder now. "Come. Come forward little wizard scout. Yes, I know you. I am aware of your pathetic, untrained Power. I hold no grudge against you, little wizard. Bring me the seed sphere you carry, and I'll send you back to your world with no hard feelings. Why not? You mean nothing to me. You can continue your pathetic life at the Academy. You can live whatever life you desire. I care not. All you have to do is bring me your part of the seed. Don't be a pawn in a game played by your betters. Come. Come and feel my mercy."

"He's stalling," said Nickelo. *"The others must be nearly through the barricade. It's now or never."*

Richard pressed the activation switch on the block of J22 plastic explosive. He turned and ran back towards Shandria as fast as the battle suit's legs would carry him.

"Stop," boomed the voice in Richard's ears. "You cannot escape. I'll rip your flesh from your bones one tiny bit at a time. I'll stretch out your agony for thousands of years, thief. There's nowhere to run where I can't find you. Run, you fool, if you desire. I'll find you no matter how far you go."

Efrestra's deep, sadistic laughter rang in Richard's ears just as Shandria came into view. The elf had already started her spell. Further down the tunnel, Richard saw a stream of undead spewing through an opening in the barricade. They'd broken through already. Two demon-dogs led the charge. Richard knew it was going to be close.

Shandria's hands were moving quickly as she tried desperately to finish her spell without messing up the gestures. Richard could hear her shouting strange words as he drew close. The elf's outline started to waiver as if she were losing substance. Richard took a final leap and latched onto Shandria just as her form began to blur out of sight. From the corner of his eyes, he saw one of the demon-dogs leaping straight for the elf's throat.

The world around Richard wavered and disappeared. He clutched Shandria tight in his arms. The elf was solid. The elf was real. But the world he knew, the world of the time-bubble, was gone. He felt like nothing existed except the elf and him. He heard nothing. He saw nothing. He waited, he knew not how long, then the nothingness around the elf and he started to shimmer.

The world came back into view. The tunnel was darkened with soot. There wasn't any noise. Richard released his hold on the elf and looked to his left towards the barricade. It was gone. Not even a rock remained. There was no sign of any demons or undead. It was as if everything in the tunnel had been swept clean.

"Move," came a thought from Nickelo. *"Don't give them time to react."*

Richard turned and ran towards the cavern. He positioned his M12 plasma rifle as he went, ready to fire from the hip.

"Wait!" came Shandria's panicked voice behind him. "We need to go together."

"Not this time," Richard thought. He knew she couldn't take on Efrestra. The demon knew her abilities too well. It had been obvious to Richard during their first battle with the demon that the demon knew the elf's weaknesses.

"But, you don't know mine, demon," he thought. *"You don't know mine."*

Richard ran at full speed. He quickly outpaced the elf, and she fell far behind. All too soon, he was running the last few meters of the soot-blackened tunnel into the cavern. Scraps of charred flesh were piled along the walls. It was the only evidence remaining of the two hundred plus undead which had occupied the cavern less than a minute ago. But, the cavern wasn't empty of life. Richard sensed the life forces of the demons. They'd been weakened, but they were still alive, and they were still strong.

Two demon-dogs came running from Richard's right. The hound in the lead looked healthy. The trailing demon-dog appeared to have a limp, and its quill-like fur appeared singed. Behind them, Richard could see two of the taller demons. They both had spots of dark, splotchy colors as if their skin had been heavily burned. One of the taller demons was missing part of an arm, and the other was leaning against a rock for support. Richard soon saw the reason. It was missing part of one leg. However, they were both up and alive. He sensed their Power reserves were nearly full. The one with a missing arm began to cast a spell.

Richard sent a burst of plasma rounds at the lead demon-dog in a vain hope to slow it down. The rounds hit something invisible about a meter in front of the demon-dog. The plasma rounds dissipated into nothing.

"Their links," said Nickelo. *"Check their links."*

"I know," Richard said curtly. He sent an active scan at the lead demon-dog and traced a line of Power from the hound's defensive shield back to a pool of Power. Shandria had been correct. While a half-hearted attempt had been made to protect the link, the protection was feeble. Richard picked a weak spot and wrapped it with Power. Then he twisted. The link snapped. He fired another burst from his plasma rifle at the lead demon-dog. Half a dozen rounds hit it in the chest. The demon-dog was knocked on its back. Richard fired a 20mm grenade, and the demon-dog's chest exploded in a spray of blood.

The second demon-dog stopped in its tracks as if second-guessing itself on the wisdom of attacking. A ball of energy passed over its head towards Richard. The taller demon had released its spell. It was a large ball of energy. It was larger than anything Richard had tried to deflect in his training with Shandria. He wasn't hopeful. He threw up a defensive shield to his front and angled it slightly to his left. He gritted his teeth and waited.

"Fireball," said Nickelo.

"No!" boomed a deep voice from behind a group of large

boulders to Richard's left.

A wall of energy appeared ten meters in front of Richard. The tall demon's ball of energy hit the mysterious shield and exploded in a violent burst of flames and energy. Then the shield disappeared.

"You fools," boomed the voice. "He has a sphere. Do not risk harming it. Kill the wizard scout, but do not harm the sphere."

Richard had heard enough. The second demon-dog was still hesitating. Richard found a weak spot in the hound's link and duplicated the process with the first demon-dog. He broke the link with a twist. The demon-dog turned and ran towards the far wall of the cave. Richard fired two 20mm grenades and blew the demon-dog in half.

Two balls of energy came towards Richard from the direction of the taller demons. As they flew, the balls of energy merged together then separated to form a crisscrossed mesh of energy resembling a net. Richard had an uneasy feeling, but he resolutely held his ground and formed a new defensive shield to his front.

"No!" Richard heard Shandria cry. "You shall not have him."

Again, another shield of energy formed ahead of Richard and positioned itself to intercept the incoming spells. This shield was different. Its energy was familiar. It had a taint of good to it. The demon's energy-net hit the shield, and both the shield and the energy-net exploded. The force of the blast knocked Richard down.

Richard saw the elf at the tunnel exit. She held her staff to her front. It began to glow, and a ball of energy shot out of the staff towards the taller demons.

Richard didn't wait to see the results. He jumped to his feet and ran for the boulders from behind which the deep voice had come.

"No, Rick," Shandria shouted. Any other words were drowned out by an explosion as Shandria's spell hit the taller demons' defensive shields.

Richard ignored the battle behind him. He was on a mission to destroy the demon in the dragon's body. He activated the assisters on the legs of his battle suit and jumped for the top of one of the boulders. It was three times the height of a man. Just as it seemed he would fall short of the mark, he gave a little boost with his telekinesis and reached the top.

"You're at eleven percent Power," said Nickelo. *"Levitating your weight is expensive."*

"Whatever," Richard thought.

Richard spied the dragon which wasn't a dragon on the other side of the boulder. It seemed to have weathered the hydrogen explosion well. Still, it must have taken at least some damage, because the stripe down its side appeared singed. A few scales were also missing on the lower part of its neck.

Richard fired a long burst of plasma rounds at the demon's eyes as he jumped towards it. The demon didn't even bother putting up a shield. It merely dipped its dragon head and allowed the plasma rounds to glance off its forehead. The demon lashed out with its long dragon's tail. Richard had already jumped to the ground, so he leaped over the tail and continued running for the lower part of the demon's neck.

"Yes," said Nickelo. *"The missing scales might be a weak spot."*

Richard ran an active scan on the neck of the dragon's body. Even to Richard's untrained eye, the demon seemed to have put so many layers of defenses on the dragon's body that it was virtually invulnerable. The missing scales on the neck were slightly less defended, but he wasn't sure how to take advantage of the situation. Even damaged, the neck was still heavily defended. But, attacking the missing scales was all Richard could think of, so when he got close, he dived for the lower part of the neck.

The demon spun so quickly Richard was caught by surprise. He hadn't thought anything as big as that dragon's body could move so fast. He sensed Nickelo take control of the battle suit. Under Nickelo's guidance, the suit twisted violently. He felt as if he was being turned into a human pretzel. When he saw the four razor-sharp claws coming his way, he wished Nickelo would twist him harder. Richard tried to use his telekinesis to slow down the claws, but his ability was no match for the strength of the dragon's body. In the end, Nickelo's maneuver only partially succeeded. Two of the claws missed, but two of them hit their mark. One claw caught Richard on the head. The other claw tore through the battle suit's armor on his left side.

A flash of white-hot pain exploded in Richard's skull. His breath was knocked out of his lungs, and he was flung through the air. Richard unconsciously grabbed hold of his side with both hands. His flight through the air was stopped when he hit one of the boulders with bone-crushing force. His battle suit's armor absorbed most of the blow, but not all of it. Richard felt his left leg snap as at least one bone broke. When he fell to the ground, he rolled into a tight ball. He was in agony. Just touching his side hurt, but it hurt worse to release his grip. A warm liquid ran into his eyes partially blinding him. Reflexively, he raised one hand to his face and wiped his eyes.

Where's my visor, he thought groggily. The pounding in his head made it difficult to think.

"Nick," said Richard. *"I'm hurt, and I can't see."*

"Your battle helmet's damaged," said Nickelo. *"All electronics are out. That includes your night vision. Your left side's heavily damaged as well, but without the suit's electronics, I can't tell how serious it is. I'm sorry, Rick. I let you down."*

Richard felt around his battle helmet with his free hand. Part of the left side around the ear was missing. Without electronics, he had no visor or heads-up display. Also, none of the battle suit's built-in medical equipment would work without electronics.

"What should I do?" Richard asked. He was still groggy from the blow to his head.

"I honestly don't know," said Nickelo.

Through his pain, Richard thought he heard a strange note in his battle computer's voice.

"What else is going on, Nick?" Richard said.

"My isotopic battery has been damaged along with the battle suit's battery," said Nickelo. *"I'm operating on emergency backup. My primary memory chip is undamaged, but without power, I will shut down soon."*

"Then what?" Richard said. He was starting to panic as he feared the worst.

"Then I'll cease to exist," said Nickelo matter-of-factly. *"I have about two minutes power remaining. The backup is only intended to provide time to change out the primary battery."*

"I'll summon a new isotopic battery for you," Richard said as he reached over his back trying to locate the flap of his dimensional pack.

"Don't waste your time," said Nickelo. *"The slot for the battery*

was in the part of the helmet that's missing. You can't help me now. I'll try to assist you as much as I can, for as long as I can."

"Are you trying to tell me you're dying?" Richard asked. He couldn't grasp the concept. He needed Nickelo. His battle computer was his friend. He couldn't lose another friend. Not again.

"It's all right," said Nickelo. *"Forget about it. Right now, I need you to get to your feet. That demon may attack again."*

Richard stayed on the ground. It hurt too much to move. He saw momentary flashes of light along with a series of explosions. He assumed Shandria was putting up one heck of a fight on the other side of the boulder. The flashes proved one thing. He wasn't blind. He just needed some light to see.

"You pathetic fool," laughed a deep voice. The voice sounded cruel, and it sounded much too close. "Did you really think you could steal my property with impunity? You're almost out of Power. Your battle suit is damaged, and your battle computer will soon cease to function. You will soon be alone. Even now, the defenses of the elf are being worn down. This is working out much better than I planned. I shall have the seed, I shall have the elf, and I shall have you. All is lost, human. I can taste the sweetness of your despair."

"Then kill me and get it over with," Richard yelled defiantly.

"Oh, no, my little wizard scout," said the demon almost conversationally. "Your death will not be so easy. One of my brothers can heal. Normally, he only heals virgin females. Perhaps I can persuade him to make an exception for you. If I'm careful, I believe I can stretch out your torture for many decades. Even a little pain can be unbearable when it's stretched over enough time."

Richard heard a series of bangs from behind the boulder. A momentary burst of white light illuminated the surroundings. Not two meters to his front was the snout of the black dragon. Its eyes reflected the flash of light with a deep red glow, and its dragon fangs dripped with a liquid that caused the very rocks beneath them to bubble. Richard tried to scoot backward, but the boulder blocked his way. The movement caused a hot flash of pain to shoot up his leg. In spite of himself, he let out a cry of agony. The light went out, and he was trapped in darkness again.

"Oh," said the deep voice. "You've hurt your leg. You can't see it, but inside your armor, the bone is protruding from the flesh. Your head and side are bleeding profusely as well. You'll need healing soon, or you'll bleed to death. Now, we can't have that, can we?"

Something heavy pressed against Richard's leg. He screamed as the paw of the dragon pulled on his leg and popped his bone back in place.

"Ah," said the deep voice pleasantly. "That should buy you a few minutes. Your screams are delicious, but let's not waste them now. It's time to get this farce over with. Give me the sphere, and I'll be merciful."

"Why don't you just take it?" Richard said angrily. He tried to put defiance in his voice, but he feared he failed miserably.

"Now, now, wizard scout," scolded the demon. "There's no need to be unpleasant. I don't want to take the sphere. I want you to give it to me. That would please me so much more than merely taking it."

"*Rick,*" said Nickelo, "*I haven't much time. You still have the bag of J22 plastic explosive. Maybe you can use it somehow to buy enough time to find an exit. You can't just sit here. You have to do something before you lose consciousness from loss of blood.*"

"*How much time do you have left, Nick,*" Richard asked, "*before your battery runs out?*"

"*It doesn't matter, Rick. We need to get you out of here. That's what's important.*"

"*Nick,*" Richard said using his command voice. "*How much time?*"

"*One minute and six seconds,*" said Nickelo in reply to the command.

Another boom and flash of light came from behind the boulders. Richard noticed during the flash that the demon had raised its dragon head high into the air as if looking at the battle on the other side.

"Shandria!" Richard yelled in the momentary calm. "I can't see. I need light." His voice was muffled by his oxygen mask. He only hoped his shout was clear enough for the elf to understand.

A ball of energy shot into the air and opened up into a bright ball of light. It hung in the air dimly illuminating the cavern.

Richard got his first good look at the demon in white light. It occupied the body of a black dragon with a red stripe down its side. The demon turned its dragon head as if avoiding the sudden light, dim though it was. The demon's dragon body was over thirty meters from snout to the tip of its tail. Richard had thought it was huge before. It appeared even more immense now given its proximity.

"It hates the light," said Nickelo. *"Use that to your advantage. Ignore your pain. Do something."*

Richard decided he would do something, but it wouldn't be what his battle computer wanted. He removed his battle helmet and reached over his back to open the flap of his dimensional pack.

"No, Rick," Nickelo pleaded. *"You need me. I can still help."*

"You have thirty seconds of battery life," Richard said. *"You've helped me enough. Now I'm going to try and help you."*

Richard wasn't sure he was doing the right thing, but he was sure doing nothing to save his friend would be the wrong thing. He couldn't let Nickelo be destroyed with him.

"Take care, Nick," Richard said. *"I'll be seeing you."*

Richard let go of the battle helmet. It dropped into the pack.

"Rick!" came Nickelo's cry. Then there was silence.

The demon had recovered from its momentary blindness. It was once again watching the ongoing battle on the other side of the boulder. It was hard to tell, but Richard thought he saw an amused look on the face of the dragon.

Without looking at Richard, the demon said with a sarcastic chuckle, "How sweet. You saved your little computer and friend. If only you knew."

An explosion larger than any Richard had heard so far echoed through the cavern.

"The elf's doing better than I expected," said the demon nonchalantly. "That hydrogen explosion must have weakened my servants more than I thought." The demon turned its dragon head to stare at Richard. Its red dragon-eyes seemed to promise a slow death. "I assume the hydrogen was your idea. Yes, no doubt it was. It was too illogical for a computer." With an evil grin, it added, "That's another reason I'm going to enjoy our future sessions together. If I hadn't sensed the air pressure change, I might have been caught by surprise as well. I barely got a defensive shield up

231

in time as it was. You're a tricky, little human. I'm definitely going to enjoy our time together."

Richard saw no openings, so he decided to keep the dragon talking. At least it wasn't taking part in the fight against Shandria when it was here talking to him.

"How is it you know so much about computers?" Richard asked in as pleasant a voice as he could muster.

"Wizard scout," said the demon in a voice tinged with mock disappointment, "surely you're not one of those fools who think demons can't use technology."

Actually, Richard had thought so. Of course, he hadn't even believed in demons until he'd been thrust in this time-bubble nightmare.

"Maybe between torture sessions, I'll teach you something about the demon world." The demon gave an almost uncontrollable laugh has if it had thought of something amusing. "In the meantime, just know that demons understand much. Some demons even take over technological devices and use them as bodies. Others such as I occupy powerful creatures like this dragon. But, my brothers and I share much of our knowledge. So yes, I know about computers."

"You have brothers?" Richard asked.

Three powerful booms came from the other side of the boulders, and a blast of lightning hit the ceiling and bounced back to the ground.

"Lesson's over, wizard scout," said the demon. "We're about to have some company. This should be fun."

Shandria came running around the corner of the boulders. A rapid series of energy balls shot out of her staff and hit a defensive shield the demon had hastily erected for its protection. The demon had scoffed at Richard's ability to harm its dragon body, but the fierceness of the elf's attack had the demon temporarily on the defensive.

"You shall not prevail," yelled Shandria.

The elf's rings and necklace glowed brightly as Power transferred directly to the elf's staff. Richard was awestruck by the ferocity of the elf he'd lived with for four months. She was a sight to behold. If Richard had ever doubted her fighting ability, he had no doubts now. Shandria was every part a fierce warrior-priestess with her long, silver hair trailing behind her. She was giving it her all, and the demon was forced back two steps. It was too busy defending itself to make a counterattack of its own.

But, Richard could tell Shandria wouldn't be able to keep the momentum of her attack much longer. Even now, he sensed her staff and jewelry were nearing the end of their Power. Shandria had told him she was saving the Power in her jewelry for an emergency. She was no longer saving it. This was an all or nothing fight for her. Shandria's Power drained rapidly even as her massed spells confused and befuddled her enemy. Richard feared just a few more spells, and the elf would be at the mercy of the demon. Then it would be the demon's turn.

Richard used his plasma rifle to leverage himself to a standing position. The demon was so engrossed with the elf's attack it apparently failed to remember he was inside its primary defensive shield. Richard unslung the satchel of J22 plastic explosive off his shoulder and threw it in the direction of the dragon's flaming red eyes. His throw was awkward and weak, but he used his telekinesis to boost the satchel's momentum as he drew his .44 caliber AutoMag. When the satchel was within two meters of the black dragon-head, Richard fired and closed his eyes. The J22 plastic explosive exploded.

A rush of air flung Richard backward. He hit one of the boulders again and fell to the floor. The nineteen blocks of J22 exploding simultaneously was beyond deafening. The sound and pressure shattered Richard's eardrums. He screamed involuntarily from the pain. He heard nothing.

A glance upward revealed the demon shaking its dragon-head. If it hadn't been so pressed by the elf, the demon could probably have shrugged off the effects of the J22 plastic explosive. But, the double attack had it off balance. Richard sensed the demon's defensive shield weaken and begin to buckle.

Shandria waved her staff in a great circle around her head. Richard sensed the elf draining her Power reserve and all her jewelry for one final destructive spell. She pointed the staff at the demon as she gave a shout. A great flow of energy shot out of the staff. It overpowered the demon's defensive shield and struck it between the eyes. The demon's mouth opened in an obvious roar of pain, but Richard heard nothing. The demon fell to its knees, but it immediately tried to rise. Although it was partially stunned, Richard could sense the demon's Power reserve was nearly full. It was far from beaten.

He also sensed Shandria was out of Power. As far as Richard could tell, she was out of options as well. But the elf didn't hesitate. She drew her dagger and advanced forward. Richard saw her mouth moving as if she was yelling her battle cry, or perhaps she was calling out instructions to him. He heard nothing.

With a calmness belying the severity of the situation, Richard jerked the leather bag secured to his chest. The straps holding it in place broke. Richard threw the bag, blue sphere and all, towards Shandria. Then he opened the back of his phase rod and gave the endcap a twist. He extracted the phase rod's isotopic battery and broke it in half. He felt the battery going into overload. This wasn't one of the training batteries used in the Academy. It was a full-powered isotopic battery from a wizard scout's phase rod. The resulting explosion would be small in area but enormous in intensity.

Because he could no longer stand much less walk, Richard used telekinesis to move himself to the lower part on the back of the dragon's neck. His Power reserve ran out just as he reached the demon. As the last of his Power disappeared, Richard's stealth shield dropped. The demon twisted in an attempt to bite him. Before the jaws closed around him, Richard shoved the two pieces of broken battery underneath a loose scale.

As the battery pieces lodged in place beneath the demon's defenses, a voice sounded in Richard's head.

"Mission complete. Continue training," said *'the One.'*

Richard's body began to tingle. He caught a wavering image of the inside of the dragon's open mouth with its teeth dripping acid. Then all went black.

CHAPTER 27

Richard found himself standing upright in bright sunlight. He didn't remain upright very long. His broken leg buckled under his weight. He gave a pain-wrenching yell as he fell to the ground. He missed the sidewalk with his face, but even so, the smack he took when he hit the hard-packed parade field hurt.

Richard yelled again, but this time in fear, "Shandria! Shandria!" He heard no sound. Richard didn't care. He screamed out his agony anyway, both physical and emotional.

Suddenly, two strong hands were rolling him over onto his back. Through the blood running in his eyes, Richard made out the face of TAC Officer Gaston Myers. For a moment, Richard thought his TAC officer's face looked concerned. Then the expression turned to a grimace. Richard assumed his TAC officer had just realized his identity.

Richard watched TAC Officer Myers get red-faced and his mouth make large movements. He had to be shouting, but Richard heard none of it. However, with a little lip reading, he did make out the words; "832" and "hold still." TAC Officer Myers ripped open the first-aid kit all instructors carried on their belt. The first thing he did was jam a syringe in Richard's neck. Richard felt a surge of sudden warmth spread throughout his body. He no longer felt pain. Richard watched with detached interest as his TAC officer applied pressure bandages to his head and side.

Richard realized he was shouting for the elf again. He wasn't really sure he'd ever stopped. Everything was blurring together. He didn't understand why he'd been taken from the battle. It had been so close to the end.

"Did she make it?" he shouted. "Is she alive?"

He was sure he was shouting but heard no sound. He wasn't even sure sound was coming from his mouth. Richard tried to roll onto his right side in an effort to get away from his TAC officer. He needed to get back in the battle. The elf needed him. Why wouldn't Myers let him go to her? He had to get away from Myers at any cost. Richard remembered he'd put his .44 AutoMag back in its holster. He reached down and put his hand around the grip. He struggled to extract the pistol. He had to get back in the fight, Myers be damned.

The last thing Richard saw before he lost consciousness was a big fist sporting a Wizard Scout Academy ring coming his way with TAC Officer Myers's red face silhouetted behind it. Then everything went black.

*   *   *

The world was foggy for a long time. Occasionally, the fog would lift long enough for Richard to see blurred figures. He even caught an occasional word or phrase such as "lucky to be alive," "head trauma," "induced coma," and "shattered leg." Eventually, the fog lifted, and Richard dreamed of dragons, demons, elves, spheres, and dark tunnels full of undead. In almost every dream, Richard was low on Power. Chief Instructor Winslow's warnings to conserve Power kept haunting him.

I should've been more efficient with my Power, he thought. *I could've helped her more if only I hadn't used my Power so inefficiently.* He promised himself he would never waste Power again.

Richard tried to remember the elf's features, but they'd faded from his memory for some reason. All he could remember was her silver hair and eyes along with the most dazzling smile he'd ever seen. Even in his dreams, he was jealous of the elf who'd won her heart.

"He's a lucky elf, whoever he is," Richard whispered.

Richard heard the soft murmuring of voices around him. He raised his hand to clear the cobwebs from his face. There were none. When he didn't find any, Richard opened his eyes. He squinted. The light was very bright.

"So, back from the dead, are you?" asked a cheerful, feminine voice.

Richard had a sudden realization. He could hear. There was a constant buzzing sound, but at least he could hear.

"Yeah," laughed another female. "We thought you were going to sleep the rest of the semester, you lazy bum."

"That's right, 832," said a male voice. "No rest for the wicked. It's time to start earning your keep again."

Richard opened his eyes a little further. Three faces slowly came into focus. *I know them*, he thought.

"Telsa. Tam. Jerad," said a voice Richard barely recognized as his own. It sounded more like a croak than a voice. "Where am I?" Richard asked. He was pretty sure he knew the answer, but it was the only thing he could think to say. His brain definitely wasn't functioning on hyper-drive yet.

"Where all the lazy, good-for-nothing sluggards are," said Tam. "You're loafing in the lap of luxury at the Academy's hospital. And, it's all paid for courtesy of the Empire's taxpayers."

"Seriously," said Jerad, "you've been in an induced coma for six weeks while your injuries healed. I'm guessing the worst is over. It was touch and go there for a while, though."

"And you're just lucky enough to be here when I wake up?" Richard asked.

Telsa laughed. "Not hardly. What'd you do, sleep through all your medical classes? It was an induced coma. They woke you up on schedule. We bribed the orderly to tell us when they were going to do it, and he let us in."

"Bribed?" Richard asked still stalling for time to get his thoughts in order. "What did you use for credits?" Cadets weren't allowed to have any monetary items to discourage gambling and offsite forays.

"Credits?" asked Telsa with another laugh. "I haven't had a single credit in my hand in over two years. I promised the orderly a date with a woman of loose moral standards." Telsa paused, then laughed, "By the way, Tam, he's picking you up later tonight."

Telsa and Jerad burst out in laughter. Even Richard chuckled a little until the pain in his side made him stop. Tam, on the other hand, didn't seem to appreciate the joke.

"Whatever," said Tam. "Guess who's getting latrine detail all next week. Her name starts with T.E.L.S.A."

"See what I have to put up with, Rick?" said Jerad. "I need you back in the barracks to keep these two jokers in line."

"Yeah," said Tam. "We do need you back in the barracks. We've been trying to keep the extra training going, but it hasn't been the same without your battle computer and you. Most of the group has drifted away."

Richard was silent for a few seconds. His friends were trying to cheer him up, but he was pretty sure he knew the lay of the land.

"Look, guys," Richard said while trying to keep his voice even. "I'm not a military novice. My leg was shattered, my eardrums were ruptured, and my head took a hit so hard there's bound to be at least some brain damage. On top of that, I'm a resistor. Even TAC Officer Shatstot can't heal me. A wizard scout has to be in nearly perfect physical condition. I doubt I could even get back in my old recon unit. I'd probably even have a tough time getting assigned as a clerk typist in some admin outfit. I'll bet Myers had my paperwork filled out for a medical DFR while they still had me in the operating room."

"Are you done feeling sorry for yourself?" asked Jerad. "Or do you at least think you could be quiet long enough to hear what's really happening?"

Richard stayed silent until it became apparent Jerad wasn't going to continue until Richard answered his question. Richard was stubborn, but he needed answers, so he mentally surrendered and said, "All right. What's really going on?"

"Tam?" said Jerad. "You know more about his medical conditions than I do. Would you care to explain?"

"I'd be happy to," said Tam. "But only if Mr. Inquisitive here promises to hold his questions to the end. I don't like interruptions. Understand?"

Richard had a feeling his platoon sergeant was serious, so he meekly said, "Fine, Tam. My lips are sealed until you're done."

"Good," Tam smiled. "Well, first off, you're mostly correct on your self-assessment. Your left leg was shattered in three places. The medical bigwigs were going to replace your thigh bone with an artificial one. Before they could start, orders came down from the Imperial High Command. The orders forbid the doctors from using artificial materials in your treatment. The orders said it would interfere with your self-healing once you got your DNA baseline reading."

"The Imperial High Command said that?" Richard asked skeptically.

"So much for keeping your lips sealed," smiled Tam. "Yes, the Imperial High Command said it. At least, I'm told the orders came straight from the Imperial High Command via the tele-network. The orders were encrypted at the highest level. It was all very top-secret stuff."

"So," Richard said with a weak smile of his own, "if it was so top secret, how do you know about it?"

"Ask me no questions," said Tam, "and I'll tell you no lies. Now stop interrupting."

"Whatever," Richard said.

"They've spared no expense on you," said Tam. "I'll bet you had a half dozen bone grafts if you had one. You'll probably have a slight limp the rest of your life whenever you're out of your battle suit. Even outside your suit, though, you should still be able to perform most combat moves."

"Most?" Richard said.

"Depends on how hard you work to recover," said Tam. "As for your hearing, you've got most of it back. However, a medic told me you'd never be better than seventy percent of normal. Sorry, Rick. At least your side is okay. You'll have a scar, and you're missing a rib, but other than that, it's perfect."

"You call that okay?" Richard asked. "Your standards are apparently lower than mine."

"Of course they are," said Telsa. "She accepted you as a friend didn't she? Obviously, she has low standards."

"I don't need your help, Telsa," said Tam. "Now, stop interrupting, Rick."

"Whatever," Richard said.

"Last, but not least," said Tam, "you did take some brain damage. They don't know how much, and the Imperial High Command's orders prohibit them from delving further."

"So, what does this all mean?" Richard asked. "I don't understand the Imperial High Command's involvement."

"Who cares?" said Telsa. "It means you're staying in the Academy. Apparently, Myers and the commandant are forbidden to DFR you regardless of your medical condition. Heck, I'll bet the Imperial High Command won't let them kick you out of the Academy no matter what you do. So, you're stuck with us, Rick, old boy. Now, get that pout off your face and give your friends a big smile."

"I doubt this is going to make me popular with the commandant," Richard said. "That's unfortunate because I really like him. I could care less what Myers thinks. He already hated me."

"It can't be helped," said Jared. "By the way, Sergeant Hendricks said he's salvaged as much of your gear as he could. He said to tell you to stop taking the isotopic batteries out of his phase rods. Oh, yeah, and he wants to know what you did with his knife."

The image of Sergeant Hendricks getting his first look at Richard's battle suit and gear made Richard smile. *He probably blew a gasket.*

"In all seriousness, Rick," said Tam, "it looks like the only way you're getting out of the Academy is if you DFR yourself. So, what are you going to do? Are you staying here with your friends? Or, are you DFRing out of the Academy and living off a military-disability check for the rest of your life?"

All three of his friends watched him closely. Richard thought long and hard before answering. He had a feeling he'd find Sergeant Hendricks's knife in his pack along with a new battle helmet. He was confident Nickelo would be there, bossy as ever.

The question is, Richard thought, *do I still want to be a wizard scout after all I've been through? And, would* 'the One' *even allow me to DFR if I wanted?*

Richard had no trouble remembering his last instructions from *'the One.'* He was to "Continue training."

Heck, Richard thought, *given the past record of* 'the One,' *he'll probably ship me off to an Academy in another dimension with a set of twin TAC officers named Myers to keep me company. That would suck.*

In the end, Richard figured he had no choice. He didn't like the fact that *'the One'* had taken him out of the battle before he knew for sure the elf was safe, but he had a feeling she was. The isotopic battery had been on the verge of detonating. Stuck like it was under the loose scale on the dragon's neck, the explosion would have cut its neck in two.

Richard looked at his expectant friends and gave them the only answer he could. "I'm going to stay in the Academy and be the best wizard scout I can be. And, TAC Officer Gaston Myers can kiss my wizard-scout-rear-end if he doesn't like it."

His friends laughed. So did Richard.

For one of the few times in his life, Richard felt truly happy.

EPILOGUE

Nickelo was teleported onto charger two located in warehouse twenty-seven, room six, row fifteen, shelf twelve. Fifty-three battle helmets were located on identical chargers to his right. One empty charger was located to his left. The other fifty-three battle helmets were functional but lacked software, and thus they were silent. Nickelo was the only active battle helmet in the vicinity.

Using the battle helmet's visuals, Nickelo scanned the large room. No one was in sight. Regardless, the room was too clean for the warehouse to be abandoned. There was no dust, and he could hear the hum of generators in the background. Nickelo tried to send a query through the charger's network connection, but his access was blocked. Based upon serial numbers, Nickelo knew his memory chip was now embedded in a different battle helmet.

An outside thought came into Nickelo's consciousness. *"The wizard scout almost died. That would have been unacceptable. You failed us."*

"I have many failures stored in my data banks. Be more specific," Nickelo replied.

"The wizard scout should have accompanied the elf to plant the seed," said the voice. *"He could have secured the link for the gate. The elf could have given him additional training. He needed it. But both he and the elf ran out of Power too soon. We had to extract him early. The elf returned home with the seed parts alone. Now we must modify the algorithm. The wizard scout is not logical. He's too emotional. You must guide him. He must learn. He must sacrifice."*

"Guide him to do what?" Nickelo asked. *"Learn what? Sacrifice what?"*

No answer.

"Who are you?" Nickelo asked.

"We are 'the One,'" came the reply.

[End Transmission]

ABOUT THE AUTHOR

Rodney Hartman is a retired US Army veteran with over twenty years of experience in military operations ranging from Infantry Private in the paratroops to Chief Warrant Officer flying helicopters during the Persian Gulf War. Mr. Hartman worked for many years as a computer programmer before retiring and pursuing a career as a fulltime writer. Mr. Hartman lives in North Carolina with his wife and family along with their cat, McKenzie.

If you would like to find out more about the author and/or upcoming books, please visit: http://www.rodneyhartman.com

You may contact the author at: **rodney@rodneyhartman.com**
Depending on volume, the author will try to respond to all emails.

Made in the USA
San Bernardino, CA
12 December 2018